ACTS OF TRANGRESSION

CORE BOOK 5

BY

MAQUEL A. JACOB

Published by:
MAJart Works LLC
2001 NE Aloclek Dr Suite 211
Hillsboro, Oregon

www.majartworks.com

ISBN: 978-1-950438-27-3

Cover Art by Dar Albert
www.wickedsmartdesigns.com

ALSO BY MAQUEL A. JACOB

THE CORE SERIES

CORE OF CONFLICTION
SEEDS OF CONVICTION
BONDS OF CONTRITION
WRATH OF ACQUISITION

CURVE OF HUMANITY SERIES

ORIGINS, SHADOWMEN OBJECTIVE
PURGE SEQUENCE, CRIPPLED EARTH
AFTERMATH

WELCOME DESPAIR
A COLLECTION OF SHORTS

THE BLOOD SAGA

BLOOD DOCTRINE
BLOOD DOMINION
BLOOD DESCENSION

COMING SOON

RULES OF TRANSITION
CORE BOOK SIX

BLOOD DEVOTION
BLOOD SAGA BOOK 4

ONE: CONGREGATION

Meeting of the Minds

Lord Pondur stared outside his office's panoramic windows watching the industrial district back in full swing. Rust red vapors drifted from the giant smokestacks, briefly coloring the sky a soft pink before dissipating. Construction rings surrounded the main refinery for the rebuilding of the upper halves, still caved in and exposed to the elements.

Every crevice on his craggy face scrunched deeper.

He straightened his stance, clasping both hands behind his back, which made the quarter length dress jacket pull tight around his shoulders. A charcoal vest and cream-colored ascot complimented his maroon matte tailored suit. The Dreridian crest etched on the vest and jacket's shiny gold buttons gleamed in the light. His collar curved up around his oval head. Casual, yet dignified. He always came prepared regardless of no scheduled meetings.

Every planet in the Dreridian system sat on high alert after an unknown enemy scourge attacked them less than a year ago. Battle cruisers patrolled the space, looking out for any vortices that may pop open. Business resumed following the disruption of trade though behavior and movement became solemn. Construction for new satellite hubs replacing the previously destroyed ones was only half completed.

A small spark of fury lingered at the enemy's audacity to strike his home. And not only his. Their relentless pursuit targeted the two most powerful races in the five solar systems, Razzna and Azrom, along with the newly formed Lassian force.

A proposed alliance between the three made him uneasy. Granted, combining their resources would make them a might of staggering proportions. That also meant they could challenge him in the future.

Maybe we throw our hat in the fray as well?

He figured having a spot in the alliance would help deter such an outcome. As powerful as they were, each race only gained their status over a millennium ago. Mere babes in the scheme of things.

The Dreridians scoured the galaxy, setting up trade systems for the past two thousand years, making them the prime industry leaders. Others tried to build similar ones, yet never achieved the same level of success. Lord Pondur snorted. The Dreridian reach was vast.

The door slid open. His head of science, Lord Graggor, entered. The portly creature moved gracefully, despite his size, to stand next to him. A dark grey tailored three-piece suit a shade darker than his cragged skin made him the picture of an aristocrat. His two stone horns were short and stubby, in contrast to Pondur's thinner, pointy ones.

"I read the reports. Everything is almost back to peak production." Lord Graggor laced his fingers in front of him and rested them on his belly. "The damage proved minimal after crunching the numbers."

"What do you think about joining the alliance with those three imbeciles?"

Lord Graggor turned towards him in shock at the sudden outburst. He drew a deep breath and reverted his gaze back to the scene below.

"We could monitor them better. Keep them at bay in case they decide to go against us." His face tightened. "I think we're giving them more credit than they warrant."

"I agree. They are still too young."

"We could," Lord Graggor seemed to tread carefully as he spoke, "mentor them. Get their leadership on track so they won't drastically trade like before."

Lord Pondur's brow lifted in surprise. He had not thought of that. Instead of the constant chastising, they would benefit from a lesson in true power. He thought about their military might. Crass and barbaric. Useful for when the Dreridians didn't want to get their hands dirty.

"Why, Lord Graggor, that is a fascinating proposal."

Lord Graggor tilted his head to one side and shrugged. "I do what I can, my Lord."

"You came for a different reason." Lord Pondur frowned. "What is it now?"

"It appears the enemy received the location of New Lassa's gate coordinates and attempted to raze the planet." Lord Graggor grimaced.

"Is that so? How did that happen?" Lord Pondur asked, not happy. He had a theory.

"Planet Barrima, under Sestis' regency, felt slighted and sought revenge. Of course, they realized their error too late."

Lord Pondur lowered his head in defeat. His fears further solidified from his mistake to not help the regency planets at the start.

"The damage?" He braced for the reply.

"Astonishingly," Lord Graggor began, "the Lassians managed to push them back. That woman," his disdain for the Lassian scientist Ganna clear, "had devised a defense system in such a short time."

"Really?" Lord Pondur replied with intrigue. "So, they learn quite fast. Good." He nodded.

"What are your next moves, my lord? The enemy hasn't unleashed any attacks in the past cycle. They are surely regrouping, as they have done before."

"No doubt." Lord Pondur unclasped his hands and tapped his chin with one finger. "Send out a message to all our posts. I want to know the whereabouts of their main fleet. We will reward any information leading to its location."

"Monetary or credit?"

Lord Pondur turned a sour expression towards him.

"This minor distraction does not warrant payment," he snapped. "Trade credit will suffice. Add in free shipping for hauls outside their system."

"Very good, my Lord. A perfect incentive."

"Now, go find out what kind of defense system that Lassian scientist has created."

"On my way for inspection in two days."

Lord Graggor exited the office, leaving Lord Pondur to his quiet observations. The Lassians. He still had little information on that race. They appeared out of nowhere. Or had they? The speed with which they learned, and the complicated nature of their cores, made him think they may have been something else entirely.

What jumpstarted their evolution?

When they came for a seat at the trade table, he was leery of them. They had not divulged their planet's location and, being new, the other conglomerates didn't push the issue since they had no intention of visiting. The gate coordinates had changed with the new planet. Lord Pondur now wanted to know the location of their original home world. Something told him it was the key to all this.

And I will find it.

⌒

The calm, yellow tone of New Lassa's clear skies added to the sun's rays. A warm breeze caressed the Eastern landscape. A large ship port housed four Lassian vessels docked on the far side, taking up its capacity. Workers from each clan did check points, preventative maintenance, and cleaning. A new skill they all had to learn after being driven into the trade industry. They used the ships for transport of goods and meetings on other planets.

This new reality made many Lassians nervous. They had never built such things, nor needed them in the past. The gate had always sufficed. Each battle meant the clans acted more like militia than warriors.

None wanted this.

On the overhead platform above the docks, Ganna stared down at the four ships, admiring their craftmanship. A labor of love, and a necessity. After sending the enemy packing only two moon cycles ago, she had a council meeting to advance New Lassa's defense system. In the north, she established another gate to lessen the burden on the two already serving as pre-check and entry.

The slow-moving breeze swished the off-white robe's hem around her ankles, tickling the tops of her feet in the leather sandals. Not ideal footwear for the docks. She had no reason for going down there. Workers loaded cargo for an order in a nearby ship. Ganna frowned. She didn't like the Dreridians' terms and would be glad when they completed the last obligatory one. She prided herself on keeping New Lassa's location from them this whole time.

Until now. The enemy had ruined that. Lord Pondur would seek New Lassa itself. An anti-tracking system built into each gate left many visitors confused as to their true coordinates in the cosmos. That method no longer provided safety for them.

She straightened her posture and turned away from the railing. A deep hate smoldered in her chest. The secret she alone kept for so long would have to be revealed sooner than planned. When the representative from the Tolitha system's royal planet showed footage of the enemy, in that moment, every fiber of her being wanted to cry out in terror. Instead, she remained calm and began a plan of action.

The Dreridians finding their home world close to where the enemy originated frightened her. She never thought in a thousand years that they would encounter those creatures ever again.

Why? Why had fate thrown us to the depths of despair once more?

The need to find an appropriate time to tell Chardon and the council about the enemy weighed on her. There would be anger, for her silence, and confusion.

Not yet.

Her first priority went to creating a weapon to defend against the enemy. She stopped walking as she reached outside, shielding her eyes from the sunlight.

Before that, she needed to diffuse the fire caused by the revelation that Hon and Mota, two manbeasts of the same litter, had ended up mated to each other. The situation escalated because she had known about it and kept Mota's promise to keep it secret.

"Everything is such a mess," she sighed.

Shaking her head at the task ahead, she resumed walking towards the main hall where the other leaders congregated to fulfill their duties.

⌣

Jaron sat at her large wooden desk inside the one hundred square foot designated work quarters. She had moved it in front of the lone picture window on the far wall with her back to the scenery, eliminating distraction. Her long-sleeved white gown dragged on the floor, the sleeveless blue overlay an inch shorter. She sat back in the hand carved chair courtesy of her mate, Modas. Handy when it counted.

Her mind raced as she thought about her children. Once again, Ganna had played God. How many secrets do you have? Jaron was beyond angry. Not because of the mating situation between her litter. No. The not knowing. Ganna could have told her about it when the case first became certain. It would have made it easier to comfort Mota these troubling days.

The muffled tap on the door let her know Ganna had arrived. She had demanded the woman come to explain herself. That she agreed surprised her.

"Come," Jaron called out.

The door opened and Ganna strolled in, a wide grin on her face as she shut it behind her.

"What a glorious afternoon!"

Ganna sat in the chair across from Jaron. "You can't possibly be still working. Get out in the fields before the day is over."

Jaron narrowed her eyes and rested her chin on the hands of her propped up arms. Ganna's expression didn't waver.

Lassa's love, I despise her!

"You know why you're here. Spit it out."

"Really," Ganna smirked. "There's no reason for that."

"You kept this from us and, as a result, harmed my family. You deserve much worse."

"I promised Mota I would never tell a soul."

"When did you do that?"

"When his core revived him. There was no way the litter would have survived. He was heartbroken."

The way Ganna delivered it with no emotion made Jaron bristle. It meant nothing to her.

"But you knew before that," Jaron spat.

"Well, yes." Ganna leaned away from the desk. Jaron raised her brow, amused that she thought she might strike. "I made that observation when Mota fell ill one day."

"So, you gave counsel to Mota and Hon without my knowledge?" Jaron dropped her arms.

"Not quite." Ganna turned her head, looking away.

"What does that mean?" Jaron placed her hands flat on the desk, ready to push herself up.

"Hon did not know." Ganna glanced back at her. Jaron froze, her eyes widening. "I had made the discovery only a few days before the blast."

Jaron slumped down in her seat, arms extended across the desk's surface. She stared at nothing, her heart aching for her poor children. Then the entirety of it struck. Mota and Hon. An unlikely match. A terrible one. As if realizing the same, Ganna turned back to her with the same expression.

"It is quite disturbing." Ganna sighed. "Hon will be more than a handful than ever before. I can't imagine his desperation for reclaiming his status and..." She eyed Jaron.

Having a litter to replace the one lost, Jaron finished in her head. Regardless of how Mota would feel about the idea. She glared at Ganna.

"Any more of my offspring with these attributes?"

"Amazingly, no." Ganna sat for a moment, appearing to contemplate something. Then she slapped her thighs and stood. "Well. That's all I have."

"That's a lie." Jaron slid her arms off the desk and let them flop in her lap. "You have so many secrets, there isn't enough lifetimes for us to expose them all."

The way Ganna tilted her head with hooded eyes before leaving solidified her statement.

What else are you hiding, you monster?

∾

Chardon stood on the platform adjacent to the docking area, watching the Barrima ship touch down onto the clamping mechanism. A loud clank resounded when they secured its underbelly. He exhaled slowly, calming his increased ire for their actions the first time they arrived on New Lassa. A dark blue trim accented the hem of his white robes, along with a sleeveless duster of the same color. He pushed the sides of his now waist long hair behind his ears in frustration.

I need to cut this mess!

It amazed him how Talas always kept his long hair in check. The real reason he let it grow so long stood beside him. Halfar found his long tresses to be some new toy to play with, wrapping his fingers in them during mating to the point of tangling. Chardon glanced over at him.

Halfar wore his signature white tunic with black leggings, boots, and coat. He focused those murky green eyes, angrier than usual, on the ship's ramp coming down..

His superior air as a former Supreme Ruler of Azrom never went away. Authority exuded from his entire being.

"Take a breath, my love. They learned their lesson already." Chardon saw the first few passengers head down the ramp. "Be nice."

"Have they?" Halfar balked. "And absolutely not."

His reply, dripping with disdain, made Chardon tense with desire. He took another deep breath. Sensing his mood, Halfar turned his head towards Chardon.

"I will remedy your ailment after this." He said it so deadpan; it caught Chardon off guard. "I won't be gentle either." He turned back to the Barrima ship. "I need release since I can't torture or kill these imbeciles."

"No, you can't," Chardon admonished him. "We've talked about this so many times."

"Still don't agree."

The leader of Planet Barrima, Master Adan, followed by his first officer, Commander Ryben, stepped onto the platform right as the ramp's edge connected to the walkway. Ten soldiers, looking worn out and dingy as usual, followed. Chardon reined in his disdain.

Truth be told, he had yet to send a convoy to Barrima to assess the planet. He also knew they were mechanics, getting dirty being part of their trade. It still irked him they used their appearance to gather sympathy from other systems.

"Regent Chardon," Master Adan greeted with a slight bow, his tone playful. "It is good to see you doing well." He straightened his posture, then flinched as his gaze landed on Halfar. "Lord Halfar." He cleared his throat and tilted his head forward. "You as well."

Halfar, not amused, let his stare burn into their guests like hot coals. Chardon let out a sigh. "Let's get this done." He walked off to the lift, sitting open at the end of the walkway.

The group in tow, Halfar tracked them as each passed before he took up the rear. Trust had to be earned. The Barrimans had ways to go, their credit already starting in the negative.

They rode the lift down to the surface and headed towards the main commons attached to the temple. Manbeasts serving as guards eyed the entourage, zeroing in on the Barrimans. When they arrived at the conference room, the already seated council members were having drinks.

"We didn't expect them to arrive on time in the first place," the head engineer said. He took a sip of his drink while sneering at Master Adan.

"There was traffic in the next system." Master Adan… pouted? "You insisted on making us hold there until you opened the gate."

Chardon felt Halfar's intensity rise. He placed a hand on his shoulder.

Easy.

The head of science gawked at him. "You dare to complain after what you brought to our home?" Her voice rose with each word.

"We have apologized thrice over," Master Adan replied.

"And it's not enough!"

Jaron walked around them as she entered.

They all sat on cushions around the large oval table. Servants arrived to dispense drinks to the newcomers, then hurried back out.

"Now," the head of science said. "What shall we do about all this?"

"Can I make a request?" Commander Ryben raised his hand at chest level.

"What could you possibly ask at this juncture?" the head of science snapped.

"It's about my counterpart on the neutral zone planet."

"Ahh, Commander Veris, was it?" Their head of politics asked, teresely.

"Yes. Can you have him and his soldiers released?"

Silence.

"That," the new liaison for New Lassa began, "is up to the planet's leaders. Have you forgotten? Your people let an enemy force ravage their world. It is only fitting they're imprisoned and forced to assist in repairs."

"I understand that." Commander Ryben's brow furrowed. "They are also master mechanics, and we need them if work resumes."

Well, damn.

Chardon had not thought about that. "Negotiating their release will not be without consequences." He leaned forward. "By taking responsibility, which would be perceived as such if we go on their behalf, would open us up for sanctions."

The mood became heavy. The liaison folded her arms and sat back against the wall behind her. She glanced over at the political head.

"This will be messy. I can go plead their case, but there are no guarantees I will succeed."

"We only ask that you try." Master Adan appeared to have humbled. Halfar snorted.

"Let's get on with the agenda for today," the political head said. "We need to get an assessment done quickly before the enemy regroups."

Jaron set the tablet in her lap on the table to interface with its system. A hologram of planet Barrima floated in midair above the center. Beside it showed a zoomed image of the surface. Chardon stared at them in awe. It appeared worse than expected.

"What a vile ecosystem," the head of science blurted out. He turned away, covering his mouth with one hand.

"No need to be nasty," Master Adan stated, rightfully offended.

"What exactly happened here?" The chief of agriculture asked with narrowed eyes.

Even Halfar seemed disturbed by the condition of the planet. The regions of extreme weather made it look almost uninhabitable. Chardon finally understood.

When they first came to New Lassa, seeking Sestis, they were out for revenge. To have an appointed Regent simply abandon them after citing hope for the future, Barrima needed help, feeling slighted. And the Dreridians gave them to the one person who would not, nor cared to.

Jaron caught his eye, and the two cousins locked into a wordless agreement. Chardon, not a skilled tactician like Jaron, could also see what they required.

"First, we need to form a blockade to prevent the enemy from reaching the planet again." Jaron placed her forearms on the table, clasping her hands. "They may have already realized your broken deal."

"Protection will be key while we figure out how to fix the planet's generator." Chardon reached over and tapped the surface image where the giant structure sat and zoomed in further. "It also regulates the atmosphere, correct?"

"Yes." Master Adan nodded. "When it malfunctioned, we scrambled to find a remedy."

"The damage was swift, and we had no time to do so. Lives were more important," Commander Ryben added. "We have been merely surviving since then."

"Question." The head of science raised her head, perplexed. Everyone gave their attention. "Why does this planet have or need a generator? What happened to its original characteristics?"

"Being a repair planet requires different biospheres for the ships we take in," Master Adan replied.

"It depends on what materials are required for the ship's build," Commander Ryben jumped in. "We try to manufacture them in the best possible arena for that technology. If a hull has a low melting point, we dock it in the cooler regions."

"And the reverse." Master Adan smiled. "We take great pride in our work and do it to the fullest of our abilities. That requires taking the material into consideration."

It dawned on the Lassians in that moment who they were in the company of. Although they implied the term on so many occasions, it didn't set in until now. These master mechanics could build, modify, and repair any ship in the five systems and beyond, as verified by the one they brought that crippled the enemy ship from the Azrom battle.

Master Adan's skills warranted arrogance.

Still don't like him.

Chardon saw why.

He reminds me of myself so long ago.

Master Adan turned to him, a smirk on his face. Yep. The man would get another rude awakening.

The experts

Ganna tracked Lt. Treshur's movements around their pristine designated lab on the science planet, Halios. His royal uniform stood out like a sore thumb in the all-white interior. Its pleated material forming the armor effect gave the black bodysuit a dull sheen. The blood red cape he removed earlier from the body armor's shoulder clasps, lay draped over a nearby chair. His boots made resounding clacks as they struck the hard flooring.

She watched him stop at one workstation and lean over a specimen in a petri dish. His shoulder length hair, a dark blue hue with sporadic silver, swung forward causing a few strands to fall against his cheeks. He suddenly froze, his eyes narrowing as he glanced sideways. Ganna didn't waver.

"Aren't you uncomfortable in that getup?" She propped the side of her head in one hand. "A lab robe would be much more accommodating." His physique she found quite pleasing. That aside, she felt the proper attire would be more functional in their current setting.

A muffled snort came from across the other side of the room. She could only see the partial left side of Lord Graggor, standing behind another workstation, walled off separating it from the rest. The bottom of his dark slacks and shined to perfection shoes were visible under the white lab coat. Part of his craggy neck peeked above the collar.

Lt. Treshur raised his head a few degrees and placed his hands flat on the surface. The way he stared at her confirmed how she had been observing him.

Like a piece of meat. An object.

"Careful, Lieutenant," Lord Graggor chided. "She seems to be on a hunt."

"Focus on the task at hand, Lassian. If you can't do that…" His expression hardened.

"Oh, pfft!"

Lt. Treshur resumed his work.

Ganna straightened her posture at the table occupied by the dismantled enemy weapon in its center. Digital tags labeling each piece floated above them. The ugly, snarled black design ruined the aesthetic. An eyesore among the purity.

"I am more than capable of getting my end of the research done." She turned sideways. The blinding white light of day poured through the panoramic windows. Shielding her eyes, she turned back around.

"Maybe we should lower the pane shields until sunset?" The Razznian scientist came out of hiding from the enclosed space for forensic analysis. The reptilian wore a reddish tan robe attached across one shoulder, leaving the other bare. Its flowing fabric dragged across the floor, making a soft shish sound. "This lab is so bright on its own, especially with the overheads."

The Razznian went to the door's side panel and tapped the window icon. Smoky grey film lowered over them, blocking the sunlight, until it whirred to a stop at the bottom. Ganna breathed a sigh of relief, her retinas still burning. Lord Graggor came around the wall towards the main table where Ganna lounged.

"Gather around, please." Lord Graggor waved them over. He assembled the bundle in his arms next to the enemy parts on the table. Digital tags popped up as he laid them. "As you know, we have replicated all the components necessary to create our counter weapon. There will be a few tweaks going forward but this will do for now."

Ganna frowned, already aware of the outcome.

Even Lt. Treshur seemed put out. Yet again, the Dreridian outshined them. It should have been me! She had the same knowledge, possibly more, yet she couldn't figure out the mechanics of the enemy weapon. Its simplicity eluded her. The Razznian's short talons drumming clicked on the table.

Lord Graggor placed on the table a cylindrical vial, eight millimeters long and three in width. The turquoise liquid sloshed gently in contrast to the enemy's thick red gel. Seeing it made them exhale with pride. A feat accomplished in record time; they had created a nullifier for the red tendrils' damage.

"And now for the delivery system." Lord Graggor picked up the first piece. "This will be our masterpiece."

The others followed suit, picking up components. Together, they assembled the new weapon, carefully connecting every part before inserting the vial. The Razznian snapped it in place, then raised the weapon. Shorter than the enemy's and lightweight. Lt. Treshur had commented on it earlier. The enemy's weapons reflected their stocky, heavy form. They could carry them with ease. For the races in the alliance, not so much. Ganna gauged the original at nearly ten kilos and it came close once they got it on the scale.

"Your verdict?" Lord Graggor's lips curved into a smirk.

"Did you really need our assistance?" Lt. Treshur asked.

Lord Graggor scoffed. "Of course! I am not omniscient. Collaboration is key with these things. It benefits all of us."

"It shouldn't be a surprise." The Razznian turned the weapon in his hands. "Dreridians are known for their products of war."

"That sounds so insidious," Lord Graggor objected.

"Yet true." Ganna took hold of the weapon as the Razznian handed it over. She hefted it a few times, then rested the back end against her shoulder while aiming it at the wall ahead. "Perfect. Even I can handle it."

"What? No rude remarks or dissention?" Lord Graggor raised his brow.

"There's no point in that."

She handed the weapon to Lt. Treshur.

Contrary to belief, Azrom used projectile weapons as well. Their expert fighting skills lie in morphed forms and swordsmanship. When it came to large-scale assault, they resembled Dreridians more than they liked.

Lt. Treshur scrutinized the weapon with those expert eyes. Lord Graggor gave him a knowing stare. A queasiness hit Ganna. Azrom didn't need new weapons. Neither did Razzna nor the Dreridians. The Lassians would rarely use this new one, since she had no intention of letting the enemy near New Lassa ever again.

In her quest for more knowledge and scientific advancements, she forgot to question her motivation. Her conversation with Chardon decades ago, where he admonished her enclosed, narrow vision that didn't allow a common sense factor, smacked her in the head. She looked over at Lord Graggor and his intense expression made her unconsciously step back. He understood her concern, and she wasn't sure if he would exploit it.

The Razznian and Lt. Treshur seemed to realize the same thing. Lt. Treshur stopped examining the weapon and set it down. He addressed Lord Graggor.

"Just so we're clear. This is not an invitation to eliminate each other. This is an alliance that we were reluctant to have you in."

"Oh, I know." Lord Graggor's beady grey eyes appeared to brighten. "The same goes for you. We will not tolerate any backstabbing. Against us or yourselves."

The Razznian tilted his head. "Are Dreridians accepting us as equals, then?"

Lord Graggor's eyes went wide. "Let's not go that far!" He became calm. "We merely acknowledge your status in the five systems."

He turned to Ganna. "The Lassians have yet to show their true might. I look forward to that."

Ganna stiffened. *What does he know?* She saw the way the Razznian and Lt. Treshur glanced at her before turning away. Her skin grew warm in the cold lab.

Have they stumbled on something I didn't keep hidden well enough?

Lord Graggor slapped his meaty hands on the table, his large talons hitting the surface so hard Ganna thought it had cracked. Looking down, she found it still intact.

"Enough chatter. Let's head to the demonstration wing to test it." Lord Graggor motioned to the enemy's weapon. "Our assistants can reassemble this and bring it to us."

"That makes no sense if we are going there now." Lt. Treshur gave him a suspicious stare.

"Oh. That's because we need to have sustenance first. Look at the time. We have been at it since the night before."

They stared at the universal time displays spanning above the entrance. The window shields held off the heat of midday.

"I guess I could eat." Ganna walked towards the door.

Lt. Treshur followed, getting close to her, and leaned into her neck.

"Be careful you don't reap what you sow, Lassian," he whispered. "I would tread carefully with the Dreridians."

"I could say the same to you," Ganna countered.

"We always do." Lt. Treshur moved past her into the equally pale corridor.

Once again, Ganna felt as if she had missed something important.

～

The Dreridian invitation listed it as a meeting of the minds. Halfar stared at the digital card with contempt. To prevent the strain on his neck, he sat upright on the bed, swinging his legs over the side. His hair splayed across his shoulders over the white tunic, almost touching his thighs. The black leggings hugged every inch. A Lassian robe would have been more comfortable, but he couldn't get used to them.

Focused back on the invite, he saw the names of the other guests. Lord Kraznan with his head of military, the lord of planet Yaos, and Emperor Calabra of planet Jiez. This was no ordinary meeting. Every one of them had conquered worlds with devastating might. He understood the reason for the secret collaboration. The thought of being in the same room as those vultures made him ill.

Along with his name were Generals Kur and Rass. They would easily deter any scrutiny from Romnus and make rendezvous point on time. Fooling Farin would be another story. His daughter could sniff out the truth instantly, yet never tell her mate. Halfar chuckled.

Serves Romnus right!

Halfar stowed the invite in his leggings' fold pocket when the chamber door opened. Chardon eyed him with suspicion while closing the door. That's where Farin gets it. He leaned back on the bed, propping his elbows. Even with that distrusting stare, he found Chardon stunning.

I love you more than life.

"What are you doing?" Chardon asked. She crawled next to him on the bed. "You look like you're hiding something."

"Hmm? Is that so?" Halfar cocked his head, smiling mischievously. "I was waiting for you." He reached out, running his fingers along the exposed skin above her breasts.

"Stop that!" She smacked his hand away, frowning. "We have more important things to do than mating."

Halfar feigned anger, narrowing his eyes at her. She didn't acknowledge the rejection.

He flopped down, lying flat.

"What could be more important than that?"

Chardon balked at him. "Have you forgotten we are in the middle of an impending war?"

"I have not." Halfar grabbed hold of her, pulling her body over his. He cupped her face in his hands. "I need you, always."

"Halfar," Chardon sighed.

He flipped her over with ease and straddled her. In the seconds she lay startled, he yanked off her robes, exposing slightly tanned skin. He really needed relief. His ire at the Dreridian's blatant display of power festered. Removing his own clothes, he smacked Chardon on the side of her buttocks when she tried to protest.

"Lay still." Halfar watched her eyes glaze over in ecstasy as he entered her. So dishonest. He opted to punish her a little. Leaning close, he whispered in her ear, "I won't let you go this day."

⁓

The second gate on New Lassa had a secondary system created by Halfar that allowed Azrom to tap into the coordinates and reroute if necessary. In the dead of night, he made his way to the site. Far from satiated after his long bout of mating with Chardon, he tried to calm himself. Anxiety crept in. Kur had commissioned a small recon ship and would pick him up at a checkpoint outside of New Lassa's system.

The darker than usual night sky marked the start of the cold season. He felt a touch of icy air caress the back of his neck. The moist underbrush muted his footsteps. Multiple presences alerted him to manbeasts keeping watch in the hills and mountains above. A peaceful planet that seemed to not have any woes. Halfar brow scrunched. *New Lassa should not be tainted by war and forced into military might!* He remained adamant about that.

Halfar stopped at the gate console, a few feet from the guardian. The man stared at him in confusion. Halfar let out a loud sigh.

"You will walk away and not tell anyone where I have gone. The coordinates are to be wiped from the system."

The guardian went into a defensive stance. "And why should I do that?"

Halfar morphed his hands into giant claws. The guardian hissed, backing away, still holding his position.

"Because it would keep New Lassa safe. Even if for a little while."

The guardian hesitated at first, then stood straight, moving to his post.

"I don't trust you. I can never trust you."

"That's fair." Halfar's arms reverted. "I expect nothing less." He motioned for the guardian to step aside. "I will set the destination myself. You only need to remove its trace afterwards."

"The less I know?" The guardian retorted.

"Exactly."

Halfar entered the points he received from Kur and activated the gate. It would alert Ganna and Chardon within minutes. By the time they reached the gate, he would be long gone. The mini vortex gaped open. Wrapping his cloak around him to stop it from being taken by the wind, he walked through the black swirling mouth that engulfed him.

The guardian stared at the coordinates before reluctantly deleting them. Right as he finished, Ganna and Chardon came running up the hill towards the gate. He hung his head, fists clenched on the console. From above, he felt a manbeast's stare burrow into him.

Planet Jiez had too many colors for Halfar's taste. The always jubilant population showed off their wealth in excess extravagance. He sat slumped against the porthole of the cruiser's main cabin. Across from him, Kur smirked, with arms crossed, at the scene below. Rass stared in disgust. Light streamers flew in the air despite it being midday. The space docks on the planet surface were close to full. When one departed, another sat not far behind to take its place.

Emperor Calabra's palace, looming in the distance, would once again accept visitors from the five systems. The cruiser approached the dock near the sprawling structure and landed with ease on the clamp mechanisms. They secured the ship, making it jolt. Halfar waited for the ramp to open before getting up, with Rass and Kur close behind.

Wearing full regal uniforms, the three stood out as they stepped down onto the ramp. When Halfar pulled out his former attire from a storage bin, Chardon immediately confiscated it for cleaning. Chemical solutions erased the scent of blood and battle. Where Kur and Rass had red capes flowing from their shoulders, Halfar wore a black full length collared coat with red trim.

The emperor's assistant, a small creature barely five feet tall, their face smooth like a child's, came up to them. The eyes brimming with joy had seen too much. A bodysuit of black and silver vertical stripes hugged their body.

"The mighty Azrom of old has graced our halls once more." He bowed. His voice, a higher register, had a strange lower ting. "Greetings."

Halfar's lips thinned. "We appreciate the hospitality."

"This way, please." The assistant led with tiny legs that moved faster than expected. "Emperor Calabra is glad to have you. The Lord of Yaos, Lord Kraznan, and Lord Pondur have already arrived." The assistant turned towards them, smiling. "Azrom always commands an entrance at the last moments, hmm?"

"I never thought of it that way." Halfar shrugged.

"We get to our destination on time. That's all that matters, correct?"

"Yes, yes."

They took a lift down to the sky bridge level and loaded into an open top vehicle. The autopilot engaged, lurching forward as it gained speed. The scene before Halfar seemed almost comical as he noticed the assistant sitting between Rass and himself in the front seat with Kur seated in the rear, his tall frame not fitting comfortably.

At the end of the sky bridge, the assistant placed a hand on the scanner set in the side panel of the palace entrance's wall. The doors slid open.

"Welcome back to Jiez." The assistant gestured for them to enter.

Down the familiar corridor, they found new artwork bursting with color, lining the already stark white walls. The conference room sat at the end. He could make out Lord Pondur delicately raising a drink even from his current distance.

The doors slid apart to each side. Emperor Calabra, dressed to the hilt in a brocaded gold and yellow robe over an azure blue suit, turned to them and smiled like an excited child. Usually timid, his attire over the top, he nevertheless resembled a respected figure in the five systems. His appearance belied his cunning and eye for revenue on par with the Dreridians.

"Azrom has arrived!" He came forward and grabbed Halfar by his arms. The look in his eyes startled him. A slight move of the emperor's gaze towards the table gave Halfar the reason for the overzealous greeting. "We have been waiting for you."

"Azrom never bothers to have the common courtesy to arrive early like everyone else." The Ruler of Yaos snorted. "Still find yourselves special?"

The way his lips curled back to reveal his shark-like teeth as he raised his drink made Halfar bristle.

The emperor let him go and glared at the ruler.

"You will not disrespect my guests. That goes for the Dreridian, too."

Lord Pondur's cup, half down to the table, halted. His craggy brow fused together, then he exhaled softly, placing his drink on the saucer before him.

"I wouldn't think of it." He glanced over at the ruler of Yaos. "We are not all so uncouth as to sling insults at another race's might."

Lord Kraznan's beady eyes opened to their fullest.

"Surely, you're joking."

It felt like déjà vu. The last time they were all in the same room, a food fight occurred. A shameful display that cost them all.

"I was merely commenting on the arrogance of a former ruler not knowing his place." The ruler of Yaos stared at Halfar in defiance.

To everyone's surprise, Lord Pondur came to Halfar's defense.

"Would you rather discuss this urgent matter with a ruler so green with less than a century of command under his name than one who has conquered worlds? One being your own that not even your army could stop from falling into Azrom's hands?"

The Yaos ruler sputtered, spraying a mist of the drink from his mouth. The assistant tugged on Halfar's cloak and motioned for him to sit. Kur and Rass went to the other side of the table across from the Yaos ruler and sat with Halfar between them. Lord Kraznan was to their left. Lord Pondur sat close to the end at a distance from the Yaos ruler. Emperor Calabra took his seat at the head of the table.

Only small platters of food spread down its length, making sure not to obscure the participants' view of each other. The tallest items were crystal-clear drink carafes filled with Jiez mineral water.

"We all know why we are here," Emperor Calabra began.

His assistant refilled a half empty glass then went to sit in the corner. "This new enemy has brought chaos to our territories."

"Yes." The ruler of Yaos, not deterred, went further with his insults. "If not for the Dreridians' misjudgment and poor assessment of the situation, we might not have had to endure such setbacks."

Halfar watched Lord Pondur's posture go erect and his eyes turn red. That's right! Halfar couldn't agree more. He also knew the Yaos ruler was in the wrong for speaking it.

"That's uncalled for!" Lord Kraznan pounded a fist on the table, shaking it. "None of us had a clue as to what kind of monsters these brutes were. We were all blindsided!"

"Hmph!" The ruler of Yaos resumed drinking.

"We are here to find a solution." Lord Pondur crossed his legs and draped his arms over his knees. "If you have nothing to contribute, then this trip was a waste for you."

"I know full well why we are here. If any of us had an answer, we wouldn't be."

Silence blanketed the room. None of them looked at each other, opting to grab a few snacks and drinks in the awkwardness. Emperor Calabra finally broke the mood. He cleared his throat to get their attention.

"I believe the first order of business is to find out where they came from." He addressed Lord Pondur. "You have some inkling of that effect, correct?"

"Perhaps. We captured their language long ago. Even then, they were too far from our system, and we had no way of tracking them." He paused. Looking over at Halfar, his expression went stern. "I believe they are somehow tied to the Lassians."

"What?" Halfar yelled. His face tightened with anger. He didn't know why, though. Something about it rang true, yet he couldn't bring himself to accept it. Not right away. "State your reason!"

"Tell me. Do you know the exact coordinates of Lassa?"

Lord Pondur's head tilted down while his gaze stayed on Halfar. "Or New Lassa, for that matter?"

"No one does, for good reason."

"Hmm?" Lord Kraznan brought out his leather fan. "Where did the Lassians come from?" He waved it slowly, creating a soft breeze for himself.

"We never established their location. They only ever had gate codes." Emperor Calabra frowned. "Lassa always traded via the galactic highways. Shipments did not come directly to or from them."

"That's fine," Halfar spat. "My question remains. How does Lassa figure into the location of our new enemy?"

"Because analysis of their stardust residue matches that of Lassians." Lord Pondur replied.

"Their… stardust… what?" Halfar raised a quarter from his seat, leaning forward. Kur eased him back down.

The other leaders looked over at Lord Pondur, confused. He reached for his drink and took a sip before setting it down.

"Surely you've heard the genetic makeup of all species contains a certain amount of stardust the distinguishes their place in the universe." When no one responded, he continued. "Lord Graggor has worked with the finest scientists in the galaxy and together created a DNA map of the known regions, along with the outskirts. The samples from the enemy spoils and those of Lassians are of the same arena, though many light years apart."

"So, they are of two solar systems that are possibly next to each other?" Emperor Calabra stated. "If that is the case, would they have not encountered each other at some point?"

That made Halfar and his generals perk up. The rage he felt ebbed, replaced by a feeling of dread and betrayal. Not from Chardon. He knew there was no way his mate had such knowledge. The other leaders eyed each other with knowing stares. Halfar sat against the back of his chair and crossed his arms.

"Someone needs to explain themselves soon."

The ruler of Yaos took a bite of the cured meat he snagged from a nearby platter. "In the meantime," he didn't finish.

"We have to work with the information at hand." Kur set his forearms on the table. "The enemy is relentless. Powerful," he said with visible anger. "Maybe even as much as we are. And I don't mean only Azrom. All of us."

"Hence our little alliance," Lord Pondur added. He cocked his head, addressing Emperor Calabra and the ruler of Yaos. "Want to join?"

Lead by example

Weather conjured up many hells on a planet, and Barrima took the prize for having all of them at once. Chardon stood on the observation deck of the Azrom armada ship borrowed last minute. Beside him, Halfar stood akimbo, staring down at the surface. Master Adan and his entourage were being held in the cargo bay until the ship landed.

Chardon's fury had not subsided from the Barrima leader's unforgivable scheme that lured the enemy to New Lassa. Luckily, the short-lived battle, thanks to Ganna adding a weapons system, didn't do much damage to the surface. As Regent, obligated to address their plight, he now felt frustrated at their home world.

From the ship's position, they saw most of the landscape. The devastation spread everywhere. No area left untouched. Across the planet, variations of the sky signaled the merciless assault on the regions below: Arctic, volcanic, tropic, and arid. It ran the gambit.

"What a mess." Halfar's brow furrowed. "Those climate stations are indeed broken."

"The surface is basically ruined." Chardon tilted his head down at the main palace and its surrounding area. He watched a small tornado pull a creature clinging to the rocks up into the air. "How does one even maneuver such a terrain?"

In answer to his question, a line of figures tethered together made their way dressed head to toe in heavy, drab garb to the palace. Their slow and steady progress lessened the power of the wind. They were the lucky ones. The volcanic region had no one traveling outside for good reason. Lava flowed, snaking along the roads, creating deep crevices.

"What do you think?" Chardon turned to Halfar. "Can it be repaired?"

"Given the resources and time permitted, of course." He uncrossed his arms. "I wouldn't make it easy for them." He gave Chardon a sinister stare. "They need to prove their worth."

"That's my plan to begin with. Their current position is their own fault."

"Are you going to plead their case with Folza?" Halfar's angry tone resonated.

"Absolutely not!" Thinking of the ambush against their daughter rekindled his rage. "They will pay for that. Once Folza is done with them, it's our turn."

Halfar smirked, crossing his arms again. The scenery closed in as the ship made its descent towards the palace landing pad. A corridor made of transparent, hardened material connected the dock to a pathway behind the palace. Sharp black rocks and rough surface blocked the wind on that side, making travel considerably safer.

The dock workers went about doing their checks once the ship landed while securing the clamps. Waiting at the ramp entrance, Chardon glanced behind him at Master Adan's group being led forward. Their anxiety filled faces gave him pleasure. When the ramp opened, everyone marched down, Halfar in the lead until they reached the bottom. Master Adan took over the rest of the way.

No one spoke. Heavy tension blanketed the procession. Two guards at the back entrance went into defensive stances with weapons drawn. Long-barreled projectile rifles instead of phasers hung from their shoulder straps. As the group got closer, the one on the left called out.

"What's going on? Are you being held hostage?"

The other raised his weapon higher.

"Did the mission fail?" His body tensed, eyes narrowing. "I will not condone being a slave. No matter what you say, we will fight."

His words surprised Chardon. That wasn't the situation at all. Then he remembered Master Adan's way of thinking. *So, it also spreads to his people.* He breathed in slowly, exhaling after a few seconds. Master Adan had both hands up, signaling an okay.

"Calm down." Adan stopped a few yards from them. "No one is being enslaved."

"More like punished," Ryben said.

Their expressions went stricken with despair. Adan sighed and gave Ryben a backhanded slap in the chest. "Don't make this any worse." He gestured to the guards to lower their weapons. Seconds went past before they reluctantly complied, the rifles still clutched tight in downward positions. "We made an error, is all. If you allow us to pass, I can explain it to everyone."

In the sky above the palace, the modified ship, used for the Barriman's failed coup, cruised made its way to a dock station further out. They would have to trek the dangerous terrain. The two guards looked up, frowning. The first one averted his gaze, landing on the back of the large group. His eyes widened in awe.

Two manbeasts, two energy users, two warriors, and two scientists stood like a barrier, blocking anyone from returning to the ship, like living shields. The manbeasts' intimidating size and demeanor made him step back. The other gripped his weapon tighter.

"I ordered you to stand down!" Adan lost his patience. Startled, the two guards snapped to attention, embarrassed. "We don't have time for this."

"Yes, sir! We're sorry, sir!" Together, they punched in the code on either side of the entry and the doors opened. "Welcome home, Master Adan."

Halfar slowed his pace to walk next to Chardon.

No matter where he roamed, the former ruler stood out. Chardon suppressed a grin.

"What do you think?" Halfar whispered, leaning close.

"That their desperation is warranted. Their remedy, less to be desired."

They entered the dark cavernous opening that went pitch black when the doors closed behind them. The group halted, unable to see in front of them. Flickers of amber twinkled in rows on each side, dimly lighting the corridor ahead. Chardon dared not make a sound, fearing an echo. To his surprise, when the Barrimans moved forward, their boot strikes were barely audible.

The thicker air explained the reason for the dull acoustics. He looked back at the Lassian scientists, their data recorders already out. They had to make thorough reports for Ganna when they returned home.

Each approach of a dark hallway triggered the motion sensor lights as the group maneuvered around for nearly twenty minutes before coming to giant doors half the size of Razznian specs, yet no less impressive. Adan presented a key card to the reader on the side panel, and the doors slid open, making a few crumbly noises. Chardon watched their motion, noticing corrosion on the edges.

They needed maintenance.

A massive hall with an equally large table in its center sat on the other side of the doors. The meeting place of old for clients and dignitaries had seen better days. Chardon saw the lack of debris tell the story of recent, rushed cleaning.

Scattered around the table were ten Barrimans, looking dour. The young man on the right end more than the others. Adan went to him and slapped a hand on his shoulders. The young man looked up at him, crestfallen.

"It's okay, Emar." Adan tried to assure him. "I don't fault you for this. You did the best you could, and I am grateful." He turned to Chardon. "This is our head of communications, Emar."

"You may think he did nothing wrong, but I differ in that opinion." Halfar's expression darkened. "Your sloppy work put MY child in harm's way."

Emar stared in fear at Halfar, then at Adan, who wouldn't meet his eyes. Adan patted his shoulder before moving to the other side of the table.

"Please, everyone, sit. I know this is unexpected. Let me explain."

A soldier came in and went up to Ryben. "I got food and drinks coming, sir." He scanned the room, his face struggling to stay neutral.

"Good. Thanks."

"We gonna' be okay, sir?" The soldier's fingers twitched at the end tip of his rifle.

"Absolutely." Ryben gave him an underhanded wave. "Get going."

Chardon felt envious. The Barrimans' were clearly on the same page. He wished his own race united the same way.

Guess I should take them more seriously.

Despite being able to defend themselves, the planet's population had no military force. Their soldiers were volunteers brought together by necessity. Chardon could only imagine the number of uninvited guests they encountered looking to salvage parts in the many graveyards scattered across the continents. And now they have a genuine threat. Chardon knew with certainty the enemy would come back.

While Adan explained the situation to his people, Chardon locked eyes with Halfar.

Are you on board with my agenda?

Chardon asked telepathically.

It's a tall feat, bringing different armies together to fight as one. He responded. *You should know that better than anyone.*

All the more reason I am asking.

Halfar averted his stare for a moment, watching the Barrimans' crushed reaction to their leader's news.

Yes, I will assist you. I really don't know why you asked.

You were going to do it regardless.

Chardon cast out matter of fact.

Halfar didn't answer right away. Then he turned to him.

I was Supreme ruler of Azrom for nearly three hundred years. You need me.

Chardon looked away. He knew he lacked experience as a leader, his expertise minimal. Barrima needed protection. More than what it had. The other worlds under his regency required some coaxing to unite under a New Lassa banner.

Adan had finished his spiel and brought his attention to Chardon. He stood with a smug expression, as if he had won a prize.

"What say you, Regent Chardon? Will New Lassa help us get back on our feet?"

"As long as you don't get in my way, I will." Chardon leaned forward on the table. "First things, first. I am assigning a battle group here."

"We can do our own fighting." His expression suddenly shifted. "Well, so long as those things don't come back."

"They will." Halfar spat. "From what I've seen of your skills, they would annihilate you within days."

"Second," Chardon resumed. "You will build five ships to my lead engineer's specifications."

"We don't have the resources." Adan arms spread wide.

Chardon's eyes narrowed. "They will be provided. How else would you complete the task?"

Adan lowered his arms, embarrassed at his outburst. His people averted their eyes, feeling the same.

"We will stay here for the next two monthly cycles to fully assess the planet. We appreciate your hospitality."

It was not a request. Halfar had taught him that decades ago. As a leader, one must convey authority and demand compliance. Chardon felt unsure of his delivery. He waited for a response. Adan seemed miffed.

"Of course." Adan gave a slight bow of his head. "We are privileged to have you."

The food and drinks arrived, carried in every which way by soldiers and non-combatants. They had jugs stuffed under their arms while balancing multiple platters in their hands. Some had large trays hefted above their heads. It struck Chardon and Halfar in that instant. There are no servants on Barrima. Everyone pulled their own weight.

A sense of awkward shame at their obvious superiority made them squirm in their seats. Chardon saw the rest of the Lassians in the room do the same. He had been called pampered and sheltered many times. Looking back, he realized every planet he had encountered had classes of servitude. This was the first time he witnessed a planet without one.

Anger filled him. He understood that other planets, including his own, would not change. *I need to do better!* The fate and wellbeing of the Lassian servants never crossed his mind. The assumption they would mindlessly continue to serve him made him gag.

He clamped his hand over his mouth. Halfar and Adan stared at him with concern.

"Are you alright, Regent Chardon?" He looked around at the food being set on the table. "Is the smell of our food making you sick?"

Horrified, Chardon removed his hand and waved it frantically. "No, not at all." Halfar placed a hand on his back. "I'm fine. Actually, a bit hungry."

"Oh? Well, dig in." Adan sat down in the middle of the row. "What do you want first? We'll get it passed down to you."

Chardon watched platters and jugs move down and across the table with practiced ease. A platter of meats and vegetables came his way, and he humbly took it. Getting what he wanted, he handed it to Halfar. To his surprise, he showed no disdain or irritation at having to serve himself. The food and drink moved on until everyone had their portions.

Adan made eye contact with him.

Seeing New Lassa solidified his thoughts regarding Sestis and her race. To the Barrimans, Lassians were entitled weaklings with no actual status in the galaxy that had the audacity to look down on others.

Maybe he's not wrong with that assessment. Chardon took a chunk of cooked vegetable resembling and smelling like Earth's green peppers and shoved it in his mouth. As he chewed, the weight of the situation blanketed him. He couldn't be ruthless like Halfar or Lord Pondur, but he would step up his game.

No one will call me weak ever again.

⸏

Soft glowing hover lamps floated above while four guards escorted the Lassians and Halfar to accommodations in a separate wing of the palace. The vast corridors puzzled Halfar. They were large enough for a battle cruiser to fit easily with a foot or more clearing space. His own assessment of the planet and its population confirmed Azrom would have taken a pass on conquest. Now, he saw the benefit of having Barrima as an asset. And they would take advantage as part of the alliance.

He monitored Chardon, feeling their desperation of acknowledgement as a leader. The elders and Sestis were to blame for his lack of skills. Instead of chastising him for doing wrong, they should have guided him better. His own journey to the throne came about through rage and bloodshed.

I have to get him up to speed.

The meeting with the other rulers made it clear. To combat the current and forthcoming threats, they had to become a united front. Without turning New Lassa into a superpower.

That cannot happen.

Extra Muscle

When Kur and Rass went over the footage from the alliance battles, the thought of grabbing one of the enemy's soldiers as a hostage became a bad idea. The way they made sure none of their soldiers' bodies or weapons were left behind gave them a clue how they would react. They would hunt their own to the ends of the galaxy to retrieve them.

"There has to be a way to communicate with these monsters." Kur towered over the round, raised platform with the information chip in its center displaying the images. "I get the silent treatment thing, but at some point, a dialogue needs to happen."

Where the platform reached Kur's waist, it came to right below Rass' chest. He leaned comfortably over the edge, his forearms resting on its surface. No one came to disturb them in the small room used for strategic consultation.

"I agree. Since they refuse, we will speak with our might. Force them to let us know their agenda." Rass let out a loud sigh. "Rather than testing the five systems to see who's the strongest or weakest."

"This isn't so much a war, but a battle of power." Kur scratched the side of his head, tangling the hair in that one spot. "Which is evident when they attacked the Dreridians."

"Without checking first. I think they got a whiff of their importance and figured, why not."

"Asinine. That is not a strategy."

"I have my plan already in mind. What's yours?" He removed one hand from his crossed arms and held it up.

"And please don't say to bring carnage."

Rass gave him a side glare, his lips thinned defensively. "I have a real battle plan. How dare you insult me." He slid his arms off until only his hands gripped the edge. "And maybe one element of assurance."

Kur's brow raised in amusement. Something resembling a pout crossed Rass' face, causing him to go speechless. His groin tightened as warmth flushed his body. An Earth term popped up in his head: Cute. The grip tightened on his biceps, nails digging into the fabric of his tunic sleeves. Rass' expression darkened.

"Restrain yourself, you deviant! We have no time for that!"

Kur smirked. "You say that." He tilted his head upward. "If we start now, you won't deny me. We have plenty of time to make our meeting with the Supreme ruler."

With hooded eyes, Rass stared at him for a second, then stopped the feed on the platform. The image froze on one of the large cannons firing red tendrils. He tapped the icon on the surface to close it. The image disappeared, and he removed the information chip.

"I'm leaving." Rass placed the chip in the storage container underneath the platform's edge where other chips lay enclosed. "Let's go."

Disappointed, Kur reluctantly unfolded his arms and followed his mate out of the room. His leggings constricted around his pelvis to accommodate the rising bulge he failed to silently talk down. At one point, Rass turned his head back and took a glance. Kur tried not to show his smugness. They made a slight detour that sent them towards their living quarters.

I win. Kur smirked.

Romnus waited with his entourage in the hidden room behind the throne. Batis sat sprawled out in the seat on the left end, his legs extended with boots on the table. He leaned back, forcing the chair to tilt at an angle while twirling one of his daggers. Biandra sat silently beside Romnus on the other end, her hands hidden within the dangling folds of her robe sleeves. The Master at Arms took position on the left, a few seats from Batis. The right side of the table lay empty, awaiting his generals to arrive.

They're late. Romnus curbed his annoyance. He could hear their approach. Ten minutes was not egregious. He merely expected their usual promptness.

The two generals came barreling into the room in a huff, visibly taxed from hurrying. Rass seemed irritated while Kur appeared put off for even being there.

"I told you we would be late!" Rass chastised Kur. "This is all your fault!"

"You could have said no," Kur replied slyly.

"Whatever this is," Romnus' eyes narrowed with the downward tilt of his head. "Save it." The two halted at the end of the table. They immediately bowed. "Sit."

They took the middle seats on the right side of Romnus. Batis gave them a playful smile. His stare averted to Romnus, causing him to flinch in surprise. Removing his boots from the table, he sat properly in his seat. The Master at Arms tsked.

"Are you all ready?" Romnus asked angrily. "Are all your reports in order? Or is this a session where you waste my time?"

"Not at all," Batis replied. "We have plans ready,"

"You will be pleased with our decisions," the Master at Arms added.

"I also have a proposal, if you would hear it." Rass got comfortable in his seat.

"Implementations are at your discretion. I only want to see victorious results," Romnus said.

"That's what Halfar would always say," Kur grunted.

The room went silent. Romnus' murderous side glare gave everyone pause. It dissolved to a lack of interest, and he looked down at his hands lying flat on the table. Batis cocked his head.

"I shouldn't be angry about that." Romnus linked his fingers. "He rightfully demanded it. Halfar also led us into senseless wars that hurt our people more than the planets we conquered."

The Master at Arms pulled a tablet from inside his long coat and tossed it on the table. He straightened it before him and tapped the screen, bringing it to life.

"We are prepared to engage on three fronts. Defensive and offensive, of course, but we also need to establish communication whether its hostile or not."

"While they refused to talk to us before, I am certain they will now," Batis said.

"I am requesting one thousand armada ships for this fight." The Master at Arms looked over at the two generals. "Is that acceptable?"

"The question should be, is that enough?" Kur leaned back in his chair. "We will grant the request." He turned to Rass. "Agreed?"

"You said three fronts. How are these ships to be divided?" Rass pointed to the tablet. "Do you have an actual breakdown?"

"It will depend on which forces are being dispatched. If we use our elite soldiers, the defensive part will not need as many ships."

Rass frowned. "That is correct." He addressed Batis. "What are your plans in this regard?"

"Not to sound like a monster, but I was going to allot only mid-tier soldiers for the task. Keep our elite at a minimum." Batis watched everyone's expression turn sour. "I have a feeling what your proposal entails, and that is all well and good, as long as the numbers are low."

Romnus let out a loud sigh and slumped against the back of his chair. He did not want another war. The enemy had other ideas. Batis had been on many battle campaigns before being assigned to the royal guard as a reward. The generals were ruthless and spread carnage wherever they went. The Master at Arms' expertise in strategy and formation made Azrom victorious at every turn.

These people I trust.

He saw Biandra's hands clenched in her lap. Her face tightened, forming creases at the corner of her eyes. They smoldered with resentment.

"Are you not in agreement?" Romnus asked her.

Startled, she looked up, her gaze landing on the others in the room.

"I don't know what you mean, my lord. I am no tactician and have no say in how Azrom goes to battle."

Batis' expression turned ugly. Kur and Rass stared at her with what she interpreted as anger.

"That is not true!" Batis slammed a fist on the table. "You know as well as I do."

"Biandra," Romnus said her name calmly. "Do you agree?"

She unclenched her hands and set them on the table's edge.

"Although I am offended by the idea, it is the correct move. Halfar did that once." Her gaze darkened. "Our lack of numbers and skills for victory resulted in an entire battalion being wiped out."

Batis went pale. "I did not know that was the reason." He turned to the generals. "Did you know?" he asked angrily.

Kur crossed his arms in defense. He seemed to contemplate hard. Rass looked upwards to the side, appearing to do the same. They both finally turned their attention to Biandra.

"It was an unfortunate decision on Halfar's part," Kur answered. "Most of the elite forces were sent elsewhere for quick resolution."

"We assigned an elite soldier to each battalion, thinking it would be enough." Rass bowed his head to Biandra. "You were one of them. I feel deeply about that outcome."

"I'll alter my original plan." Batis locked eyes with her. "Will you assist in my decision?"

Biandra nodded, sliding her hands back into her lap. Romnus realized what the moment meant. They were going to avert war. Not a mere fight, but nothing that would warrant a large part of their forces to be dispatched. One thousand ships. Less than a quarter of a percent of the Azrom armada.

"Let's hear the rest of these plans of yours," he addressed them all.

The meeting resumed uninterrupted as Romnus sat mulling over his reign.

Romnus adjourned the meeting after two hours of heated arguments. The whole mid-level assignment issue irked him. Still part of Batis' plan, it would need serious over-haul. Rass hoped Biandra reeled him in. He stood and waited for the Master at Arms to leave before following. With all their cards laid out, Rass decided to act fast on his agenda.

"Are you frustrated?" Kur asked, coming up close behind him.

Rass tensed.

I forgot he was there! He relaxed and kept walking, not slowing his pace.

"More determined."

"Romnus said it was at our discretion. Are you really going where I think you are?"

"This solves the greater problem. We need elite soldiers," Rass explained.

"And the only ones Azrom deems as expendable are them." Rass halted at Kur's venomous tone. His face scrunched, baring teeth. "We have done wrong by that clan. They have no obligation to help us."

"They are of Azrom like any other." Rass turned his head towards him. "Expendable as they may be, they always come back unscathed."

The two generals continued walking. Royals nodded to them as they passed, a few greeting them in the usual terse manner. They headed outside to the transport bay and commissioned one for the journey to the other side of the planet.

Streams of grey smoke from the village ahead snaked up to the sky. The tops of houses became visible amid the dense forest surrounding it as the transport got closer. Two sentries stood on either side of the entrance, their eight-foot-tall frames covered in black robes over ribbed, dark blue body suits. Wild black hair sprouted from their heads down past their shoulders. Their very demeanor instilled fear.

Kur tried to ease his nerves. His stature was nothing to sneeze at, yet the barbarian clan made him feel small, weak. He heard Rass grunt in amusement at his plight. The sentries waited for the transport to stop fifty yards away and the two generals to get out before addressing them.

"What business does Azrom's generals have this day?" The one on the left asked.

"Speak so that we may know your intentions and act accordingly," the other said.

"This is an official visit," Rass replied. "We request the leader and his commanders to gather for a meeting in the common hall."

The sentries glanced at each other. Kur knew that look. They understood what it meant. The rumors had spread. Their clan would be out of the loop. Extending one arm toward the entrance, they gestured for them to proceed. As Kur and Rass stepped over the threshold of the clan's territory, Kur saw the first sentry tap behind his ear and speak. *When did they get those?* Ahead of him, he watched another clansman get up from a stoop, nodding with one hand on his ear, then made a mad dash to the center of the village.

Mountains of clansmen doing daily chores towered over the two, not giving them much attention. Kur kept close to Rass. A few young ones and runts like Rass, standing at barely six feet, ran around the area. A clanswoman lumbered across the road carrying a basket full of produce the size of a small vehicle. She glanced down at Kur and smirked.

I'm only a foot shorter! Give or take.

He couldn't fathom mating with a brute like her. She would break his delicate bones. Rass gave him a haughty stare before glaring at the behemoth. A menacing electric vibe between them surprised Kur. Rass basically told her with one stare to back off.

"Be reasonable, my beloved," Kur laughed. "I would not stray from you for that."

"It's not you I am concerned with." Rass broke his gaze.

True. He had no faith in his ability to fight her off if she desired him.

Commotion at the commons let them know the clan council had gathered. A young soldier, a teenager by clan standards, an inch taller than Kur, came to escort them. Inside the hall sat ten members at a long hand carved wooden table. Thick ornate legs nearly the width of Kur's torso handled its massive size. He marveled at the craftsmanship.

The leader and his mate sat in the center with his personal entourage of leaders on his right and his commanders on the left. Rass' father, Abras, sat third in. No recognition registered on Commander Abras' face. Kur remembered him saying official business. There would be no joyful greetings until after the meeting. The leader's stern expression darkened the mood.

As if we came to declare war on them.

Kur moved forward towards the two seats set in the middle of the room before the council. Rass went ahead, sitting in the chair closest to his father's position. Which left Kur staring directly at the leader. He had never personally talked to them. Only relaying their orders via messenger.

"You want us to fight." The leader's voice boomed, sending shivers down Kur's spine.

"I am sure you have heard from Commander Abras the state we are in," Rass said.

"This enemy. They are a menace." The head of resources sitting second from the leader's mate said. "Tough. Merciless."

"You can defeat them with ease." Rass stared him down.

"Is that your take, Commander Abras?" The head of resources asked.

A long pause followed. Kur sat nervously, meeting Rass' concerned stare.

"No." Rass' father replied bluntly.

Rass sat stunned. Kur did not voice his agreement of the response. He had a feeling the Commander would see it that way.

"But, you…" Rass sputtered.

Commander Abras raised one hand to stop him from speaking. Another commander spoke.

"Our track record may be flawless. That does not mean we are invincible." Her voice boomed equally yet had a soothing tone. "We are your best choice."

"How many?" The leader asked his commanders.

Kur heard a pattern from the whispers in the room and how the council responded. The females spoke fluently, almost in full sentences, whereas the males went with one or two words, sharp and to the point. Interesting.

"To conquer," replied the first commander next to Abras.

When Azrom needed brute force to take control of an entire system to snatch one or more planets, they sent out three ships with one thousand clansmen aboard each. For them to say it would take that much meant Rass, and he had underestimated the situation.

Kur remembered hearing Talas always guaranteeing no casualties at every battle. He kept his word to this day.

Can I be just as bold? To ensure such a thing?

He hung his head with eyes closed as he pondered what to do. The room went silent. He could feel Rass' unease. Opening his eyes, he stared the leader down.

"Then we conquer and drive them back to where they came from. I will not allow one death from your clan."

Startled gasps filled the air. Rass turned to him, eyes wide in horror.

What are you saying?

His voice invaded Kur's mind like a knife. The rare occurrence of telepathy usually required mutual consent.

"I'm sorry," Rass whispered, still enraged. He grabbed hold of Kur's sleeve. "But you can't say something like that on Azrom and mean it."

"You will ensure our victory and safe return?" The female commander asked.

"I will." Kur clenched one hand. "I'm tired of losing our people to battles we could have easily won if we weren't so…" Kur struggled to say what he wanted.

"Arrogant." The leader boomed. His voice reverberated, causing a soft ringing in Kur's ears.

"This time, we will let you do what is required and back you with Azrom's might."

"As you shall." The leader stood, prompting the others to do the same. "We are done."

The council dispersed, and with them, the staunch atmosphere. Suddenly, a festive mood took over. Food and drinks flooded the common hall and the noise decibel rose. Commander Abras spoke briefly with the leader outside the threshold, then turned back towards Rass.

"Are you well?" He asked his child, yet his eyes narrowed at Kur.

"I am, yes." Rass seemed to fidget. He too glanced at Kur. "Keeping my mate from doing anything rash has its challenges."

"Is that so?"

Kur felt his body heat with anger. How insulting! Abras' hand slammed down on his left shoulder, the weight and force making him wince in pain. He endured it, looking stubbornly up at the massive beast.

"Be more careful." A calm underlying an authoritative tone. Kur understood. He removed his hand and sat at one of the nearby long tables. "Come. Drink."

Rass slid onto the bench opposite his father. Kur joined him. A clansman slammed three giant mugs down before them, their content sloshing over the rims to fleck droplets everywhere. Kur glanced up and saw the basket hauler from earlier. She gave a sinister grin, not paying Rass' wrathful glare any mind.

"I told you I have no interest in others," Kur said to Rass as the female left. "Why do you try to intimidate every being who looks my way?"

"And you don't do the same?" Rass snapped.

"No," Kur replied sweetly. "Because there's no need. All of Azrom knows I would cut down anyone who dared."

Rass rolled his eyes upwards in exasperation. His father lifted his mug, an irritated expression locked on Kur. The generals used both hands to raise their mugs, the circumference twice the size of them. They carefully tipped the wide brims as big as their heads to their lips and captured as much as they could while letting the rest dribble down the sides of their chin and onto the fronts of their tunics.

Lack of Trust

The noise from Folzian dock workers going about their tasks ground on Chardon's senses. Compressed air and spent exhaust hissing nearly drowned out everything else. She looked around at the massive hangar where the Barrimans' ship and hers sat ready for boarding. Armed guards waited at each ramp to ensure both races left without issue.

Her gaze came back to the group before her. The female leader and her two aides stood patiently, a soft peach glow emanating from their bodies. *They seem happy.* Chardon knew a change in their color signaled a warning.

Chardon scrolled through the document on the tablet the Folzian leader handed to her on arrival. The form listed sanctions and other legalities associated with taking responsibility for the Barriman prisoners. Coming to the end of the document, she exhaled softly.

Loose strands of hair fell forward as she stared at it. The wide sleeves of her white robe, with a sleeveless sky-blue overlay, brushed against its sides. From an inside pocket, she took out a tiny electronic square and placed it on the tablet's data platform. A ping sounded when it connected. On the bottom of the screen, the Lassian emblem, newly revised, attached to the signature line.

Chardon tried not to crane her neck when she handed the tablet back. The leader, standing a foot taller, turned to give it to an assistant behind her.

"Thank you, Regent Chardon, for your cooperation in this matter. Please keep better vigilance over your charges."

Her condescending smile had Chardon suppress the urge to snap back with a few harsh words. Beside her, Lassa's head of science placed a hand on her back. She understood what he conveyed with the gesture. Steady. *I know!* Chardon chastised herself. Having an outburst would negate her competence as a leader.

"No, thank you for not having them executed. I am forever grateful."

"Of course." The leader beamed with eyes shut and lips pressed thin.

Behind the trio, a lift arrived. The doors slid open to reveal the Barrimans surrounded by more armed guards escorting them out. Commander Veris, second in command under Ryben, looked dejected. He held his head low, not taking stock of the area. His men acted similar, ashamed.

As you should be.

"I leave you then." The leader bowed her head, then raised it with a smile. "I trust you to depart in a timely manner. My guards will assist. Good journey, Regent Chardon."

The trio left the hangar via the same lift, leaving Chardon with the Barrimans. She took a deep breath, calming herself before addressing Veris.

"Whatever you have to say for yourself, I don't care. You will do as I ask. Is that clear?"

"Of course, Regent Chardon." Veris' tone equaled his defeat.

"Your task is to head for Razzna and negotiate raw materials for ship builds. We uploaded the details to your ship's database. I expect a successful outcome."

This time, Veris raised his head in surprise. His men looked around at each other dubiously.

"You're entrusting us to negotiate with Razzna?"

"Are you planning to betray me?"

Horror crossed his face. "No! That is not what I meant." He raised his hands in defense. "We will do your bidding,"

They all dropped to one knee and bowed their heads.

Chardon's mouth twitched in disgust. She didn't like that sort of gesture. On Azrom and the other powerful races, it was acceptable because of royalty. She was none of those things.

"Get up!" She snapped. "Get on your ship and leave at once. I want a report of your arrival on Razzna and when you are done with your task."

She watched them rise to their feet and scramble towards their ship.

"Well, at least they are obedient and raring to go," the head of science laughed.

"You better hurry and get on board with them before they take off."

"Yes, you forgot to mention that to them."

Chardon's eyes widened with fear. Then she sighed, her shoulders slumped. The head of science patted her on the back.

"No worries. I will explain it to them." He clasped his hands together and gestured towards Chardon. "Safe journey home, leader."

She waited for him to reach the top of the ramp; it retracting as he went until he stepped inside, and the hatch sealed. Her whole being became exhausted. As if she had been in a mini battle. Chardon went up the ramp of her ship and headed straight for the main cabin.

"This is ridiculous."

⸜⸝

The dead of night on New Lassa came with the absence of sound, heightening the slightest noise. Kelin crouched further down into a thicket of brush near a clearing deep in the forest. He slowed his breathing and reduced his presence. He had done this a few times over the decades, getting better with each instance. Moonlight shed a soft glow on the open space ahead.

Within minutes, he heard the familiar sound of Talas creeping silently through the foliage, then enter the clearing.

Despite the chill in the air, he only wore a thin leather waistcoat over a white tunic, dark leggings, and boots. His solemn expression hid the real reason for it. Both hands held a longsword, identical in design, forged together of equal weight. Talas swung them once in full rotation, then began combat maneuvers.

Kelin watched Talas handle each strike with ease, knowing any enemy on the other end would meet their demise. Such precision. He almost appeared to dance the way his body transitioned between moves. Thirty minutes went by before perspiration beaded his brow. A sadness filled Kelin. This secret he must keep at all costs.

Dual sword wielding, a forbidden art locked deep in the warrior soul, would only unleash when the end of the fighter's life became imminent. A last-ditch effort to kill the enemy without prejudice. Kelin could count on both hands how many times it had happened in the past.

Yet, Talas can still do so with no limits.

He felt the difference in his mate from the start. The unconscious confidence beneath his over-the-top airs. Talas backed up every claim. That part turned many of their people off. Talas, the walking contradiction, perfect with visible flaws.

After an hour of intense movements, Talas finished his training session by swinging both swords into neutral down positions at his sides. He sniffed hard, tilting his head back, as he breathed in the cool air before exhaling slowly, lowering his head. With a deep sigh, he sheathed the weapons in the slits on the back of his jacket where they crossed, forming an X.

Kelin flinched at the sorrow mixed with anger on Talas' face as he turned to head back home. Seeing it over time never got better. He waited in hiding for another ten minutes, collecting his thoughts while making sure Talas traveled a suitable distance. His knees ached as he stood, the sensation traveling to his lower back. He stretched his body backwards, raising both arms up to the sky. Shaking off the stiffness, he walked along the narrow trail leading to the village.

A rustling sound, barely audible, made him pause. He scanned the entire perimeter, concentrating on any sound. Hearing nothing, he resumed walking, but remained leery of what may be lurking. For all he knew, it could be a forest creature searching for food. He didn't think so. Someone else had been watching Talas.

You have to be more careful, my love.

~

Wet leaves covered in trapped moisture, slick with their natural oils, made Ganna lose her footing as she tried to sneak off from her position on the other side of the clearing where Talas trained. She had created a shield to eliminate her essence, hence able to bring a portable chair that folded into a four inch by two-foot panel. No reason to crouch in the elements like Kelin.

She got to her knees and wiped her hands off on the front of her now filthy robe. The moisture seeped through, making her knees and feet soaked. *Disgusting!* Up ahead, she saw Kelin stop and look around. Ganna ducked her head, waiting for him to move on. When he did, she stayed put for a few minutes before grabbing the panel and used it to stand.

Talas. A problem that kept arising. She had tried numerous times to tether him to the locked restraint embedded in every warrior. It never took. There was a valid explanation. One that meant she could no longer hide the truth. *Not yet. I need a little more time.* Another session to try again. If that didn't work, she had no choice. She made her way back to the lab.

Kelin's hunch paid off as he watched Ganna emerge from the forest. He stood on the outskirts, hidden in the dark shrubs. Ahead of him sat the vast fields of tall yellow grass. Even in the dim moonlight, he could see her dire expression, lips pursed thin. It signified how much she knew. Kelin clenched both hands at his sides. One more reason not to trust her. Talas had nearly reached home, so he walked a bit faster once Ganna had gone far enough not to spot him.

⌒

Multiple red eyes from rows of battle ships blending with the darkness greeted the Barriman ship upon its entry into Razznian space. Veris felt his insides churn with dread. The communication board lit up as the tech patched it through the system. An image of a Razznian soldier appeared on the main screen.

"State your reasons or be eaten for payment," the guttural Razznian voice demanded.

"At least they're upfront about it," the communications tech said.

Veris cleared his throat and motioned for him to open the channel.

"I am commander Veris of Planet Barrima. My reason is by request of Regent Chardon of New Lassa."

The audio feed went silent. New Lassa's head of science stepped forward.

"As the head of science for Regent Chardon, I can confirm the request."

The feed lit up again, showing the Razznian hiss.

"Permission to land near the palace is granted."

"That is most gracious of you." The head of science bowed. Veris realized he should do the same a few seconds after. The feed cut out. They both stood straight. "Most are not permitted to dock near the palace. Not even the heads of their military."

"In other words, if they don't like us…" Veris trailed off.

"Correct. We state our case and hope for the best. They trust Chardon, but not necessarily you or your race."

The glowing red eyes parted before them, and a guiding strip of lights formed towards the planet's surface. After breaching the clouds, the palace loomed ahead. Veris took a sharp breath at the unexpected magnificence of its structure.

"They're a reptilian race, right?" He asked the head of science.

"They have visions of grandeur."

Veris noticed the giant doors on approach. He gave the head of science a puzzling stare.

Ten armed guards waited at the end of the ramp when they landed. Veris could see the bloodlust in their beady eyes. *They can't wait for us to slip up and get a free meal.*

"This way," the one in the rear said. They turned around, putting themselves in the lead. The rest spread out around Veris and the others. The head of science walked beside him. "Any weapons drawn will be considered a hostile act towards our empire."

"We are unarmed." Veris said proudly.

"You lack common sense."

The insult stung Veris. He looked over at the head of science, who shrugged. *Of course, he doesn't need a weapon.* He already was one, being an energy user. They entered the palace and Veris once again marveled at the sheer size. The lift ride jarred his senses, going up then sideways. After what seemed like an eternity, it finally stopped, and the doors opened.

Lord Kraznan sat at the end of the long hall on a throne of dark marble carved with a crude design fit for a reptile king. His large alligator-like form filled the seat, his thick tail swishing along the side. He held a leather fan stiffened by chemicals that he used to cool his face. Scholars, military leaders, and servants slithered about doing tasks. The guards led Veris and his group a few feet from the bottom of the throne, bowed, then left.

Veris stared up at the Razznian Emperor and met his yellow eyes. The deep green slits appeared black, depending on how the light hit them.

"So you say Lord Chardon has sent you here?" He addressed Veris yet glanced at the head of science. "What reason do you come for?"

"My name is Veris of the Barriman…"

"Yesss," Lord Kraznan hissed as he cut him off. "The race of fools who made a deal with the enemy." He leaned forward, his eyes narrowing. "We lost ships and soldiers because of it."

"I…" Veris struggled to say anything more. He understood the emperor's reluctance to hear him out. Then he remembered the stare Regent Chardon gave him before leaving. Gathering his resolve, he met Lord Kraznan's gaze. "Regent Chardon has declared the alliance requires new ships. To make the core materials, we need raw resources. Razznian mines produce the finest ores."

Lord Kraznan's expression became whimsical. He snorted, as did his advisors standing nearby. One of them looked Veris over.

"You dare ask for favors after what your kind has done?" He turned to the head of science. "What are you Lassians thinking, bringing these miscreants into the fold?"

"Simple, really." The head of science tilted his head. "They want redemption and have promised to change their ways."

"Nonsense!" another advisor scoffed. "They will betray all of us the first chance they get."

"I assure you," Veris bowed his head. "That is not the case. We have seen the error in our ways. The enemy has no honor. They will come for us all in the end."

The first advisor raised a hand to stroke his chin, staring at Veris.

"How were you getting raw materials before? If you know of our ore, then it has been acquired at some point."

"Oh, we had to negotiate with the Dreridians, which included an up charge fee plus delivery."

Movement inside the hall seemed to halt. Lord Kraznan

sat back against his throne, a look of disdain on his face. The advisor dropped his hand.

"That would be close to a thirty-five percent markup from our costs. They are cheating us out of profits."

"That shouldn't surprise you," the other advisor said.

"This is why Regent Chardon has entrusted us to come directly." Veris spread his arms wide. "We wish to pay you fair pricing and eliminate third party dealings."

"It would also mean first in line for upgrades to your ships as part of the alliance." The head of science added as he produced a tablet from inside his robes. "This is their workmanship on one of the more advanced ships in the galaxy."

He brought up a holographic 3D image of the modified ship. The second advisor slithered closer, scrutinizing every angle. "Impressive."

"What say you, Lord Kraznan?" The head of science smiled. "Would you be willing to work with New Lassa and planet Barrima? For full profit shares?"

The gleam in the emperor's and his advisors' eyes gave Veris the answer he needed. A huge relief came over him. He did not want to die getting eaten. He had seen their variety of teeth and wanted no part in that. The head of science looked over at him and grinned.

The Dreridians won't be happy about this.

⌒

Dual screens on Ganna's work bench had similar images frozen in place. One from New Lassa's battle with the enemy on planet Andal displayed on the left. The much older one on the right appeared slightly grainy with multicolored striations. Ganna sat with her seat swiveled towards the door, her face crestfallen at the sight of Chardon and Jaron staring at the screen. Rage took over Jaron's shocked expression while her cousin merely looked deadpan at Ganna.

"What is that?" Jaron demanded as she approached, pointing at the older image. "Where did that come from?" Her yelling made Ganna flinch.

Chardon came forward and calmly said, "You better have an explanation for this. So help me, Ganna. I am in no mood for theatrics from you."

Ganna surprised them by giving them the nastiest glare she could muster. Chardon stepped back from her. Jaron got closer. The two women locked eyes, their hatred for each other on full display.

"Enough!" Chardon grabbed Jaron by the arm and pulled her away. "Tell us what's going on." Ganna huffed. "Right now." Chardon's chilling tone forced her to comply.

"Fine," Ganna replied through gritted teeth. "I didn't want to alarm anyone until I was sure. I guess there's no mistake now." She pointed to the second image. "This is a core memory from the time of Lassa before we took physical form."

Jaron gasped. Chardon's head reared back in surprise. He swiped a hand over his face and let it drop. "What do you mean?"

"Our original essence had no form. Yet we could communicate through emotion, color, and thought." She saw their astonishment. "These… things. They came to Lassa and ravished it. Wiping out most of the planet's resources."

"And with no bodies to combat them." Jaron's rage subsided for a moment. "We did nothing to stop it."

"They didn't even acknowledge our presence. Not knowing the lights floating around were sentient beings that they destroyed when firing their weapons at them."

Chardon's anger rose. "You kept this from us." Ganna frowned. "The moment you saw the enemy, you knew what they were and where they came from."

"Like I said, I had to be sure…"

"Stop lying!" Jaron erupted.

Ganna stood. "What would you have me do? I barely

found out a way to access these! We need more information. Our ancestors had the advantage of observing these monsters for years. I will not let us be wiped out because we didn't know!"

Jaron stared wide eyed at her, conflicted about what to do next. Chardon hung his head and breathed deep. To all their surprise, a voice from behind chimed up.

"That's fine and all." Talas stepped into the room. "But you should have at least given us a heads up on your theory." He stood next to Jaron. "I understand your reason. It just isn't valid at this point."

Jaron seemed to realize something. She crossed her arms. "Did you say years of observation? How long were they on Lassa terrorizing its surface?"

"From what I can tell from some of the core data, at least a decade."

Chardon seethed. Talas nodded.

"With no one to stop them, they took their time. Lassa had to rebuild somehow."

"Which meant we needed physical bodies to protect ourselves." Chardon said.

"I get it!" Jaron snapped. She gave Ganna a dirty look. "I still don't like that you kept it from us. We could have planned better and not had so many wounded."

"I didn't know about the red weapon. How could I?"

"Fair enough." Talas nodded at the screens. "How far have you gotten? Is there anything we can use now?"

"Not much. They had no reason to fight really except amongst themselves after awhile. They were cruel in their destruction, obliterating entire forests, killing nearly all the wildlife. Tapping the core for energy and leaving it half its size."

Ganna felt hatred creep inside her, and she forced herself to stifle it. No time for that. She looked over at the others and saw shock on their faces. *Oh no! They saw.*

Chardon cocked his head and grinned. "So, you do get

angry at the way things are. Maybe if everyone knew, we wouldn't be so upset by your actions."

"No," Talas said. "We would still be angry. Just more understanding."

"Speak for yourself!" Jaron pointed at the screens. "There has to be something to pull from those ancient cores. I will wait for a report." Jaron turned and left the room.

"Even if they only had infighting, these memories can shed some light on how they operate." Talas patted Chardon on the shoulder and left him with Ganna.

"Tell me there's a way to stop them." Chardon placed a hand on a nearby table and leaned on it. "That we can win against them."

"I'm not sure." Ganna slumped in her chair, suddenly feeling defeated. "They are worse than what these memories hold."

"Do they know who we are? What we were?"

The fear in Chardon's voice made Ganna perk up. She sat upright.

"No. I don't think they do."

"That means," Chardon smiled slyly. "We have an advantage, unlike the others."

"Why, my dear leader," Ganna cooed. "What do you have in mind?"

A sense of pride filled her as she watched Chardon's expression turn devious before her eyes.

###

Getting Talas to visit her personal lab required a bold sense of cunning. With Chardon and Jaron upping their game to ensure New Lassa's safety, Ganna saw the opportunity arise to abduct Talas while preoccupied setting small game traps in the forest. She launched a tranquilizer dart. With no wariness of an enemy, he wasn't prepared when it hit the back of his neck. He froze. His hand struggled to reach towards where it sat stuck in his flesh. The automatic plunger went down, injecting the powerful sedative.

Talas went down with a thud.

Ganna approached him, a hover stretcher in tow. She used the remote fob to lower it and used for feet to roll him onto it before raising it again. Talas always took a back trail to avoid others, which she also took. The stretcher floated behind her as she headed back to her lab. The sun had not begun its ascent, meaning she had maybe an hour or two to fix her mistake.

If the procedure took, that would give her more time to help New Lassa thrive. If not, she had to figure out an excuse as to why Talas laid in her lab unconscious. She could say she found him collapsed in the woods. Not a complete lie. No one would believe it. At the doors, she squinted to find the side panel. She had disabled the motion sensor lights to avoid being seen.

The entrance opened from a swiped of her hand and entered, making sure it slid shut once the stretcher cleared the frame. It settled on a nearby platform. Ganna went to her console and booted up the system. The scanner came online and mapped Talas' core system. She pinpointed the top branch at the base of the skull.

"Now, let's bring you down a peg to be just like everyone else."

Selecting the block sequence, she hit the upload icon and watched Talas' reaction. At first, he twitched violently as the sequence struggled to attach. Then he went into full convulsions. Ganna stood from her seat and hurried to his side. She saw the sedative levels taper off at an alarming rate on the monitor.

Oh Lassa's stars! He's waking up!

Talas' body arched off the platform as he screamed. An unseen energy made the hover lights flicker. A glow of pale yellow, pink, and orange lights emanated from his chest, surrounding him, and filling the room. Ganna hit the sedative button to get him back down, but the light rejected the tubes, never reaching his body.

Wide beams formed, then shot out piercing the walls of the lab. Ganna looked at the ceiling, expecting to see damage. Not a scratch anywhere. The light subsided and Talas slumped onto the table, silent and covered in sweat. The sedative tubes latched on right as he struggled to rise, his eyes full of rage landing on Ganna. He went down, and she sighed in relief. Then she panicked. What if someone saw those lights? She went to one window and raised the panel.

Daybreak had begun.

Workers headed for the fields stared at the beams of light speeding across the sky. The manbeasts climbing to the tops of the hills and mountains followed their path to find the origin. Jaron shielded her face with one hand to see them better. The council members beside her continued to chat away. Jaron stopped in her tracks as she saw one beam heading straight for her. She lowered her hand, then tried to outmaneuver it. The council members realized what was happening and cried out in vain.

Regardless of how many ways she tried to dodge it, the light struck Jaron like a homing beacon in the solar plexus where her core resided.

"Ahh! Ahggh!" She choked on her own saliva. Her body went stiff, falling hard to the ground. Modas came instantly to her side. With eyes wide, she grabbed the front of his robe. "Awg."

"What's happening?" Modas turned to the council members. They gathered around kneeling, then shook their heads. "Jaron!" Modas took her hand. Light pulsed from her center as drool spilled from the corners of her mouth.

Trinon knew he couldn't dodge the beam of light. It felt non-threatening, yet fear gripped him as it got closer. Ponnae tried to pull him away, her yelling muted. He pushed her aside and braced himself for impact. The moment it hit his core; he went down.

Not from any physical strike, it being only light. It engulfed his insides and invaded his mind. He could do nothing except lie on the ground, stricken with terror. Ponnae rushed over and started shaking him.

Chardon created an energy shield to block the beam of light. He had seen the direction it and the others had come from. Once again, one of Ganna's experiments had gone awry. The servants attending him cowered behind under the alcove of the recreation center. *Can I really avoid it?* He could tell by the way it seemed to adjust its trajectory to his movements earlier.

The beam went straight through the shield and into him in a flash. His whole body lit up, the rainbow particles buzzing in the air. *No!* As if understanding his plea, it complied and eased back. He dropped to his knees and slumped forward, landing face down in the dirt. *What?* That's all he could think before pain seized him.

The villagers ran about in a panic, not sure what to do and had no explanation for the beams of light. Hon stood outside the family commons staring at the sky watching them go to their targets. He knew who had been struck. What awful timing. With arms raised at his sides, he welcomed the chaos. There was no reason for one to target him. His true core remained intact. He almost felt sorry for Ganna. She had a lot to answer for.

He lowered his arms and smirked, turning from the sight of the sky. A beam of light hit his core from behind, striking the middle of his back. He gasped in surprise, his mouth unable to close as he gurgled. The last thing he saw before hitting the ground was Mota running towards him. *Why? What could I have possibly not anticipated?*

News of the incident reached Ganna. She sat in her lab, confused and frightened. She couldn't figure out what it all meant. Think! Her mind went through multiple scenarios while she ignored the calls for medical assistance. Then it came to her. *Oh no!* She stared at Talas' sleeping form. This isn't how it was supposed to turn out. She had every intention of telling the ones involved the story of Lassa while never restoring their original cores, thinking it unnecessary.

The alert on her console screen told her medical technicians were on their way to the main lab. Letting out a heavy sigh, she rose from her station and headed out to greet them before they came barging in. A thought came to her. Going over to Talas, she hit the fob to release the floating stretcher from the platform. It rose, the sedative having stopped being delivered, as the tubes detached.

"Come along. Let's see if this farce works."

Ganna left with the stretcher floating behind her. Villagers at the medical bay entrance stared at them with suspicion. Her assistants were already bringing in the other victims. Modas, Mara, and three council members gave her angry stares.

Kelin rushed over, breathing hard.

"I heard there was some sort of attack. Talas went out to set traps and hadn't returned, so I," Kelin's eyes fell on the stretcher next to Ganna. "Came to see if he was helping," he trailed off slowly, his tone turned venomous. "What's going on?"

"Oh." Ganna gestured with one hand towards Talas. "I followed one of those lights and found him unconscious in the forest. I couldn't very well leave him there, now, could I?"

She turned to the assistants. They nodded to her, then proceeded to carry their charges inside. Ganna followed, guiding the stretcher.

Kelin clenched his fists. Modas slapped a hand on his shoulder. He looked up at the manbeast and their eyes locked.

Mara became tense. A beam of light did head towards the forest. And passed right over it. No way did one of them strike Talas.

"Those lights came from her personal lab's location," one councilman said.

"What did she do to him?" Kelin seethed. His eyes squinted as he bared teeth. Electricity buzzed from his hands. "I swear." He didn't finish the threat.

"Yes, I concur. Mother will probably kill her when she regains her senses." Mara grinned.

"She'll have to get in line," the other council member snapped.

"Why?" Modas slid his hand from Kelin's shoulder. They all turned to him. "Why has this affected my family more than any other?"

"It is curious." The third council member tilted his head back. "Jaron, Trinon, and Hon. There must be a reason for such a connection. And we still don't know what those beams of light were."

"Until their awareness returns, we can only wait." Kelin stepped back a few feet, then turned around to leave.

Modas and Mara lingered a while longer with the council members before they too left. In the sky, the beams dissipated, leaving pale streaks amongst the clouds.

TWO: LASSA'S LIGHT

The Beginning

Two Thousand Years Ago

A shimmery orb of colors floated down a well-trodden animal path in the forest. Its translucent prism form swayed with the gentle breeze that swept through the area. The being exuded a sense of calm and elation, admiring the silver flora that sparkled like stars winking amongst the fluffy, yellow underbrush. Small creatures scurried up the trunks of trees covered in red fern that dotted the dense forest to hide from birds of prey screeching in the skies above.

The being had parted from the others of its kind for some alone time. Its colors flickered like static when they changed. As the original incarnation of the planet's soul, it had a duty to make sure all things stayed connected. After interpreting the planet's designation, it had given itself the name Lassa which meant being of benevolent light. The others saw no qualms with the nature of the situation, not caring that it alone had a name.

Through a clearing ahead, it could see more of its kind congregating by a river. The hush enveloping the land made its prism flicker into a more dominant blue color then back again. It floated farther up above the forest to get a view of the entire landscape. The planet's multitude of colors greeted it. Lassa became a mere outline in the sky as They blended in.

There was peace. As it had been for thousands of years.

From higher in the clear sky came a glitch in its fabric. Lassa tilted its body upwards, curious to what would cause such a thing. Clouds parted as if hands came down to push them apart. Inside the fissure, darkness peeked at the planet, forming a vortex that turned in on itself, swirling madly, expanding. It ripped open, bringing the view of space.

An unseen shadow dwarfed the stars one by one. Black, angry objects spewed forth, raining down to the surface, spreading across the horizon like a plague.

Lassa had not ventured too far from their home but knew that weapons covered the nearly black hulls, blotting out the sun as they cruised across the land. Over two hundred ships dispersed to every corner of the planet. Their weapons' hostile glow told Lassa what would happen next.

Lassa sent out a silent scream to the others. Too late.

The weapons unleashed fire and destruction. Mass infernos obliterated beings caught within. Sadness and fear gripped Lassa, for it could do nothing to prevent the carnage. It felt the anguish of the others as they too cowered in fear. The invaders relentlessly continued their assault. Lassa felt the planet burn, giving up most of its flesh to smoke and ash.

Each ship landed in the quadrant it razed and the planet beings watched ugly, thick bodied bipedals in dark armor march out from the extended ramps. They blanketed the planet in a swarm, tearing up the already scorched soil, killing the animals, and taking as much of the natural resources as they could find.

Drilling into the center, the invaders found the planet's energy source and attached rods down to siphon it. The surface slowly died.

Whenever they encountered any of the beings, they attacked them with the long projectile weapons they carried that dispensed darts of light. When that proved futile, since the laser rounds passed through the shimmering lifeforms, they gave up trying to destroy them.

Lassa struggled with whether it should use the only method of defense it had. A power that, when unleashed, would decimate the entire planet, killing everything. It didn't want to do that. This transgression on its precious mass and namesake was awful, but it also knew the invaders would not stay long. The planet would endure. It would survive. The invaders would get bored.

The others sent their support of Lassa's decision. For now, they would wait.

Other beings had visited to explore or make repairs and never bothered the ecosystem of the planet. In the entities thousands of years of existence, they had never been invaded.

For ten short years, the beings on Lassa watched helplessly as the invaders ravaged their home until, as predicted, they grew angry with disappointment. By depleting the planet's core, life and all resources became scarce. They could no longer take anymore. The planet had nothing left to give.

One by one, the invaders went back to their ships, loading up the spoils of their deed, and left the planet the same way they came. On the day they boarded the last ship, Lassa hovered nearby. It had deciphered the enemy's language early on and wanted to hear the commander of the ship's conversation.

"This place had nothing of value." The dark behemoth lobbed purple spit from its mouth onto the dirt. "What we collected amounts to almost no profit. This was a waste of our time."

"And," the one that always stayed by the other's side. "No inhabitants to trade for slave labor or anything else. Just a worthless planet of trees and floating lights." They propped the wide mouthed flame thrower cannon and held it up with both hands. "Should we scorch the rest of it?"

Lassa bristled, its shimmery body flickering through every color.

"No." The first one replied. "Leave it. Not worth our time, like you say." They walked over to a tree burnt beyond recognition and scraped blackened scabs from its trunk, exposing a pale-yellow layer. "Guess this planet will eventually heal itself."

The invaders finished boarding the ship, lifting off into the vortex left open for them. Once the ship's aft cleared the edge, the vortex snapped shut. The grey, darkened sky cleared two moon cycles later, returning to its original pastel green and pink.

Lassa's shimmer fluctuated between red, dark blue, and orange. Rage consumed it. The others floating nearby came towards it and in a silent communal, clustered together to ease their pain. They vowed to never let this happen again. A new plan to survive flowed between them.

They had consciousness, but no physical bodies to defend themselves. From what they had learned from the invaders, bipedal beings dominated the galaxy. To compete, they would need to find a form that suited their unique construct.

Lassa sent the idea to the others. It received perplexing responses.

-But we are what we are!

-Why must we change for the universe? There is no guarantee that those beings will return!

-And there is none for them not. Lassa retorted.

-Then what do you propose we do?

Lassa went a soft pale blue, contemplating.

-Cores. A vessel for our true forms when our physical bodies are not in use. Tethered to the soul of the planet, keeping us safe in a deep sleep.

-Ahh!

One of the others floated forward.

-We will need to create a field large enough to hold them.

Lassa looked out at the nearby landscape. Most of the forest in the East lay destroyed, a vast wasteland scorched black and appeared unrecoverable.

-There will do.

The beings floated to the desolate area and surrounded it with tendrils of light connecting them to form a glowing circle. They began channeling their energies into the ground, gaining help from what little energy the planet had left, and leveled it slowly by breaking down the elements. Time of no importance.

After thirty years, thick roots broke through the new soil and giant translucent buds bloomed from their tips, covering the entire area. They stopped working the soil and broke their connection. The die now cast, Lassa sent out their decree.

-And now, my beloveds, our evolution awaits.

⌒

Year One hundred of Evolution

Selections for vessels were underway while a third of the beings volunteered to venture out into the darkness of space for clues on how to utilize their alternative forms. Hundreds of colored orbs filled the sky, disappearing into the stratosphere. They spread throughout the solar system, watching, learning; sickened by what they observed.

They had never left their home. No reason to seek the unknown. No reason to communicate with other beings. Their peaceful existence did not warrant such things. Those times had ended and their need to defend became the goal. Seeing the chaos of war between other worlds made them cringe. Must we become like them? The way each hostile race progressed towards their corner of the galaxy; they knew there would be no choice in the matter.

As they came back, handfuls at a time, depending on how far they traveled, they gave a report on their findings and transferred what they learned to the others. When all the vessels were ready, the beings occupied them and tested their movements. Blank canvases at the start. Each vessel changed to complement its core.

Over time, the previous orbs of colored energy became a race of diverse features. Some gained a talent for harnessing their energy to use as weapons. Others chose to arm themselves with handheld ones. They implemented a combination

ACTS OF TRANSGRESSION | 71

of their multiple species' fighting skills. It would take time to master them all. That was fine. Their determination to be ready for the next invaders fueled their resolve.

Year Two hundred of Evolution

Rows of people wearing white robes fluttering in the wind stood six feet apart before giant stones set at the head of each line. The yellow grass bristled around their ankles. Lassa's host, with dark strawberry blonde hair flowing down their back against the white robe, scanned the group with dark blue eyes. Their sensuous mouth spread thin in a mischievous smile.

"Welcome to your advanced training grounds. This is where you must hone your fighting skills to defend our home. I wish you success. May my light shine upon you all." Lassa saw pride on each face, then turned to the instructor standing beside them. His large, muscular frame and dark hair cropped short made him appear formidable. And he was. "You may proceed."

"As you wish." The instructor addressed the group. "First in line, ready yourselves!"

They did as instructed, stepping into an offensive stance, their hands raised chest height in a cupped position as if about to catch a ball. Soft blue light formed into glowing orbs between them.

"Aim for the center of the stone!" He waited until all of them were ready. "Begin!"

One by one, the trainees unleashed their balls of energy towards their respective stones. Two-thirds of them hit and of those, only a handful shattered the stone. Lassa walked away, satisfied that the training went well. The trainees were the last round of their race to inhabit vessels. No one floated along the surface in their original form.

Lassa made their way to the temple built next to the core fields. A place of spiritual guidance, learning, and medical research, the temple's plain grey stone structure didn't stand out. Lassa felt it needed to convey simplicity. With physical bodies came the required task of maintaining them. They kept half the population in their cores, the field beyond ablaze with a rainbow of glowing buds that spanned miles.

They rotated out for training and social events when needed. They would plant every core in their vessels if an attack occurred.

Lassa strolled along the temple's corridor, through an archway and into the main courtyard. The head of the temple, Mercan, bent over a flowerbed, scrutinizing its bounty of colorful petals.

"A new species of plant life, I take it?" Lassa went to stand by the entity in a male form.

"Hmm." Mercan grumbled, dissatisfied. His black and silver hair brushed atop the shoulders of his plain beige robe, whose hem grazed the garden floor. "I was trying to create an additional food source, not something to place on a viewing ledge."

"You can't win all the battles." Lassa reached down and plucked a leaf from one flower.

Mercan scoffed.

"Then what's the point?"

"You're too ambitious." Lassa smelled the flower's center.

"I am making sure we can defend ourselves next time!" Mercan seethed.

Lassa flinched from him, seeing the rage in his eyes.

"I know that."

"Then don't ever question my ambition," Mercan's grey eyes grew dark. When he saw the look on Lassa's face, he stepped back in shame. "I am sorry. I know you want this more than any of us."

"No, you're right. Whatever is necessary."

Lassa looked out past the fields onto the horizon. They glared at the sky, remembering the invasion.

"Not this time."

Mercan stared at Lassa with interest, making them uncomfortable.

"How are you handling the duality? It seemed a good idea, yet you never gave me any feedback on your experience so far."

"Having the option to change my sexual orientation is a bonus. I think we should structure more of the population this way."

"Oh?" Mercan raised his brow. "But, you haven't procreated even though you identify as female more than the other. That will be the true test."

Lassa frowned at the thought. Physical body aside, they did not relish having another touch them in such a way. They had seen the new mating ritual implemented and found it disturbing.

"When I find the right mate, I will let you know."

"Yes, we previously exchanged energies to create new ones for increasing our kind. This next step is messier, by far."

"And the rest of our quadrant in this galaxy appears to be like that."

"It's barbaric, in my opinion." Mercan went back to examine the flowers. "I found a mate." He looked up at Lassa with a crooked grin. "She found my proposal quite intriguing."

"I hope you didn't tell her she was a steppingstone in your research." Lassa frowned.

"Of course not!" Mercan snapped. Then he smiled. "I simply suggested she was the best candidate for my superior genes."

Lassa sputtered, letting out a short cough.

"I'm leaving." Lassa turned and headed back through the temple halls.

Personalities had changed drastically since the evolution. They could still communicate telepathically, but for some reason, most chose not to. Facial expressions and body language replaced mood, previously conveyed through light and color.

Which could easily deceive, putting out false feelings, in Lassa's view.

Using their energy as weapons gave Lassa a scummy feeling in the pit of their soul. Why? Why had those ugly creatures invaded? It would be unusual for a planet not to be discovered over millenniums. Being attacked never occurred to them.

I wish we had more time.

Upping the Ante

The next race that arrived, attempting to invade, appeared not aesthetically ugly. Instead, their viciousness showed as they bombarded the planet with no warning. Lassa stared at the sky in anger. As the smaller ships came down to cause havoc, energy users blasted them into oblivion. They would not let the enemy touch Lassian soil.

More emerged from the clouds, firing at anything that moved. Lassa frowned. A third of the ships reached the surface and engaged the energy users. Hand to hand combat wasn't a major part of the training since utilizing their powers took precedence. The Lassians' numbers, though outmatched, did not prevent them from decimating the enemy.

Energy users pushed back the enemy with sheer will to stop another razing. A sense of foreboding filled its namesake. They felt the wide beam of destruction before it shot down from space towards their home. Power welled inside Lassa's body.

Multicolored speckles of light shimmered around them, pulsating out. They focused on the beam. Lassa's eyes glowed white hot as the shimmers expanded, meeting the beam halfway. The two forces collided, boomeranging the beam back to its origin. Shimmering lights spanning miles across the surface obliterated everything.

A group of energy users caught in the aftermath had their bodies destroyed. Thankfully, the cores remained. The enemy retreated, seeing no way to victory. They left destruction and despair in their wake and planet Lassa, once again, would need time to recover.

Mercan went to retrieve the cores, along with any damaged bodies he could regenerate. The beauty of having interchangeable vessels. No soul would be lost. Lassa felt sorrow as they surveyed the damage, especially their part in it. They had never used such an amount of energy and it only reached less than half its potential.

I could destroy a planet if I so desired.

Lassa found Mercan in his outdoor lab, observing a cage full of wilderness creatures. They didn't want to know what he planned to do with them, but curiosity called. After ten years, the planet had repaired itself by seventy percent. Giggles came from inside the main building behind them. Mercan's little one, Ganna, ran out into the open yard.

Silver curls bounced along her neck while grey eyes, like her father, shone bright with joy. Still an infant at five years old, she seemed cute by Lassa's standards. In her hands, she held a measuring tool. Mercan turned to her and reached for it. She slapped it in his hand.

"Here you are, father!" Her high-pitched voice grated on Lassa's ears, diminishing the cuteness.

"Aren't you useful?" Lassa said, approaching the two.

Mercan rubbed the top of Ganna's head.

"She sure is. Right, my daughter?"

"Yes!" Ganna replied gleefully.

"Want to go back inside or stay and watch me?"

"Stay! Here with father," she grinned.

"What, exactly, are you doing?" Lassa asked him.

"We need more fighters." Mercan replied bluntly. "Our energy users can only handle so much. And our hand-to-hand combat is nothing short of lacking. You saw the way those invaders fought."

Lassa nodded.

They didn't factor in having to actually touch the enemy. Their focus on long range combat took priority.

"I agree. That said," Lassa pointed to the caged beasts. "What are those for?"

A sinister grin spread on Mercan's face, causing Lassa to step back.

The beasts were a little over twenty-five centimeters long, their width half that size, with squishy bellies. A closer look at their spiky coat found the quills soft. Pink snouts sniffed the air as they climbed around in the cage.

"I am going to make new fighters. Unparalleled in strength. These creatures are quite vicious with a tenacity for survival. They will do nicely as specimens for the cause."

Lassa raised their brow, dubious about Mercan's plan.

"As long as you aren't torturing them to meet your end." They saw Mercan's disappointed expression. His daughter pouted. *What have they been doing?* Lassa cried out in their mind. "While you do that, I have researched a particular weapon one of our scouts reported on in the early days. I didn't think it useful until now. Our kind who can't use their energy would benefit."

"Oh?" Mercan raised his head from observing the beasts to look over at Lassa.

"They are long metal blades attached to a single grip. There are variations of one or both sides of the blades being sharp. I saw some of the first invaders using them."

"Proper handheld weapons, huh?" Mercan's face scrunched.

"I don't particularly like it either. We have no choice if we want to defend ourselves. I will have the original scout work with your science team."

Mercan let out a loud sigh. He moved Ganna to the other side of the cage, then handed her the tool.

"Get the data for me, my light."

"Okay, father." Ganna's tiny hands worked the tool with expert precision.

Lassa found it disturbing. Mercan wasn't raising a child. He had procured an assistant through birth.

"You go your route, and I will go mine. Having three ways of fighting is better than what we have now."

"How long will it take to perfect your project?" Lassa eyed him coyly.

"Maybe twenty years. Fifty at the most. You?"

Lassa smirked. "Give me half that and I will have elite warriors."

"That would be ideal." Mercan's eyes grew dark. "I feel more invasions are coming."

"Yes, I think somehow our planet is being targeted." Lassa glanced down at the beasts, squirming to get out. "I'll leave you to it, then."

Lassa tried not to hurry away from the lab. Mercan's projects were becoming scary. Bordering on the unethical. They decided not to ask any unnecessary questions in the future. Other work had to be done, like creating a working forge.

‍

Hundreds of the new weapons lined the training field opposite the energy users. The warriors who would wield them used that section of the region to learn their techniques. A few practice demonstrations proved successful. Time to fully implement the plan. The top warriors stood in a single horizontal line, awaiting permission to choose their weapons.

During the demos, Lassa noticed some of them were capable of dual wielding. One, in particular, stood out among the others. The original scout who discovered the weapons. Lassa eyed them with intrigue.

Laxis' body defied beauty. Dirty blond hair, slightly wavy near the ends, fell past his shoulders. Lean muscles perfected his lithe frame of just over six feet tall. Perfect lips, not too thin or too plump, held a playful tightness.

His charm and demeanor oozed sexuality.

Every warrior present had no qualms about not being able to use energy. When the last invaders came, they were the ones who took the initiative and fought with whatever could be used as a weapon. Their quick thinking partly gave Lassa the idea.

Beating Mercan by two decades also made Lassa smile. His project, close to completion, hit a recent snag. He allowed them a peek at his progress of beasts manipulated and bio-engineered with artificial cores and bodies. Huge beings with many that stood well over seven feet, a stark contrast to their original forms, frightened Lassa.

Stepping before the row of warriors, Lassa locked eyes with Laxis.

"Since you have mastered these weapons and provided the best techniques on how to use them, I am appointing you as an instructor. Teach them well."

Laxis bowed his head then went over to the weapons. He perused the different styles of hilts. Towards the center, he stopped and slid two swords off the platform. One had a simple ribbed design while the other had an image of tree branches etched along it. Holding both, one in each hand, he swung them to gauge their weight. Satisfied, he turned around to his students.

"Let us become a force that brings our enemies to their knees," Laxis shouted.

A loud roar erupted from the warriors contorted faces.

Lassa's eyes went wide. They never imagined the warriors would feel such rage at the planet's invasion. To defend was all Lassa thought about, not domination. They wondered if Mercan had the same way of thinking as he planned to unleash those creatures into the world.

The invasions flashed in Lassa's mind. They tilted their head. Frustration. That's what they felt. All of this being a means to an end, they shouldn't dismiss everyone's efforts.

Lassa walked away from the training grounds. They were

tired. More accurately, their body felt tired. The energy of their core buzzed ferociously. Their vessel barely contained it, exhausting the biological system. It calmed whenever they slept.

Back in their quarters, Lassa laid on the bed and rested both arms across their stomach. In ten years, the warriors would be ready for battle and Mercan's beasts added to the ranks. Lassa closed their eyes. They dreamt of the planet being at peace again.

Mercan stared at his creations in awe. One hundred manbeasts stood before him. Another thousand were ready to be created after this batch completed their combat training. Taller than the rest of the population, with muscled frames and sharp talons, they were a formidable sight. Their manes hairline reached the midpoint between the shoulders and back.

He admired the smooth tanned skin varying in tone from light to dark. The majority had dark hair, while others were different after manipulating certain pods' DNA. When it was all said and done, the project satisfied him.

Off in the distance stood a giant black monolith reaching five hundred feet in the air. Its sleek surface would normally be impossible to scale. His manbeasts could with practice. Observing the small creatures for decades allowed him to assess their strengths. Now, ten times their normal size, they could deal optimal damage.

He heard footsteps crunching the dried leaves scattered across the ground of his outdoor lab. Lassa came up behind him, then stood at his side. They gawked at the manbeasts. Mercan smirked.

Impressed yet? He mocked her inwardly.

His daughter, Ganna, fifty years old and as tall as her father, came out of the main building carrying a new device that scanned the body and did analysis.

She went past Lassa and her father without acknowledging either.

"They're huge," Lassa exclaimed.

"Well, yes. They will be our frontline."

"There was no need to make them so big."

"It would have been a waste not to." He called out to Ganna, already done with the first row of manbeasts. "Make sure their vitals are stable. We don't want any of them to over clock themselves."

"Okay, father!" Ganna never looked their way.

Lassa appeared miffed by the snub. Mercan let out a snort.

"What's amusing?" Lassa lashed out.

"Ganna remains focused when scientific research is involved. She's not rude. I'm sure she will come by later and talk to you."

"Hmm. I still don't like it."

Mercan sighed. "Well, do you want to see them in action? I found so much combat footage when I combed the nearest solar systems feeds we archived."

"You had them watch all that?" Lassa asked, astonished.

"What? No." Mercan gave her a dirty stare. "I embedded the information in their cores." He watched Lassa's eyes go wide. "All they have to do is train their bodies to move like what they see in their minds."

"Deadly from the start," Lassa muttered.

"Absolutely."

"I guess we will see who rises to the top."

"Oh, and why is that?" Mercan felt intrigued again. Even Ganna stopped for a moment.

"I plan to have a sort of council. The energy users will be led by me. I found one for the warriors and now need one for these manbeasts."

"To coordinate strategies for future invasions?" Ganna asked, having to yell, being so far away. "That makes sense."

"Why are they so quiet?"

Lassa scanned the row of fighters.

"What do you wish for them to say? Unless being spoken to or giving directions to each other, speaking is unnecessary."

"I suppose you're right." Lassa frowned. "What about the other thing we discussed years ago?"

"Ganna is working on that. We should be able to hide our location soon. Only those who stumble into our system would see us."

Lassa nodded. Mercan felt the same. The frequent invasions stemmed from vortices tapping into their region. Some new galactic trade sprouted in the next system over. Mercan was certain the random coordinates occurred when merchants ventured off the path, since every invader came from a different race. Ganna had mapped out their own system and found where the origin of the signals.

Although Mercan enjoyed his new role as a science officer, he still wished they didn't have to evolve, forcing themselves to be like other races in the galaxy. In his opinion, they had in fact devolved, stooping to the invaders' levels. The planet's technology in a brief span of three centuries had jumped exponentially.

He called out to the manbeasts.

"This is your chance to hone your skills. Go out and become stronger than you imagine. We will assign a leader after the trials."

"Understood!" the manbeasts replied in unison, their voices booming in the air.

Lassa moved back, stunned at the audible assault. Mercan smiled with pride, watching them move out towards the monolith set in the center of a new training ground.

With law defying speed, they all leaped and ran across the terrain, focusing on their destination. Mercan watched Lassa clutch at their stomach as if trying to knead out a knot.

Invaders, battles, war. They wanted none of those things. If it weren't for those first creatures coming to their planet and ravaging it, they would never have thought of vengeance. Yes. They would meet any race that came to harm them with equal ferocity.

There was no other way.

⤳

Five years after the manbeast training, one showed more promise than the others, her prowess unmatched. Lassa, Mercan, Ganna, and Laxis had gone to observe the manbeasts' training and determined she would be their leader as part of their council. Lassa approached her during an afternoon break.

The manbeast sat on a large boulder, sharpening her talons with a piece of thin stone. They made a high-pitched twang with each stroke against it. She stopped when the group got close and looked over at them with disinterest. Lassa noticed not all the manbeasts were huge. This one stood around six feet two inches tall.

Lassa marveled at the chiseled arms exposed by the sleeveless robe over a simple tunic and woven pants. Her boots were muddy from the fields. Dark, wavy hair touched her shoulders, and amber eyes stared back at them.

Beautiful. Lassa heard the word echo in their mind and realized Laxis had thought the same. His gaze seemed fixed on the female Manbeast, exuded longing. He appeared enchanted.

"What do you call yourself?" Lassa asked her.

"Mandra." She set the stone down.

"You will lead these manbeasts. Nurture, train, and discipline if needed. Can you do that?"

"As you command. I will fulfill my duty." Mandra stood.

"Good. Come," Lassa gestured with one hand, waving it towards the newly built council chamber. "We have much to discuss. Another invader has been detected. Let's form a strategy before they arrive."

Mandra's eyes lit up with fervor. Lassa approved.

The group walked to their destination, with her following close behind. Out of the corner of their eye, Lassa saw Ganna frown at the manbeast. Mercan noticed as well.

Restraints

Land to air weapons powered by energy users struck down enemy fighter ships that dared to enter Lassa's atmosphere. Dual sword wielding warriors and angry Manbeasts met the enemy that evaded the first round and reached the surface. Smoke from downed ships and burning trees mingled with the scent of ash as it rose, clouding the sky.

The third attack in under forty years saw the population becoming accustomed to war. Their daily lives comprised training, to hone their skills for total victory, eating, and resting.

From a distance, Lassa watched the fight, not joining in the fray unless an enemy got close to them. As an energy user, they were not helpless. They deemed their power too great, only to be used as a last resort.

Lassa watched Mandra fly into the air, her body twisting into a somersault before landing feet first in an enemy fighter's chest. The weight of her blow sent her opponent crumbling to the ground, where she unceremoniously ran her talons through its abdomen. A fountain of orange-colored blood spurted as she wrenched them free. Lassa stared mesmerized by her movements, at the ease of her devastating might. Whenever they witnessed it, their core seemed to pulse, like a heavy thump lasting only a second.

To their right, the warriors pushed back the enemy, cutting down each row as they advanced, forcing the horde into an enclosure to make quick work of their demise. Laxis stood in the center of it all, a force of nature wielding two swords, never leaving his circle of defense. Not one enemy budged him from his position.

A different core pulse filled Lassa as they observed his ferocity equal to Mandra's. Such fierce fighters made them proud, yet something about the two of them stirred a feeling within them. They couldn't describe what their core coveted.

The enemy began their retreat, collecting the wounded and dead as they headed to their ships while others came down to retrieve them. The Lassian fighters let out a collective celebratory roar that reached the sky. Lassa smiled. Another victory without casualties, all because of Laxis and Mandra's planning.

Warrior and Manbeast met halfway on the battlefield and laughed, embracing each other before heading towards the rest of their group waiting for praise. They walked side by side, comfortable in their own bubble. Lassa felt the uneasy pulse, glimpsing a soft red glow from inside their robes.

Lassa cared deeply for them both. They would not wish harm ever. *What is this then?* Laxis and Mandra were the most fearsome fighters of their race. In that regard, Lassa worshipped them, not wanting to take their status. Lassa despised fighting, refusing to get their hands dirty. Even selfishly sacrificing others to maintain their stance. The council occasionally chastised them for it.

With their eyes tracking the two, Lassa made their way to the main hall to see how many wounded were being brought in. Mercan and Ganna directed the newly assembled medical staff to tend them. Those who didn't want to fight anymore switched to learning medicine and healing. A few in the council turned their focus to other issues, such as technology, spiritual guidance, and agriculture.

Is this what evolution is supposed to look like? Lassa frowned. They felt unsure.

❧

When it became clear, over time, that the warriors outperformed the manbeasts in battle, Ganna and her father brainstormed for a solution. The manbeasts were created to limit the use of the main populations' core bodies. They did their job of maintaining the front lines with cunning efficiency. No problems there. By keeping them in that role, the manbeasts could not branch out.

"As much as I despise those things, we have to make sure we put them to full use." Ganna stood at her workstation, raising a test tube filled with a yellow liquid to inspect. "Our warriors are too good." She frowned. "Laxis has made them deadly."

Mercan snorted at that. He turned to stare at her and flinched at her expression. She helped him create the manbeasts, and now she wanted to see them harmed.

"Daughter, what seems to be the issue again?"

"The manbeasts have become prideful, secretive, while the warriors continue to develop their skills, getting wounded in the process. Those beasts should be the ones taking the brunt of the fight." She returned the tube to its holder, clinking it hard against the others.

"And what do you propose?"

"I'm not sure. We need to keep our warriors at their level."

"Hmm." Mercan walked past her to stand in the lab's open doorway. The field of cores lay before him on the other side of the plot. He leaned against the frame. "Maybe we should limit the warriors' dual wielding abilities. That wouldn't strip them of their skills. Make it so they only use that technique if there is no other way."

"Like their last dying act?" Ganna's brow furrowed.

"Something of the sort," Mercan leaned back, tilting his head towards her. "They usually don't display it unless they encounter a worthy opponent. It would not be noticeable."

"How will we get them to comply?"

Mercan stood straight and came back into the lab. He

cupped her face in his hands.

"Comply? No, my dear child. We will manipulate their core matrix at the next checkup session. This is not a request."

The corners of Ganna's mouth twitched until they curved slightly into a devious smile. He dropped his hands and went to his own station. A talk with Lassa would be necessary to allow for easier transition. That way, they blamed Lassa and not him.

###

Rows of warriors filled the training grounds as Lassa stood before them atop a raised platform. Laxis, positioned directly below her, had a wary look.

This could go badly. Lassa steadied their stance and addressed them.

"My warriors. Your skills have surpassed our wildest expectations. So much so that we feel your full might is no longer necessary." A hush fell on the crowd. Laxis stared up at her with fury. Lassa could see he felt something ominous in their tone. "From now on, dual sword wielding will only be permitted as a last resort. Training for that skill is forbidden."

The loud uproar of angry warriors assaulted Lassa. They stepped back in terror, not sure where to run if the crowd moved towards them. Laxis went around the side of the platform and ran up the ramp to confront them.

"What is the meaning of this, Lassa?"

"It's…" Lassa clutched their hands against their chest. "as I said. There's no need…"

"Is the goal not to eliminate our enemy?"

"Of course." Lassa stepped back more. "Which we do, with extreme prejudice. Like," Lassa glanced away from him, "animals."

Laxis' head tilted back as his eyes went wide. He understood exactly what Lassa meant, unsheathing his sword on instinct, ready to strike Lassa down. A manbeast dropped between them, blocking his swing.

The crowd turned their attention to the platform.

Oh no!

Lassa didn't want this. They went to the edge and raised their hands, palms up.

"Please, stop! My intentions are pure, I promise you!" They looked over their shoulder at the manbeast. "Stand down, Mandra. You too, Laxis."

The two eased away from each other, Laxis sheathing his sword, Mandra retracting her talons. Tension choked the air. Lassa didn't realize they would react this way. What was so wrong with their suggestion? It benefited their race.

###

Laxis felt a difference as his body screamed to move like a dual wielder, yet his mind kept shutting down the notion. He couldn't figure out why accessing his skills seemed so hard, even though he didn't need them at the moment. The enemy went down despite that.

Across the surface, enemy fighters tried to bring Lassians to their knees. At every turn, the manbeasts denied them. The way they dominated the battle made Laxis feel the warriors' role had rolled back into an assist status. The longer the battle went on, the more he sensed it. He cursed Lassa and Mercan, knowing the two had something to do with the situation.

A guttural yell from behind made him turn to see a warrior, badly wounded, bring out his other sword and attacked his opponent with such fury that his movements blurred. With each strike decimating the enemy, their core got dimmer.

No!

Laxis sped towards them and knocked the already dead enemy out of striking range and hit the warrior in the solar plexus. He dropped to the ground, his eyes two glowing pools of white. His core pulsed a faint green light that emitted from his torso, then winked out.

Cries from the battlefield let him know other warriors were suffering the same fate. Mandra came to him and met his gaze. She caressed his cheek, then flashed back into the fray. The manbeasts forced the enemy off the planet while the energy users pummeled their ships until they left Lassian space.

Mandra grabbed the front of Lassa's robe with both hands and brought them close until they shared the same breath. They were the only ones in the small quarters Lassa used to be alone before the evening meal.

"What have you done?"

Lassa struggled to understand her rage. They had not tampered with the manbeasts. Why would she be so concerned?

"I wish you wouldn't be so rough with me. I've done nothing wrong."

Mandra let go and shoved them away from her. The act hurt Lassa's feelings. They only had admiration and love for the leader. Why was it never reciprocated?

"What you have done is indeed harm. Stripping away a part of their souls to make my people look superior? That is unforgiveable!"

Lassa became angry. Red, pink, and orange light glowed from their body.

"I stand by my decision. I didn't know until after what Mercan and Ganna had done." Before Mandra could ask, Lassa huffed. "And I would still approve it if I'd known."

Lassa watched Mandra's horrified expression turn from them as she left the room. A heaviness weighed on their core. Then it hit them. Of course, Mandra would be angry. Her mate was the leader of the warriors. It affected her and their offspring.

I've messed up again.

Lassa loved them both. That felt correct. Losing either would break them. Their affection steered more towards Mandra. Confused by their emotions, Lassa went to the window and rested their head against the pane.

The reports from the medical bays were dire. Warriors who used their forbidden skills had their cores dimmed to the point of being extinguished, many resulting in death. Mercan removed the cores and buried them in the fields, feeding them energy. Multiple wounds covered all the bodies.

Was the enemy fiercer than the previous ones?

Lassa couldn't tell anymore since their race had perfected defeating any who dared engage them. Nonetheless, warriors on the brink of death would not do. The limiters needed to be adjusted to eliminate dual wielding as an option.

⌒

Tall trees became mere shadows against the dark sky as Laxis walked deeper into the forest. He had gone miles away from the territories to where only wild creatures roamed. Both of his swords lay crossed against his back in his jacket's loop holders. Dried leaves crunched under his boots with each step. He stopped at a small clearing drenched in black. The moonlight barely penetrating the space.

Good. No one would see.

He reached back and gripped the handles of each sword. His body revolted, not knowing which one to pull out. A battle of will inside his mind became fierce. He struggled, not letting go, determined to force his desired outcome. His core flared, a golden light glowing from within, causing excruciating pain. He dropped to his knees, gritting his teeth, still holding on to the sword hilts.

A deep growl escaped his lips. The soft breeze cooled the sweat dripping from his brow. Inside of him, electric buzzes scurried until a cracking, like glass shattering, erupted. Laxis' eyes glowed with the same golden hue as he unsheathed both swords, swinging them forward. He took a deep breath and relaxed, letting his core settle down.

The glow dissipated.

A secret.

Laxis would tell no one how he defeated the limiter.

92| MAQUEL A. JACOB

Even though he knew many of his warriors could do the same, he decided to let them be. Mercan and Lassa would win for now.

Transcendence

Clear skies greeted Lassa, Mandra, and Laxis while they waited on a hilltop for the enemy ships to appear. Mandra sat perched on a boulder that reached Laxis' thighs, making her appear a few inches shorter than him. Lassa stood next to him, their white and blue robes flowing in the wind. Animosity still lingered between them, but they always brushed it aside for battles.

Laxis rested one foot on a small stone mound and leaned forward. Lassa glanced over at his lean body with dark blond wavy hair that touched the middle of his back. The rust-colored leather suited him. Envy crept inside. This is who Mandra cherished.

But so do I.

"They look formidable," Laxis said.

They had all watched the feed during their briefing with Mercan and Ganna. The enemy ships were three times the size of previous foes and seemed to have a larger force.

"We just have to fight a little harder to make them see the error in their destination." Mandra reached down and found a piece of rock to sharpen her talons. "No need to hold back."

Dark flecks littered the clouds above. Energy users blasted a few out of the sky while others sped towards the surface. Like locusts, smaller ships swarmed out of them. The sound of their propulsion engines droned out the shouts of rage from the Lassians running to engage them.

"Here they are." Laxis removed his foot.

"Time to send them back."

Mandra rose, balancing on the boulder. She squinted, her expression turning dire.

More ships darkened the sky. A wide beam of pale-yellow light spanning nearly a kilometer shot down and scorched a swath of land in the territory to the East. Lassa's mouth went wide in an O.

"Not this! Why do they have something so horrid?"

"You may have to fight this time, Lassa," Laxis chided.

He turned and left the hilltop. Mandra leapt towards the surface to engage the enemy with her fellow manbeasts. Lassa scanned the planet with their mind's eye and felt foreboding. This enemy, they were on a different level. One that would make the Lassians prove their worth.

The beams rained down from the heavens onto the surface, forcing the energy users to form a tighter dome shaped block so they could bounce them back to their senders. A handful of enemy ships came out of the clouds and hovered over the forests, the lands, and in the sky, searching for their next targets.

The battle went on for weeks, with the Lassians keeping the enemy at bay. The goal was to push them off the planet, but they were relentless. Reports from the communication center showed no reinforcements enroute. This enemy force was all that there was.

Lassa dared not use their full power to get rid of them. They were certain the Lassians would be victorious as always, with minimal casualties. Lassa realized war had no guarantees to ending unscathed. The percentage of vessels lost came out to less than one tenth of a percent. The number of cores zero.

The battle took an ugly turn as it hit the next moon cycle. The bigger enemy ships only used the beam weapons if they saw no other way to take control of a territory. Their goal appeared to preserve Lassa's resources. Destroying the very thing you came for would prove counterproductive.

Lassa searched for Mandra and Laxis and found them both engaged in fierce battles.

Blood painted Laxis' face and tunic with splatters, much of it his own. Deep gashes crossed his torso, the jacket ruined. He still fought with no signs of fatigue. Lassa knew better. Four other warriors assisted him, and they, too, were on the verge of death. With horror, Lassa saw all of them release their second swords. They spread out, pushing the enemy back while annihilating them. Laxis, although a deadly dual wielder cutting down his opponents, was outnumbered.

On the Western border, a sea of enemies had cornered Mandra and her group. No matter how much they fought, the manbeasts were matching their strength. Above, an enemy ship moved towards them, the weapons bay of its underbelly glowing. Lassa reached out, knowing their actions were futile, with Mandra's location too far away for them to help.

"No!" Lassa screamed.

The beam of light shot down, killing manbeast and enemy. Mandra and a few others leaped from the center, but their bodies were still hit. The beam continued sweeping as the ship moved across the lands. Lassa went down the mountain they had kept from enemy take over to a lower section. In the North, they saw Laxis struck down and his body, along with his four warriors, stabbed repeatedly until another group of warriors descended on the enemy and killed them swiftly.

The beams obliterated the temple and laboratory. Ganna's cries of despair at the loss of her father, whose core light disappeared in an instant, slammed into their being. Lassa saw everything in their mind's eye, felt every pain, every death.

"I'm sorry," Lassa said through tears and gritted teeth. It must be done.

They gathered all their energy, tapping into the planet's core. Multi-colored shimmers of light enveloped them, forming a wide halo around their body. It pulsed inward, as if sucked in. Lassa looked up at the enemy as a beam came towards them.

"This is your end."

The energy burst out of them, spreading like a blanket across the entire planet. The enemy ships not yet caught by it fled into space. The ones on the surface scrambled back to their fighters, abandoning their comrades. All life Lassa deemed unworthy succumbed to their wrath.

The shimmering lights ate their fill of enemy hulls and the ships' occupants. Lassians in the area went down, their bodies melting. Before destroying too many cores, Lassa reined in their power. It came back into them in a rush, knocking them off the mountain. They fell into the sea below, the water like concrete. They felt their skeletal integrity compromised as the cold wrapped around them, dragging them down into the water's depths.

Grainy steam rose from Lassa's body into the air, now filled with debris and smoke. With their last breath, they used mindsight to seek every living being on the planet and found a quarter of its population had perished.

I can live with that for now.

Lassa closed their eyes and let themselves sink.

Ganna crawled out from the membrane she had enclosed around the medical staff and herself when she realized Lassa would use their power on the enemy. Not yet perfected for mass production, the gelatinous shield blocked the effects. Since Lassa using that energy rarely happened, developing it took a back seat.

She chastised herself for not creating a better shield for the temple. So many lives lost. Father. Her fury flared once more. The membrane protected a small radius. A handful of assistants survived. Her Father's shattered core lay at her feet.

She had gathered up pieces and fused them together before Lassa's final blow.

Selfish being.

Despite her disdain for Lassa, Ganna knew she had to find the body eventually. With so many vessels and cores destroyed, she had her work cut out for her. The long gone enemy was no longer a threat. She went to task with the help of ten scientists she personally trained.

Before finding Lassa, she needed to restore the cores of the temple workers and cabinet members. She required their expertise the most. The task would take minimal time using the newest machine in her secret lab below.

Hidden from everyone, including her father, Ganna had tapped into the planet's core and created a device that took small amounts and amplified it in a storage unit. That way, the core would not be depleted. The stored energy doubled or tripled depending on the set output. That is what the planet infrastructure used for power.

Ganna constantly had to adjust the flow when that being relied on the planet's core for sustenance and fighting. *Why am I the only one who understands how precious our planet is? Even those ungrateful manbeasts wanted autonomy. Looking down on the rest of Lassa as inferior beings compared to them.*

She hit a panel on the edge of the far wall and it parted open, falling away to make room for the secret lab below to rise. Its doors slid open and Ganna turned to her assistants.

"We shall start with our own, then work towards finding the council."

"What about the being Lassa?" One of the female scientists asked.

"That thing is not a priority and unnecessary for the revival process."

"Of course."

Ganna stood out of the way, letting them file in. She went last, heading straight for the station that monitored the planet's core. The levels had depleted more than she liked. *May Lassa's wrath come upon you*, she cursed the being. That wouldn't happen, of course. Ganna had a feeling that thing had probably survived. She could hope for their demise, though.

While her assistants worked on finding vessels and cores, Ganna went to a different station and pulled up the project she had been working on before detecting the enemy. A gateway system she wanted to install right near the moon and behind them. Any ship trying to pass by would unknowingly enter the gate and be deposited on the other side of Lassa, not having seen it. Their communications would be unable to pick up on its signature either.

She estimated it would take another two decades to get it in place. A few tweaks were required to make sure the gate remained stable. Ganna glanced over the side of her station at the one monitoring the core. Deep in the sea near the North, she saw a tiny energy dot pinpointing the location of Lassa's vessel and core. She wondered if she could create a new vessel better than the one her father had made the planet's consciousness.

That is, if the first one was not salvageable.

A sheet of white light filling Lassa's vision hurt their eyes. Dull pulses of pain throbbed behind them. The sound of soft dragging made them listen for its origin. Their eyesight finally adjusted, and they found themselves staring at the medical bay ceiling. Overhead orbs floating in the corners were too bright. The smell of burnt metal, dust, and antiseptic invaded their nostrils.

"Ugh!" Lassa raised a hand to cover their mouth and saw some fingers fused together. "What is this?" They cried out in a panic, trying to sit up.

"Oh, no you don't."

Ganna came to their side. Looming over them with a

handheld scanner, the scientist looked haggard. A closer inspection of their surroundings and Lassa saw part of the far wall missing. An energy field crackling with webbed fractures kept the bay from exposure to the fields.

"You are still reassembling yourself." Ganna dropped her hand, holding the scanner down. "I am amazed you are recovering so quickly."

"The leaders!" Lassa struggled and sat up against Ganna, trying to hold them back. "Mandra. Where is her core? Her body?"

Ganna raised her brow. A glare formed as she pursed her lips in disgust.

"That is your concern?" Ganna let out a sigh and turned away. "Most of the bodies are still where they fell in battle years ago. I haven't the resources to go scouring for survivors. You," she pointed accusingly, "are a priority, yet you nearly squandered your power."

Lassa's body glowed red, their eyes turning silver.

"You will take me out there to retrieve them. And you will help me fix this."

Ganna reared back from them, a terrified look on her face. Lassa had always suspected the young scientist felt a sense of unnatural loyalty to the planet. That translated to a lack of empathy for the ones protecting it. As if that was their duty and they should never question or think of anything else.

For the love of Lassa.

"Fine." Ganna relented and found a clean robe for Lassa to wear. "The weather is out of season. You'll need this." She handed it to Lassa and waited for them to dress. "Please be careful."

Lassa followed Ganna out of the medical bay via the sliding doors. Outside, snow fell in patches while other areas had rain or sunshine. *What have I done?* A multitude of colors filled the sky. Debris from enemy ships and the damage they caused covered the surface. The air smelled awful. Stale blood and smoke. Lassa's energy destroyed, yet some things lingered.

Remembering Mandra's last location, Lassa sped towards that region. They encountered bodies everywhere along the way. *This won't do.* They focused on finding Mandra and finally came to her body. A large chunk missing from the right side of her torso, along with a severed leg and crushed arms. Her eyes were still open, yet no life remained.

Lassa dropped to their knees beside her and screamed. They slammed their fists onto the dirt below, letting the tears fall. The light pulse of red from her exposed core made Lassa look over in awe. They used their fingers to rip the torso all the way and pulled it out, cradling it.

Pieces of it had broken off and fractures covered it. Lassa turned to Ganna.

"We have to save her!"

"That core is practically dead." Ganna protested.

"There has to be a way to do it." Lassa glared at her. "It doesn't need to be intact. As long as most of her remains." Lassa hugged the core. "I can't lose her." Their head suddenly snapped up. "I can't lose either of them." Laxis. That pain in their core spread like fire. "We have to find Laxis as well."

Using their mind's eye to search, Lassa found Laxis and headed that way. Ganna again followed close behind, though not as urgently. The warrior's body lay in a mess. Stab wounds rendered it almost unrecognizable. Even Ganna gagged at the sight, covering her nose and mouth to prevent the smell and not retch.

"My sweet Laxis," Lassa bent down, still holding Mandra's core. They stroked an unmutilated part of his face. "Take him back to your lab." Ganna stared at her with indignation. "I won't ask you again."

Ganna went to the other side of Laxis' body and hefted it over her shoulder. A transporter sat empty five hundred yards away. The outer hull, though charred, still appeared operational. Ganna deposited Laxis in the back hatch.

Lassa stood.

"We must hurry before it's too late."

Lassa climbed into the passenger seat as Ganna hit the power button. The transport sputtered, the dash lights flickering, until it came to life. They rode in silence to pick up Mandra's body before heading back to the medical bay. Instead of entering the main doors, Ganna carried the pieces of Mandra's body into a side entrance. Lassa sucked air through clenched teeth as they came to a wing with a different setup. They knew instantly this is where Ganna and Mercan manipulated cores.

"I can split the energy. The body is simple enough to regenerate, although it can never house that core again. We will need to create another. The core will have to be buried for protection. It may take decades for recovery." Ganna arranged the body in the cryochamber. "It will never be complete."

She left the room and came back hauling Laxis like a sack of meal. Lassa suppressed their displeasure at seeing her handle him like that. Ganna deposited him in another cryochamber and removed his core through the largest gash in his abdomen.

"I don't want this," Lassa blurted.

Ganna sealed the two chambers and carried Laxis' core to an empty cube on the shelf with rows of them. For Mandra's core, she placed it in an organic webbing for burial preparations.

"What?" Ganna asked, confused.

"This power. This body." Lassa hung their head as they sat in a seat by the console. "I'm tired. I don't want it." Lassa looked up at her, pleading. "There has to be a way to take this from me!"

Ganna's sinister stare made Lassa flinch. Before she could think of some horrific experiment, Lassa beat her to the punch.

"It just needs to be handed down to my lineage. Blend

our essence so that we will remain bonded."

Ganna's mouth gaped open. "You would have to procreate first."

"That's an easy feat. It doesn't matter who it is, so long as our offspring mates with one or more of Mandra and Laxis' children."

This time, Ganna came upon her in fury.

"That's disgusting! How could you suggest something so…"

"Genius?" Lassa's eyes sparkled with heinous joy. Then they softened, filled with sadness. "How else will I keep them safe? I told you. I can't lose them. I won't."

Lassa stood and went over to the cryochambers. They caressed the tops. Ganna stayed clear, not wanting to be near them. Lassa understood her hesitation. They also knew the young scientist never passed up the chance to do something unprecedented. One thing Ganna cherished above all else was scientific exploration. With her father gone, she would take up the helm.

"When the time comes, take my power and give it to my heir. Find a compatible vessel from Mandra's bloodline for what's left of her core." They glanced at Laxis. "He should recover with no memories. You must lock them. And his dual wielding."

"What about Mandra's vessel?" Ganna asked cautiously.

Lassa thought for a moment. Their affection for Mandra and Laxis knew no bounds. If they could have even one of them…

"Give it to me. I will no longer have the planet's energy and since that vessel cannot hold its original core again, there's no need for it to be wasted."

"You selfish, narcissistic…" Ganna admonished them.

Lassa turned around and grabbed the front of her robes. Tears stung their eyes as they bore into Ganna's.

"I will do as I please! I am the embodiment of Lassa! No other is above me. My existence is to bring light to my people, this home." Their eyes narrowed. "You will spread my words of blessing and preserve my legacy."

Ganna wrenched from Lassa's grip and stepped away from them. Such fury and sadness rolled together, consumed Lassa. They could see the way Ganna's expression changed from horror to resolve. She would do as they asked. Reluctantly.

That didn't matter. As long as she did impeccable work, Lassa had no interest in Ganna's feelings. They had an inkling she would become a nemesis in time.

"Let us finish this and start collecting what vessels and cores we can recover. The quicker we get back on our feet, the faster I can find a mate."

Ganna placed Madra's broken core in the cube next to Laxis' and let it seal shut.

"The warriors and manbeasts will need new leaders."

"I will let the council take care of that." Lassa made their way to the exit. "I have a feeling we will not be seeing anymore invasions for a while. News will spread to avoid this quadrant."

"That won't be necessary." Ganna walked past her and stopped at the start of the grass scorched in sections all the way to the forest ahead. "No one will know where we are from now on." Ganna turned to look back at Lassa. "I will make sure of it."

Lassa smirked. The planet's technological evolution jumped tenfold in the past century. They had faith in Ganna's words. It gave them time to regroup until the need to search for resources came upon them.

Planet Lassa would be safe and its vessel, a new life.

Three: Déjà vu

Awakening

Talas jolted awake from a deep sleep, lurching forward until his head hovered above his knees. His eyes moved rapidly, trying to regain focus while a smoky haze surrounding everything blurred his vision. He clutched the front of the robe he wore.

Where am I? His name kept eluding him even though he could hear it linger in the back of his mind. His core's light blossomed, making him double over. Memories flooded through him. Ancient ones from multiple cores that merged with new ones brought anger.

All the lives he led mingled together. Love. Children. Kelin. He did not negate any of it. Talas. That is what they call him now. Still a Lassian warrior, except with diminished power.

I am Laxis.

Remembering the demise of his true love, Mandra, the strongest manbeast ever to wield talons, caused him pain. The shock of feeling her core dim took the fight out of him as he lay being impaled by the enemy. He had lived for her majestic being. Then it hit him as the current memories made themselves clearer. Her body! Another inhabited her form. Why? Who would dole out such cruelty? More of the jumbled memories unraveled.

The doors on the other side of the room slid open and Ganna stepped in. She caught sight of him and smiled.

"Oh, you've finally awakened…"

Talas had his hands around her neck in an instant,

squeezing. He heard her gagging, struggling for air. His eyes glowed amber. She locked onto his stare and her own widened in terror.

"Talas!" Kelin ran into the room and tried to pry his hands from Ganna's neck. "You can't! I know you're angry. We all are. Please."

Talas ignored him at first, then realized the hurt in his tone. He turned to Kelin. This is my new mate, who I love dearly. He took one more look at Ganna, then released her. She fell to the floor, landing sideways on her knees.

"What happened?" Kelin asked. Talas walked over to the bin where Ganna stowed his clothes. He slowly dressed. "Please tell me what's wrong."

"Everything," Talas said. He glanced over his shoulder. "And nothing at all."

"What?" Kelin searched his eyes and flinched. "Why are you," his voice hesitated, "different?"

Talas turned and cupped his face in his hands.

"My beloved, I'm sorry. Don't abandon me."

"That's how I feel about the way you're looking at me."

"I will explain. But first." He went over to Ganna as she clawed her way to a console and slumped in the seat. "You will tell me why." Fuzzy recollections aside, he wanted…no, needed to hear her say it. Explain it.

Ganna stared fearlessly at him, her demeanor changed to haughty.

"It was their idea, not mine. They didn't want their old body. But they didn't want to lose any of the original beings."

"So you chose to do Lassa's bidding? The consequences be damned?" Talas' voice rose with each word.

"Lassa's light…" Ganna prayed, not finishing.

"To hell with Lassa and their tainted light!" Talas suddenly reared his head up and stared at Ganna. "Lassa took her body." His face contorted. "You really did what they asked and put that parasite in Mandra's body!"

"Can you please tell me what's going on?" Kelin demanded.

"No." Talas replied bluntly. He saw Kelin look defiant. "Not yet. This needs to be sorted out before that." He returned his attention to Ganna. "Isn't that right? Head scientist?" He vehemently spat out her title. "Where are the others?"

"You were the last to wake up." Ganna rubbed the bruise forming on her neck. "Come, Kelin. We must leave before my hands do more harm to this woman."

"Not that I don't mind," Kelin said. "But you're correct." The two left the medical bay. Outside, Kelin halted for a second. "I will wait for you to explain it. I trust you, Talas."

Hearing his new name, he cringed inside. Then he remembered his time on Earth. Better than Sarah.

⌒

Jaron kept her distance from everyone, hoping it to be the best action. Memories long forgotten filled her mind, the guilt weighing on her like a boulder. She had not told Modas the reason for her last-minute dash into hiding. The empty abode, newly built along a row of housing, blessed her with silence. She sat on a stoop in front of it, her head tilted back, and her eyes closed as a soft breeze came through.

With it came the familiar sound of Talas' footsteps. She knew them well. Her body stiffened as she opened her eyes and brought her face down to see his approach. Even from afar, she saw no felt his anger. To her horror, Modas and Chardon came up the hill on her right.

No! Please!

Talas noticed them yet didn't slow his advance. He got within ten feet of Jaron right as Modas and Chardon came to stand next to her. Chardon moved to her left when he saw Talas' expression.

"This is not how we are going to handle it, Talas."

"Shut up," Talas snapped. Chardon blinked back in surprise. Modas stepped closer to Jaron. "You need to move." Talas stared the manbeast down.

Jaron leaned forward.

"Don't you dare speak!" Talas ordered her.

"Please, listen to me," Jaron begged.

"How could you?" Talas stood with his arms at his side, fingers twitching against his thighs. "What you've done is monstrous. I will never forgive you for this!"

"What is going on?" Chardon demanded. "I won't tolerate your behavior."

Talas whipped his head towards him. "Tolerate? You're going to do more than that." He turned to Jaron. "Was this also part of the plan? You give all your power to a descendant, so you don't have to deal with the responsibility?"

Chardon's face went slack. Then he frowned, addressing Jaron.

"What is he talking about?" Then his eyes widened. "Those memories. They're true?"

"You need to explain," Modas said, his tone terse.

Jaron finally stood. "I didn't want her body to get destroyed. You have to understand." She took a step closer. "I cared deeply for her, too."

Talas drew his sword with lightning speed, the blade stopping short at the side of Jaron's neck. She could have easily avoided it yet chose not to. Modas extended his talons while blue spheres of electricity formed in Chardon's palms.

"Tell your mate to back off. You know I'll kill him." Talas and Modas locked eyes. The manbeast wavered. "That goes for you too," he glanced at Chardon. "Leader."

"I know you're upset. I won't ask for forgiveness. You loved her." Jaron clutched the front of her robes. "I wish I knew how to fix it, for your sake, Laxis."

Talas lowered his sword, letting its tip touch the ground. Tears threatened to well over, so he wiped them away with one hand. "Where is her core?"

"It's why I did what I had to. You saw. Her core was fragmented. Ganna took what we had, and force fused it with another vessel."

"That's not what I asked." His anger briefly flashed back.

"I," Jaron swallowed. "I have an idea, but uncertain. They would only have a few deep memories, but mostly." She stopped.

"Mostly what?" Talas yelled.

"Her talent and strength."

Talas' eyes went wide. He stared at her for a moment, Jaron appearing wary, not sure if he would resume his attack. Then his eyes narrowed, glowing softly in the daylight. He sheathed his sword and turned away from her.

"That makes it that much worse," he said, walking back through the fields.

"Jaron." Chardon let the energy dissipate from his hands. "You need to tell me what's happening. I feel my energy surging exponentially and I'm not sure how to control it when it gets too much. And you called Talas, Laxis. Is it truly him with his original core intact?"

"It's," Jaron leaned forward as she sat back on the stoop, "hard to say." Jaron tried to hold her tears at bay. "It hurts so much."

"Try." Modas did not sound amused. "Talas just said he would kill me."

Jaron simply nodded. "This body. It belonged to the great manbeast." Modas stepped away from her in disgust. "Along with her mate, the great warrior, Laxis, the two were Lassa's cornerstone of defense."

"Your core lives within a manbeast?" Modas seemed to struggle with that revelation. She knew why. He never understood his attraction to her, or how he couldn't shake his blind loyalty to Chardon. "Then who are you?"

"I can't tell you that. I won't. Please, not yet. There is so much that needs to be done first. More dire things than this." Jaron looked to him then Chardon. "Afford me more time."

Chardon gave her a piteous stare.

I know. You're disappointed.

"Fine. I will let it slide for now. But we need to rein in

Talas before all hell breaks loose, as they say on earth."

Jaron nodded again, defeated. Her whole body sagged. She leaned over, settling her head onto her lap. She didn't dare look at Modas, who walked away without a word. Chardon placed a hand on her head.

"This will work itself out."

When Chardon became a tiny figure in the distance, Jaron burst into tears.

I'm sorry!

Hon stood off in the shadows of the hill near the row of houses, watching his mother fall into despair. *Serves you right, you selfish monster.* He sympathized with her not having genuine memories for so long. Parts of her original core imprinted on him at birth. The only two people who knew her real identity at the time were Ganna and himself. He smirked. He could only imagine what Ganna tried to do to Talas for all this to happen.

That woman will get her due for this!

Out of the corner of his eye, he saw his father walking aimlessly towards the hill on the other side. That part he didn't like. Not one bit. Sadness hit him.

Make it right? Fix it? Easier said.

Ganna sat leaning over her station with her head buried in both hands. Sadness and rage filled her.

This isn't how I wanted it!

And there was no one else to blame. She had not expected the outcome from multiple attempts at manipulating Talas' core. Laxis. Oh, he will be a problem if he retaliates. She lifted her head. Maybe. Ideas on how to reason with him flooded her mind.

The lab door opened, breaking her concentration. Ganna turned to see who had entered.

Looking like a predator who had finished devouring its prey, Hon stood in the entrance, eyes locked on her slumped frame. She straightened her posture, making eye contact. The two stared at each other, not speaking yet, saying everything they needed to. Hon finally smirked. Ganna's eyes narrowed, and she turned away.

"You've made such a mess. And for what?" Hon pulled an empty rolling seat towards her station and plopped down. Ganna stared in awe at his audacity. "Now my family is having a worse time dealing with yet another crisis. Are you proud of what you accomplished?"

Ganna had him by the front of his robes in a flash, her face looming less than an inch from his. The young manbeast's smug expression turned to fear. She couldn't control her anger at that moment.

"I don't ever want to harm our race!" Spittle flew from her mouth. "Everything! Everything I do is for the sake of Lassa's people!"

Chardon came into the room and stopped short, gasping at the sight of Ganna holding Hon in place. She didn't acknowledge him, her focus on Hon.

"If other planets would have left us alone, we would still know peace and not have to defend ourselves like this!"

"Let him go, Ganna." Chardon spoke softly.

Something about the tone of it snapped Ganna out of her rage. Her eyes widened and she let go of Hon's robe. She stepped back from him.

I've shown weakness!

Chardon turned to Hon. "Stop antagonizing everyone. It serves no good. Nor is it amusing."

Still awestruck, Hon slowly rose from the seat and went around Chardon to exit. He took one look back. Ganna gave him a pain filled side glance. He nodded to her and left.

"I get it, I really do." Chardon stood inches from her. "But your methods are detrimental to our people's morale. What benefits our fighting amongst each other?"

Ganna made fists at her sides. She bit the corner of her lips, not daring to answer with one of her glib remarks. *I need to fix this!* Her original plan's timeline blown to smithereens, she had to factor in a new one.

"I can see what you've been doing to your core," Chardon said. Ganna went stiff. "That will only work for so long, and it seems to have reached its limit." He placed a hand on her shoulder. "Blocking off your essence to make yourself an enemy is never ideal."

Ganna frowned, smacking his hand off her. "If I hadn't, we would never have advanced this far! I am the one entrusted with guidance for our kind. Nothing gets done if everyone is just content with the present."

Chardon let out a heavy sigh, turning away from her. "You never asked us, Ganna."

The doors slid closed. Ganna backed into the wall and slumped. It's true. She never once initiated any collaboration with the others. She merely dictated her plans and ordered each division to implement them. It worked for centuries in her mind. Now the cracks in her plan were showing. She slammed a fist against the wall.

"Why? Why am I wrong?"

Loyalty

The five systems deemed Azrom Trade merchants on par with Dreridians. A third of them derived from the fourth royal house. Their talents leaned more domestic than military. Which seemed fine until they affected Azrom's status. Rumors spread of their dissatisfaction regarding how the Supreme Ruler dealt with the Dreridians and other major factions in the trade industry.

Romnus tried not to let them antagonize or goad him into undesirable positions. Another plot to assassinate him and the Queen came to light. Spies were everywhere on both sides. This time, the plots felt more emboldened. He had not yet found the origin of that sentiment.

In his private study, with the hover lights on dim, Romnus sat wearing a simple cream-colored tunic with black leggings and boots. A black cape fastened with a short silver chain at the clavicle draped over his shoulders. One hand cradled a cheek as he leaned against the side of the curved high-back chair. The servant came over to refill the chalice on the table before him. Only a few drops lingered from the first round.

"Would you like anything else, my lord?" The servant asked, softly.

His gaze slid over to scrutinize every inch of her. Her hands tightened on the carafe, her body going stiff. She tried to shrink her presence. Ample bosom, the smooth curves of her hips and backside. Nicely shaped pink lips, perfect for suckling his hard nipples. Healthy. That was a good thing after decades of near starvation following the last war.

"No. That will be all."

He averted his gaze, sensing her relief as she hurried out.

"Don't ever do that in front of our Queen," Batis said, passing the servant on his way in. "Or Biandra, for that matter."

"What are you talking about?"

Batis stopped halfway, sitting in the seat across from him, and stared at him in awe. He then shrugged and settled down. He propped his legs on the table opposite the glass on the other side of Romnus.

"Never mind. I have an unpleasant report." Romnus glared at him. "Unless you'd rather not hear it at this moment." Batis reached over and took a small fruit from the tray that always stayed stocked in the study.

Romnus let his hand drop into his lap. The sole reason for being in the study alone was to avoid any news. An hour or two of solitude, that's all he wanted. Getting close to two-hours before Batis showed up surprised him. He lucked out.

"It's fine. What now?"

"A communication." Batis took a bite of the fruit.

"Hmmm."

"In an outer region language. Encrypted." Romnus' eyes burned bright upon hearing the last word. "I have one of our spies trying to decipher a copy. Unfortunately, it had already gone out. We were too late to intercept." Batis looked over at him.

"Where did it come from?" Romnus asked calmly.

Batis became alarmed. Romnus knew what he'd say.

"Before we jump to conclusions and start executing royals, we need to confirm these things. We still don't know what it is they hope to gain from such a deal, whatever it may be."

"And the royal council?" The last two Supreme Rulers had little luck in loyalty with royal advisors. "What are they saying in the midst?"

"So far, nothing. And yes," Batis chewed before continuing. "It seems odd that they are silent. There's no way they haven't heard even a murmur."

Romnus lifted the chalice and drained it. He set the empty glass back on the table and stood.

"I'm leaving."

Batis gave him a knowing stare. "Feeling out of sorts?"

Romnus stopped at the entrance, turning his head towards him.

"I'll be away for the rest of the day."

"I'll keep the Queen occupied for you," Batis replied, smiling sweetly.

His expression fell as Romnus' face scrunched with hostility. He walked off, not wanting to ask what he meant by that. His visits to the brothel were no secret, but he saw no reason to announce it for the Queen and everyone else to know.

Farin. She acted differently towards him after the birth of their twins. Did she desire him to abstain from releasing his frustrations on the sex slaves? If that's the case, she should tell him so. Until then, he needed it.

Batis contemplated the new wrinkle concerning the fourth royal house. Cowards! A cunning bunch of entitled parasites. They demanded recognition of status and consumed mass amounts of the amenities offered. He knew why the lower houses opted to make a move. Azrom had met its match in their eyes, and they wanted to be on the side of the victor.

But you're wrong! We were simply caught off guard.

He dropped his legs and leaned over to hit the call icon on the side of the table. The servant returned; hands clasped tight in front of her below the midriff. Can't blame her for that. He too had previously delved in sexual depravity, although he ceased doing so over the years.

"What would you like, Commander?"

"Some of that wine and dried meat."

"Anything else? Will you be here for a while?"

"Hmmm." Batis grinned. "Send for Queen Farin. I believe she is strolling the halls. Bring enough for two."

"As you wish, commander." She gave a bow and left.

Swinging his legs back onto the table, he let his head fall back against the chair. He closed his eyes and took a deep breath. Like Romnus, he was aware the times of leisure were ending soon. If the enemy doesn't show up first, Azrom would see infighting again.

The servant came with the wine and food, startling him upright. He had lost track of time and fallen asleep.

Was I that tired?

"Aww." Farin came into the room behind the servant. "You looked so sweet, too. Shame."

"My lady Farin." Batis wiped his face with both hands and removed his legs so the servant could set down the tray. "You should know better." He lifted the carafe of wine and poured some into the two chalices. "I am anything but sweet."

"Hmph! Liar."

Farin sat across from him instead of in the seat Romnus previously occupied. Dressed in a dark blue robe secured at the waist with a wide black sash, she was the image of royalty. Her jet-black hair hung loose, flowing over the shoulders.

"Will there be anything else, my Queen, commander?" The servant kept her head low.

"That will be all, thank you," Farin answered. When the servant left, she raised her drink. "To your transparent attempt to keep me at bay while my mate goes to desecrate the brothel."

Batis glared at her. She pursed her lips, not meeting his gaze.

"Don't." Batis rested his arms on the sides, letting them dangle. He refused to pick up his chalice.

"Fine." Farin's expression went slack. "For being my friend after all this." Her sorrowful tone, barely a whisper, hit him. "Is that better?"

He reached over and cupped her face with his hands. They stared at each other for a long time. Seeing her on the verge of tears, his hands trembled a bit before he let her go.

"I will always be on your side." He raised his glass. "To friendship."

They clinked them together and drained the wine. Batis poured a second round.

"By the way," Farin sat to the side, one elbow on the armrest. "Did you know someone from the fourth house pushed me down the stairs and doused water on me?"

Batis froze. He slowly lowered his glass to his chin, not quite sure if she jested or was completely serious. A rage lit within him.

"What did you say?"

"No one else was around." She took a sip of wine. "I slit his throat."

"Farin," Batis said through gritted teeth, setting the glass down.

"Don't worry, he lives. I sent him to the medical wing."

"That's not the issue!" He leaned forward.

Farin turned to him with fury. "Why are you angry? I said I didn't kill him! It would take more than that to get rid of me."

"You should have reported it. We would have handled the backlash."

"Do you think Romnus would be rational?" Farin cocked her head. "Like you are now? Do you see that royal rat telling anyone what he did to deserve that wound or my wrath?"

Batis sat back, staring at her in disbelief. Yes, a tumble down some stairs wouldn't kill her. She surely had bruises on her body. How would she explain those to Romnus? As if reading his mind, she chuckled.

"I'll just tell Romnus I wasn't paying attention, and in my usual clumsiness, mis stepped. It sounds comical, me taking a header."

"No, Farin. It doesn't." His eyes narrowed. "They've gone too far."

She gave him a side glance to deter his next action. That won't work this time. He planned to head for the medical wing after leaving their small snack session to pay the fourth royal house slime a visit. And dare his counterparts to try worming him out of the punishment he deserved.

"You can't kill him." Farin took a longer sip of her wine.

Batis smiled widely, his expression borderline evil.

"Oh, I won't, dear Farin. I promise."

∿

Batis' plans for torture deflated the moment he arrived at the medical wing and caught sight of the culprit lying unconscious on a gurney in the private sector reserved for royals. The man's throat had indeed been sliced deep. The other injuries gave Batis pause. Both arms and legs were broken, and the left arm nearly crushed. A wide, horizontal puncture wound in his abdomen appeared to come from by fingers held close together.

Blood dribbled from the corners of the royal's mouth. The doctor on hand stood repairing his throat with a laser suture. A teary-eyed royal female stood close by, watching. Must be his mate. She turned hateful red eyes towards Batis. He smirked in amusement, remembering Farin had a guardian more dangerous than Trinon. And twisted. Batis realized the incident went down after all with a witness.

"What has happened here?" Batis asked sweetly. The woman's face scrunched further. "Surely this was not the doing of another royal member." He cocked his head back. "Unless, of course, this outcome warranted such an attack."

The woman's eyes went wide in fury. "How dare you give such smug remarks to my mate's condition!" She stepped forward, getting a few feet from him. "You find this funny? I demand retribution!"

"Ah," Batis smiled. "You don't know why. He's not awake to tell you."

"It doesn't matter!" She swiped her right arm to one side. "I want whoever did this to meet their judgement in public." Drool formed around her exposed teeth.

The doctor moved on to the abdomen. He tsked, shaking his head. "Barbaric."

I concur.

Batis stared down at the mess covered in black blood oozing onto the gurney. The level of hate needed to do that kind of damage frightened him while admiring the work.

Couldn't have done better myself.

"I think you should wait until he revives to hear his reason." Satisfied with the royal's swift treatment, he turned to leave. "Oh, I wouldn't broadcast this incident until you have the facts of the matter." He tilted his head to glare at her over his shoulder. "No need to cause a royal mess."

He watched her balk at his suggestion before averting his gaze and went out into the hall. Midway to the fields where Biandra surely strolled, he clenched his fists. On second thought, it had gone too far. If Farin sent the royal to be treated herself, he doubted she would leave out the rest of his injuries. No. She left it up to her guardian. The father of her first child. A menace within the royal house, exiled from the public eye.

Chastan.

Batis released his fingers and wiggled them to get the feeling back. Tiny half-moons from his short talons digging in his flesh turned dark from blood filling their form.

You monster.

Nightfall had already consumed Azrom when Romnus returned to his throne room for any current updates from the royal council. Only two were still working and advised him there was nothing to report. The lateness tugged at him as he made his way back to his chamber. Farin lay sound asleep. He undressed quietly and crawled into bed, careful not to jostle her.

Seeing her serene face brought guilt. *Yet, I have no reason to feel this way.* He wrapped his arms around her and fell asleep. His dreams were ugly.

At daybreak, Romnus woke breathing in Farin's hair. He pulled her tighter, feeling the warmth of her body. She pressed against him, smiling with her eyes still closed.

"How was your day? Anything fun?" He asked playfully.

"Oh, nothing. I lounged with Batis and drank wine."

"Hmmm. Is that so?"

His hands roamed her hips, gathering the fabric up. She tried several times to push his hands away. Not forcefully, but enough to make him suspicious. They locked eyes. Farin turned away, her body going limp in defeat. He raised the sheer fabric and saw the first edges of a dark bruise. He pulled the blanket away and saw the others on her sides and legs.

"What happened?" He demanded.

Farin looked over at him and grinned. "It's nothing, really. Just me being clumsy as usual. I fell down some stairs." She laughed nervously.

Silence engulfed them. Romnus stared at her until she met his eyes again.

"Farin," he warned. "You have never been clumsy a day in your life."

"It doesn't matter. Me tripping on my own two feet and tumbling down a flight of stairs isn't going to break me. I'm not some fragile being."

Romnus gripped the side of her buttocks.

"That's not the issue. Where was your shadow?"

Farin pursed her lips. "He can't be that close to me, so it wouldn't have mattered." She gently yanked her gown back over her hips. "I took care of it."

She swung her legs over and got out of bed.

His guilt from last night bloomed. On most days he strolled the palace with her. The fall would not have happened. Something about it struck him as wrong.

She's lying to me. It's been taken care of? No. I won't accept that.

He watched her get dressed, the bruises more disturbing in the light.

"I'm going to head over to see the twins." She stopped at the entrance and smiled brightly. "Are you coming?"

"I will later." Romnus mustered up the energy to rise from the bed. He leaned against the headboard, taking in her silhouette as the sun peeked over the outer balcony. "Shower them with love for me."

"See you at morning meal." She walked down the veranda, leaving him to his own thoughts.

Now to find out what happened. He flung the rest of the covers off and got up.

###

Romnus first needed to find Chastan. Farin's mood, despite asking in such a sweet tone, forbade him from following her to the twins' chamber. He walked into the common hall of the first royal house. The last time he visited being before his wedding. The place, though dimly lit, still seemed dark, resembling a charcoal drawing. All grey and black, with two hover lights in the far corners of the ceiling. No one had used it in a long time.

Chastan blended in the shadows as he stood before the giant hearth. His appearance startled Romnus, yet he kept his response in check. No longer the royal playboy chasing every piece of ass he could get his hands on; Chastan became a menace. His blond locks hung past his shoulders, the bangs obstructing his eyes. The black cloak over a black bodysuit secured with a black sash intensified his ominous presence.

"I woke to my Queen covered in bruises. Care to explain?" Romnus stopped a few yards from him. "You should know lying to me is not ideal."

"My loyalty…"

"Is to me and the empire…"

"To Farin. As it always should be."

"What happened to Farin, Chastan?"

"She fell down the stairs."

Romnus came at him with lightning speed, his hand getting around Chastan's neck. To his surprise, Chastan bent backwards, leaping out of his grasp and landing above the hearth, all four of his limbs' pincers embedded in the stone wall. He hung like a spider, his eyes glowing with fury.

"You trust me to act as her shadow, then question my loyalty? I took care of it after Farin slit his throat."

"So why have I not heard of a funeral rite?"

"Because Farin said not to kill him. That with the current atmosphere in the palace, it would make things worse."

Romnus balled his hands into fists. That was true. Still. Chastan unhooked himself from the wall and landed on his feet. His agility made Romnus think twice about coming for him again.

You've changed greatly, cousin.

He turned and left the commons. The small fruit Biandra left on the side of the bed while he slept burned an imaginary hole inside his robe. He pulled it out and popped the whole thing in his mouth, chewing slowly. The juices flowed, calming his nerves.

Chatter amongst the fourth royal house traveled to Romnus by mistake when two royals whispered about the current events near an alcove where he stood hidden, again, trying to have a moment of solace. When the first royal talked about one of their members being in the medical wing, he listened more closely.

"Can you believe what was done to him?"

"It was uncalled for. And his mate is livid."

"That cretin Batis had the audacity to tell her not to pursue justice."

"The culprit should pay with their life."

Romnus waited until they moved away, still talking about retribution, then headed for the royal medical wing. Everyone gave him a wide berth while bowing and giving morning greetings. He addressed none of them. His laser focus on his destination.

Inside the royal sector, he came across the so-called victim lying sedated while his mate paced the small area at the edge of the bed. She stopped short and inhaled sharply, seeing Romnus.

"Unless you are here to decree justice for this travesty, get out!" The mate screamed.

Romnus ignored her.

The doctor turned, stricken with fear from checking his patient, and bowed.

"My lord, what brings you here?"

"Wake him. I have questions to ask."

"He's in excruciating pain. Bringing him up would…"

Romnus morphed his left arm into giant pincers and slammed it over the royal's head, engulfing it. The tiny, serrated edges would sever it clean if snapped shut.

"Or don't," Romnus deadpanned.

The victim's mate pressed both fists to her mouth, then lowered them.

"Please, my lord. I'm sorry! Don't kill him!"

"I warned you not to spread this incident to anyone," Batis said as he came into the room. He addressed Romnus. "That won't solve anything."

"Are you taking care of it as well?" Romnus turned his head towards him.

"My lord." Batis got closer. "I need you to listen to me." He glanced at the pincer.

The doctor went over to a side table and came back with an injection gun. He turned the dial at the bottom.

"Please, I will wake him now." He gestured at Romnus to step away.

Romnus retracted the pincer, reverting it to a normal arm. The doctor gave the royal the injection and within seconds, he was awake, yowling in pain.

"Is this your idea of justice?" The royal's mate yelled. "No matter what he's done, this was over the line. I demand the one who did this be punished. They must pay for this!"

The royal gave his mate a sorrowful look, then cringed in horror as Romnus glared at him.

"Go on. Tell your precious mate what you've done."

"I…" He looked around the room. "Please, my lord. It was an accident. I had no intention of doing harm," he stuttered.

"Well, that's not true," Kur interjected, walking in to stand by Batis.

"The consequences of lying to me will be worse than anything else you do." Romnus said.

"I didn't." The royal clenched his fists. "It wouldn't have killed her. It was just a push." His indignation grew. "You want to punish me for giving the Queen a few scratches? Her leashed pet did this to me after she slashed my throat."

His mate gasped, her body going rigid. She dared not look at anyone. A pained expression filled her face.

Batis crossed his arms and smirked at her.

"Will you still want vengeance after this?"

"You stupid mongrel!" She spat at her mate. "This makes things worse."

"Indeed." Kur nodded.

"Give me a reason not to kill him." Romnus' eyes burned with intensity.

"He didn't kill her. That was never his goal. He's not a murderer," his mate replied.

"She's right about making it worse. Fourth house relations are in the decline." Batis glanced over at the woman. "This hurts us all. What do you think would happen if the people found out about your house causing harm to our Queen?"

The royal and his mate went pale. Romnus could tell they were only thinking of their agenda being impacted. They won't back down from their position. As much as he wanted to tear the royal's limbs off, he stepped away.

"I will let this slide. Know this. Anyone who tries to harm her again," he glanced over at them, "dies."

He brushed past Batis and Kur as he left the room. They followed him in silence. Good.

Don't say one word to me right now. I'm angry at you as well.

He could feel their anxiety.

A Bad Scenario

Debris lay scattered along the center aisle of the fifty-foot-wide bay. Containers sat randomly crooked or damaged on each side of the giant shelves. Further in, broken canisters of explosive gels oozed out on the floor. At the end of the bay, a gaping tattered hole the size of a city block loomed dark, the smell of charred metal drifting in the air.

"They blew the vault," Batis said deadpan.

Rass seethed at the sight of his weapons bunker in disarray. Its sole responsible for it lay with him for good reason. That vault stored the most dangerous weapons in the known galaxy. Planet bombs. A selection of various strengths depending on how much devastation one wanted to administer. The blast itself from the bunker would have been deafening right before the alarm.

"I need to get this sealed off before bringing in the technicians for an inventory count." Rass started walking down the center. He touched some of the damaged pieces along the way, bending down for the smaller ones. "How many injured?" His eyes scanned the area, and he noticed where bodies had once laid.

"They had to have a spy within the bay for them to toss the first round of smaller explosives. Looks like it harmed every guard. No casualties."

"The spy probably realized his error too late and tried to save them."

"The rebels turned on him once they had access. They would be wounded the worst."

"Such stupidity." Rass stopped in front of the hole with Batis next to him. "They have no idea what they've done."

Shimmering lights flashed inside the black hole, signaling rifts on the verge of forming. Several containments showed cracks. Rass pulled out his portable commlink and tapped it to open a channel.

"I need emergency bomb technicians at the secondary weapons bay." He paused as he stared into the abyss. "We have planet bombs unaccounted for."

"Well, that will get the scientists up and running," Batis said tersely. "Romnus is going to lose his mind."

The alert of a massive dimensional force spilling out then leaving the planet sent the entire military into action. Rass couldn't believe it at first, hoping for a glitch. Confirmation of its origin solidified his rage. To raid the secondary weapons bay took more than a few days of planning. It would require months, years, to pull it off.

"Where would they store them?" Batis asked. The two of them turned from the disaster. He glanced over at Rass. "Depending on how many they took, send them to another location would be no simple task."

"Yes, they used the gate system to hide them in a secure space. My guess is the bombs are floating around an uninhabited planet in case they become unstable."

"That's just reckless!"

Footsteps approaching made them look up towards the entrance.

"I couldn't agree more," Lieutenant Treshur said. He walked deliberating down the aisle, avoiding the pieces of debris yet scrutinizing it all. "We will get this mess cleaned up and contained. You can go quell the Supreme Ruler's wrath."

Rass snorted. "Who's stopping him again?"

"At least make an effort." Treshur met his gaze. "You know what will happen if he's let loose. I don't want that any more than you."

"He has a point," Batis stated. "The last thing Azrom

needs is a river of royal blood."

"It would be acceptable this time." Rass felt his body heat with fury. "Round them up. I want every fourth house royal accounted for."

"This could get messy," Batis laughed.

"That's the way I prefer." Rass gave a half grin, its crookedness conveying his thinking.

A group of scientists arrived at the bunker and took collective sharp intakes of breath. Their faces scrunched in fear and anger at the sight of the blown vault. Treshur motioned for them to follow him into the containment area.

"Come. Let's get this hole repaired and those bombs sealed before Azrom becomes floating fragments of sand."

Rass left the bunker and headed towards the main palace while Batis went to the fourth royal palace. The afternoon sun had not reached its peak yet and already chaos had fallen on the planet. He knew Kur had given chase to the fleeing ship that accompanied the missing bombs. Rounding the corner that led to the courtyard, he glimpsed Kur's mother, Emalli, playing with the younger children.

Emalli raised her head and met his stare. She knows what happened. He sighed inwardly. Her network of spies never ceased to amaze him. A large dark cloud the color of charcoal drifted angrily across the sky, forcing its way past soft white ones. Its span covered the entire town below. No doubt Romnus had seen it.

In the distance, he heard the yelling start in the fourth house. People engaged in their leisure after morning chores halted their activity, not sure if they were under attack or in battle training. Batis would not be cordial or gentle.

Rass stopped at the door of the war room connected to the throne's. He took a deep breath, then barged in with an air of authority. Romnus sat at the end of the table, Biandra by his side, feeding him those small orange fruits. From the looks of it, they weren't doing him any good. The toxin's effect barely contained his rage.

"My lord! I have sent Batis to round up the fourth house. Kur is in pursuit. We have the situation under control." He didn't really believe it, but showing uncertainty would mean death. "Please give me your decree and it shall be done." He bowed slightly.

When he finally looked up, Rass flinched, clutching the front of his tunic. His eyes narrowed and his lips pulled back, baring teeth. He could feel his insides squirm, instinctively warning him to flee—RIGHT NOW!

Romnus' eyes were glowing bright, making them seem like they didn't belong to him. Juice from the fruit dribbled down the sides of his mouth onto his black robes. A blank expression slowly gave way to a burning fury. Biandra, help-less in the situation, eased away from him so not to alert him of her own fear. Rass shifted his gaze to her, and she held up three fingers. Rass turned his attention back to Romnus. Three fruits would do nothing in his state. They would kick in later and still only slightly abate his mood.

"I want," Romnus rose from his seat, "every missing royal hunted down and brought to me."

"Of course." Rass fought to stop his voice from wavering. "It shall be done."

"Never mind." He wiped the juice from his face. "Track the enemy. If even one of our planet bombs falls into their hands, our doom is sealed."

"We will not let that happen. Have faith in our resolve."

"It's not lack of faith." Romnus walked past him into the main corridor. His entire demeanor oozed malice. Those in the vicinity hurried out of his way. "I am merely addressing the reality."

Rass and Biandra followed him out into the courtyard. Emalli pushed the last child back into the palace, turning her head to give Rass a knowing look before going in herself. Rass kept himself in step with Biandra ten feet behind Romnus, who headed straight for the fourth royal house palace.

Oh no! Rass glanced over at Biandra. Her pained

expression said it all. No one around could stop him. Rass' father was too far away in the village and even then, probably couldn't hold Romnus back. It would take many. They closed in on the main entrance.

Batis shouted out orders to his unit in the process of dragging every royal member inside of the fourth house out onto the lawn. Yelling, crying, and curses made the rounds. The only ones spared were the children kept at bay in the commons.

Everything seemed to go still as Romnus came onto the scene. Batis took one look at him and backed away instead of addressing him. The soldiers did the same, not wanting any part of what may happen. There would certainly be blood.

One soldier unceremoniously hauled the head of the fourth house, Lord Elendar, on his knees towards the front, then went to stand with his unit. Lord Elendar rose his head, the light brown strands of hair falling around his shoulders and reared back in terror at seeing Romnus. His green eyes went wide. He didn't move from his position, despite the insult of being on his knees. Dirt and grass stained the various shades of mustard-colored sashes of his black robe.

"Lord Elendar." Romnus towered over him like a giant staring down at an insect. "Explain this to me. Do you not have full reign of your house?"

Lord Elendar's tanned face went flush, turning a deep pink. He looked over at his entire house, held captive in their own courtyard. He noticed some of them attempting to cover their faces. His own contorted, seething, while Romnus' presence pressed down on him. He forced himself to stare up into those glowing eyes.

"As you too know, I cannot keep tabs on every being inside my house." He gulped.

"Are you telling me," Romnus leaned over a bit. "That you had no idea about the disrespect and acts of transgression that your house has been responsible for over the past centuries?"

Lord Elendar struggled with an answer. *Of course, I know! How could I not?* At one point, even he had gone against the reigning emperor and for good reason. Halfar was a menace like his and Romnus' father. Tyrants, all of them.

"That may be, Romnus." Lord Elendar could hear the gasps at his casual address. "But what would you have me do? These are trying times." He held up his hand. "I am not condoning any of this. I am appalled, just as you are."

"Then you sanction my decree of punishment for the guilty."

He didn't ask, making Lord Elendar immediately nervous. Romnus' arms morphed into giant claws, his height extending as his legs became those of a praying mantis.

"Wait! Do not kill my people!" Lord Elendar cried out.

He watched in horror as Romnus flashed forward and went for the first row of royal house members kneeling in the grass. Less than a foot away from his prey, six arms wrapped around Romnus, stopping his advance to strike. Lord Elendar's expression turned to awe as he witnessed the arm muscles of three warrior clan members bulging while they tried to restrain their emperor.

Rass mustered the courage to take advantage of the opportunity to talk Romnus down.

"As much as I enjoy indiscriminate killing, it would be best if we identify the actual culprits and not wipe out an entire royal house."

To Lord Elendar's surprise, Lady Emalli came into view behind him.

"It would cause more strife than necessary, my lord. Please reconsider." She bowed deeply.

For a split second, Romnus faltered. His claws snapped open and shut a few times. He glanced over his shoulder at the warrior clansman on his right. The two stared at each other. Romnus turned away and let his claws retract. His legs went back to normal.

"Release me." His glowing eyes dimmed. The moment

they let loose, he accosted Lord Elendar before anyone could stop him. His hand embedded deep in his abdomen past the wrist. "This is a reminder to do better." Romnus leaned close and whispered in his ear. "Cousin."

Lord Elendar clenched his teeth hard as not to show how much pain he endured. They met each other's gaze. Romnus smirked. Then ripped his hand out, causing a splatter of black blood to fly out onto the grass. He stepped away to avoid it. Lord Elendar clamped a hand over his wound and glared at him. His vision blurred.

No! I will not fall in front of him!

"Very well." Romnus flicked his hand to remove the excess blood. "I will stand by my first decree. Send every royal involved to me." His eyes flashed bright for a nano-second. "I will administer their reward personally."

Lord Elendar watched Romnus leave with his entourage in tow. A medical attendant ran from the palace and slid across the grass to his side.

"My lord! Be still. I have you." The attendant injected healing gel into his wound.

"Thank you." He placed a hand on the man's shoulder. "I think I may lie down for a while."

"Yes. I'm giving you a sedative."

Lord Elendar felt the second injection. Before he fell under, he took stock of his house members' faces and made a mental note of who he would send to their deaths. This time, his brood had crossed the line.

Another balmy Azrom sunset greeted Halfar as he stepped out the gate onto the main palace roof. The royal guards standing at attention bowed low, then turned towards the steps to escort him down. *They don't need to bow anymore.* Their gesture made him uncomfortable. He ruled for less than three hundred years, like his father and uncle before him.

Our bloodline doesn't last long, huh? At least I wasn't murdered or died in battle.

At the second landing, the group moved onto a separate corridor privy only to the emperor and his party. No need for anyone to know he had arrived. Romnus' cryptic message alerted him something had gone horribly wrong. His escorts led him inside the palace to the supreme ruler's private study.

"Do you always huddle in the dark at nightfall, cousin?" Halfar emphasized cousin. The guards bowed and left him at the entrance. "Brooding doesn't become you."

He sat down across from Romnus at the small table between them. Even in the dim lighting, Romnus appeared tired, angry, and hurt. The smell of hard liquor from his half empty crystal tumbler invaded Halfar's nostrils. It must be bad.

Romnus rose the glass to his lips and took a small swig. He set it down on the table and met Halfar's gaze. Darkened skin around his eyes aged him.

"It's too much." Romnus' body seemed to sag a bit. "The chaos."

"Tell me. I can't help you if you don't. What other reason would you summon me?"

Romnus' anger grew deeper, then deflated the next instant.

"A fourth royal house member pushed Farin down a flight of stairs two moons ago."

He said it so nonchalantly that at first Halfar didn't register his words. Then it hit him. Rage welled up.

"Were the death rites made public?"

Halfar barely contained himself.

"There was none." Romnus reached down and retrieved his glass.

A servant came carrying a full carafe of the same liquor and another glass. She filled it for Halfar and exited swiftly.

"Why?" Before he could continue, Romnus lifted a finger off his glass. "Explain."

"They stopped me."

"Who?"

"All of them. The generals, Batis… Farin."

Halfar snatched up his glass and tossed a good amount down his throat. The burn made him wince. "Then he went unscathed and unpunished."

"Of course not." Romnus half smirked. "Farin slit his throat." Halfar halted the second swig of his drink. "Her shadow did worse."

Halfar's grip tightened around the glass. He never liked the idea of Chastan being his child's security shadow. Not after what he had done to the women of another royal house.

"Is that why the mood is somber on Azrom? I noticed the sky has a dark tinge, despite the sun still setting."

"No." Romnus finished his drink and set the glass down hard, making a loud thump. He sighed, letting his head fall against the seat. He brought it back up. "A rebel group of that house blew the planet bomb containment and fled in a cruiser ship."

"What?" Halfar yelled, leaning forward, smacking his hand onto the table. "Tell me you jest!" He could feel his eyes burn with fury. Romnus merely stared emotionless at him. He had become numb. Halfar eased back into his seat. "I don't know what…"

"How did you do it, cousin?" Romnus slumped forward, his forehead resting on the table. "How did you handle your reign without madness?"

"I didn't," Halfar answered. "Did you forget? I did go mad. You forced me to abdicate."

"How did you not kill everyone?"

From his view, Halfar could see, through the space between Romnus' neck, his eyes glow then dissipate.

"That is a valid question. It's not like the thought didn't cross my mind." Halfar drained his glass and refilled both glasses from the carafe. "What did you do?" He already knew Romnus would not have had the mental fortitude to stay still.

"I had Batis round up the entire house for execution." Romnus lifted his head.

Halfar once again paused his drinking. "That is not the answer, cousin."

"They stopped me." Romnus sounded like a pouting child. He sipped his drink.

"Who this time?" Halfar couldn't picture anyone in Romnus' entourage capable of such a thing.

"All of them. Again. Even the warrior clan came."

Halfar exhaled with relief. "Good. You know why."

The murder of an entire royal house would turn the population against Romnus. Assassination would be the least of his troubles.

"I never wanted to be Supreme Ruler. I don't," he stopped.

Romnus kept his glass halfway to his lips before taking another drink.

"What do the royal advisors say?" He knew the answer. He wanted Romnus to say it.

"They feign ignorance." Halfar nodded. Romnus ran a hand over his face. "I promised you I would keep Farin out of harm and love her for eternity. I feel like I failed." He sniffed hard. "I'm sorry."

Halfar frowned. "Which part? Cousin?" Romnus stared at him. "If your love for my child has faltered, then release her from your bond. As for her safety, she is more capable of that herself."

"I didn't say I fell out of love," Romnus seethed. "I just… when she looks at me after… I don't know what…"

Romnus gripped his glass.

"She knows about the brothel. I can only imagine what she thinks of you visiting the way you do." Halfar's eyes narrowed further. "And what you do in there." He felt a small amount of pity for his cousin. "That, you need to fix on your own. As for the matter at hand."

"I need you to tell me what to do." Romnus sat back in his seat. "I'm all out of pride. I can't do this alone."

Halfar's brow rose in astonishment. For the mighty Romnus to say such a thing. To admit defeat and ask him, of all people, for help stunned him. He regained his composure.

"No, you can't. I will do what I can." Halfar raised his glass. "First, you cannot start executing royal house members."

"What about the ones who assisted in this mess?"

"Hmmm." Halfar drew it out. "Imprison them. Then wait and see."

"For what?" Romnus seemed confused.

"How the enemy moves." Halfar's expression darkened. "I think the rebels will be in for a rude and bloody outcome."

Romnus gave him a disturbed look. He understood the way his cousin shrunk back from him even though he could go no further in his seat. Halfar had heard it many times whenever he made a certain face. He looked diabolical; evil.

Rotten Fruit

With planet repairs complete after the enemy surprise assault, Lord Pondur once again stood at the panoramic windows of his office overlooking the industrial sector. One hand lay on the curve of his back while the other held a small ornate cup he sipped hot liquid from. He wore a dark brown tailored suit with an ascot of teal and gold swirl design. The heavily starched peplums of his jacket were like sharp weapons.

The crags on his face relaxed as he watched transport vehicles delivering goods. Trade flowed with ease. He turned away and went to his desk. Tapping the display icon, he brought up the holoscreen across the room on the far wall filled with overlapping images and data feeds. He had his research teams collect every bit of information they could find on the enemy's neighboring system, then sent to him directly. A nagging hunch kept him on edge the past few years. He used the navigation pad and swiped through most of the useless stuff, focusing on anything that didn't make sense.

After collating over twenty pieces, the scenario became clear. He stood awestruck at what he stumbled on. Slowly, he slid back in his chair and leaned against it. He raised one hand, setting his elbow on the armrest, as his fingers rubbed together. The soft, shiffing clack of his talons intermittently hitting together calmed his nerves.

So that's it.

His beady eyes narrowed at the holoscreen.

He knew with certainty that Lassian scientist, Ganna, recognized the enemy, yet kept that information to herself. He came to that conclusion because Lord Graggor, in his need for understanding his rivals, had taken a sample of her DNA without her knowledge. Ganna's age surpassed centuries, nearly a millennium.

The cores.

Lord Pondur got the gist of how the Lassians survived for so long. He needed clarification. Leaning forward, he tapped the commlink. A soldier manning the communications hub came on screen in a smaller one at the corner.

"My lord, what can I do for you?"

"Send for our head geneticist and Lord Graggor."

"Of course, my lord. Right away."

The image blinked out. Lord Pondur patiently waited for his two subordinates to arrive. Ten minutes later, they entered his office. They both immediately looked over at the holoscreen and took in the same information. Lord Pondur didn't move or address them. He let them come to the same conclusion.

"My, how persistent they are," the geneticist finally said, turning to bow.

"Yes, such tenacity." Lord Graggor bowed, then approached the desk along with the other. "You want to know how."

Lord Pondur crossed his forearms on the desk. "I'm sure it's something we have not encountered. First." He pointed to the enemy data.

"Hmm." Lord Graggor nodded. "It seems Lassa and the enemy inhabit the same quadrant. It would take no time for those creatures to hop over into the next solar system."

"From their movements, they had been collecting resources for centuries in the opposite direction. When running out of planets to desecrate became an issue, they turned to the other side where Lassa sat." The geneticist scratched the side of his round, craggy chin.

"This is the part you want." He leaned over the navigation pad. "May I, my lord?"

"Please."

The geneticist turned to the screen while moving a few data feeds to the front. "Census scouts categorized Lassa as uninhabited simply because they detected no physical forms besides wildlife."

"That is a failure on the census bureau," Lord Graggor huffed, his mouth down-turned in disgust. "Incompetence."

"I agree. They should have done their due diligence and sent a research drone at a minimum." The geneticist zoomed in on a feed from the first round of scouting. "See those colored lights floating about?" He turned to Lord Pondur and saw he already knew.

"Cores." Lord Pondur stared at the image. "I saw that same glow emanating from some of the Lassian energy users." The crags around his eyes accommodated their widening. "That's why! They swap them out."

"This is their true form." The geneticist's tone suddenly became full of sorrow. "A sentient being of energy with no hope of defending itself."

Lord Pondur also felt a sense of pity for the original Lassians. They had no choice but to evolve. To create a physical form to defend their home.

"That woman knew all along." Lord Graggor sounded angry.

"I can't blame her." The geneticist shrugged. "She would have to be sure. And when she confirmed it, more research had to be done. They would have no more knowledge of the enemy than we do now."

"Lassa became hidden centuries later." Lord Pondur raised his arms and rested his chin on the tops of his steepled fingers. "And New Lassa as well. That is a significant jump in technology."

"And they had no ships until recently, relying on gates for travel." Lord Graggor seemed to ponder on something, tapping his chin. "How many original cores would have survived over time?" He pointed to two other instances of attempts to invade Lassa.

The geneticist frowned. "Not as many as you think. And Halfar didn't make it any better."

Lord Pondur let out a loud sigh and stood. He went around to the other side of his desk to stand between the two.

"We will sit on this for now. I want to see what that Lassian witch has up her sleeve."

The commlink pinged and a voice came through.

"My lord, there is a message coming from the outskirts of the next system over." There was a short pause. "It is the enemy, my lord. They are requesting a meeting to negotiate."

They all scoffed in unison.

"The audacity!" The Geneticist cried out.

"Such foolishness," Lord Graggor added.

"Yes, they have no intention of doing so." Lord Pondur's eyes narrowed. "This is a trap. They want something we would never give them." He tapped the reply icon. "Send a message telling them we will speak on this at the end of this weekly cycle."

"Yes, my lord." The commlink turned off.

"You're going to entertain them?" Lord Graggor asked incredulously.

"We don't want to disrupt trade again, do we?" Lord Pondur gave them a sly smile. "I will hear what they have to say. For now."

⌒

Diplomats from each of the five systems sat in their war rooms awaiting the connection to the enemy feed Lord Pondur prepared to broadcast. From his own conference room, he stared at the slew of faces on the holoscreen. Not one nervous bone in any of their bodies. If anything, they were hostile towards the idea of even listening to them.

Lord Pondur had the same sentiment. This small stint won't last long.

"Ready to transmit, my lord," the communications technician announced via the commlink.

"Open the channel. Mute the others and make sure they are unseen."

"Yes, my lord." The technician signed off. Another screen added to the array.

Lord Pondur stared at the enemy leader, taking in every inch of the creature's face and body language. Crude, shifty, and without honor. That was his take at first glance. The other leaders on the feed appeared to rear back in disgust, gauging the same.

"You attack my home world without provocation and now you want to, what? Negotiate? For what reason?" Lord Pondur stood before the holoscreen with both hands clasped behind him.

The enemy, scoffed? The translator kicked in and the enemy's words filled the feed.

"Planets that look weak deserve to be razed. We only want your resources. The population can die."

The other leaders, though muted, were visibly yelling at the screen. Lord Pondur remained calm, not letting the enemy on to them having an audience.

"Is that your grand plan?" Lord Pondur tilted his head, amused.

"Only those who conquer all can claim themselves master."

"Then what are you negotiating? Continue to try taking whatever you want."

"You control five systems. I want to talk face to face. About trade." The enemy's facial expression had a tiny twitch Lord Pondur found disingenuous. "Willing to meet in the neutral zone on the edge of the second territory."

How specific.

Lord Pondur locked eyes with the enemy leader.

"That would be impossible. The zone would never allow you in." The enemy leader seemed to struggle with the dilemma. "Your actions have made you," he paused, "a liability to their location."

"Neutral ground means no bias. Why do you not urge permission?"

"I have a better idea." Lord Pondur's gaze didn't waver. "I would feel much safer if we held the talks here instead."

Disappointment, then something sinister crossed the enemy leader's face. A long silence ensued before he replied.

"If that is your wish. I will comply." The enemy leader, smiled? All Lord Pondur could see were rows of sharp teeth. "Please send the details. We are open to any date."

Of course you are. The only thing you're doing is attacking worlds.

"Yes, my assistant will get back to you."

"I look forward to it." The enemy leader's image winked out, then the screen disappeared.

Lord Pondur tapped the commlink. The technician came back online.

"Unmute them, full feed."

"Here it is, as you wish, my lord." He signed off again.

Multiple voices heated with rage reached high decibels, filling the room. Lord Pondur curbed the urge to wince at the onslaught as he addressed them.

"My friends, please. Calm yourselves."

Realizing they were being heard, most of them did so. A few others did not.

"Preposterous!"

"I will not be silent on this!"

"How dare they!"

"I said," Lord Pondur lowered his head, still staring at the screen. "Calm yourselves."

Silence blanketed the room. Sitting out of view near the windows were Lord Graggor and his military head. They both had thinned lips and furrowed brows.

"Destroy a neutral zone and there is no obstacle between the systems," one of the other leaders stated.

"Yes, I am well aware." Lord Pondur unclasped his hands and sat in the highchair at the end of the long table.

"They're not imbeciles." The Lord of Planet Yaos said tersely.

"No. They are quite intelligent." Said Emperor Calabra.

"And that means they are more dangerous than we thought." Lord Pondur rested his arms on the side bars of his seat. "This does not bode well."

"How could you invite them to the home world after they attacked?" Lord of Yaos yelled. "What are you thinking?"

"A show of force," Lord Pondur replied calmly.

Looks of confusion met his remarks. The military general caught on.

"They only saw a glimpse of our planetary defense. They haven't done their homework."

"That is correct." Lord Pondur gazed at the other leaders. "I will need your assistance to show them this won't be easy for them. Actually, near impossible."

The acknowledgement of what he implied crossed their faces. He smiled.

"I will assume your full support." He didn't need a reply.
\###

The enemy ship eased out of orbit and descended towards the primary hub of the Dreridian home world. Two large armed forces awaited them on the platform. A mix of soldiers from the five systems swearing allegiance to fight for the Dreridian conglomerate made up each battalion. The moment the leader and his entourage stepped off the ramp onto the dock, they trained weapons on them.

In turn, the leader motioned to his rear guard, who produced one of the red tendril guns. When not one Dreridian soldier flinched or moved, the leader gestured for his own to lower it. The rear guard turned back into the ship and came out without the weapon.

Lord Pondur saw the scan report from when they crossed the checkpoint. The enemy ship came fully armed, ready for combat. Even with one, they would cause damage to the planet once again. He noticed the change in plans when the enemy realized they were not intimidating anyone. They run tail whenever they deemed a fight not an easy win.

"Trade negotiations, my craggy hide," his secretary of defense said. His imperial uniform hugged tightly to his frame. The seams and buttons appeared ready to burst apart as his chest heaved. "That they had the nerve to brandish that damnable weapon as leverage is distasteful."

"I agree. They have no tact or common sense, yet they're not stupid."

"A contradictory species," Lord Graggor said as he walked up to stand beside the other two. "My lord, I have faith in your decision."

"But?"

"This is a tad risky," the secretary of defense finished.

"Let's hear what they want first." Lord Pondur went to meet the enemy leader halfway for a greeting. He could almost smell the dishonesty.

\###

"Give us information to conquer Azrom. You don't like them. We take over and double trade for you, combining our resources with theirs."

The enemy leader's outlandish proposal rang out like a siren.

Lord Pondur, along with Lord Graggor and his secretary of defense sat dumbfounded. At first, he thought maybe he heard wrong. When nothing else came forth from the enemy leader's mouth, he understood they had indeed heard him.

"I'm not sure why you have targeted them. We don't stop trade just because we don't like a planet. On the contrary, we want more from them." Lord Pondur took a breath. "Please explain."

"Azrom is considered a mighty power. Their time is up. Not as mighty as they claim."

Oh no. Lord Graggor looked over at him in astonishment.

"Tell me, have you ever considered attacking Azrom?"

"No need. We have intel."

"Then you don't need us to provide anything." Lord Pondur seethed.

"Not true. Only limited information. Need all their military stats."

"Haha! Ha! Ha!" The secretary of defense burst out laughing. He regained his composure and locked eyes with the enemy leader. "We would never give you such a thing. What guarantee do we have that you won't turn it against us?"

"None. Why should we not if it warrants it?"

Lord Pondur had enough of their farce. "The answer is no."

"That is unfortunate." The enemy leader set his brawny fists on the table. "We will take it by force and show you true might."

"You will have a rude awakening." Lord Pondur stood. "This," he waved a hand in the air, "meeting, or whatever false pretense this was, is over."

The enemy entourage rose, followed by the secretary of defense.

"Oh, and if you try to use force on your way off our planet, we will obliterate you from the stars." He gave a wide smile, making sure they understood.

Instead, the enemy leader humphed and left the room.

Lord Pondur, Lord Graggor, and the secretary of defense sat back down. A servant came to replenish the drink carafes that sat empty from the enemy ceremoniously draining every single one, the Dreridians getting one glass of it the whole time.

Greedy. They all agreed on that.

"They have no idea." The secretary of defense took his

newly full glass of spirits. "Azrom is indeed mighty. We can never deny them such a title."

"The inside contact bothers me," Lord Graggor said.

"You think the Supreme Ruler of Azrom doesn't know there are spies within?"

"I am sure he does. But it would be negligent not to address it with them."

Lord Pondur tapped the edge of the table with a talon. "It stems from the defeat of the three ships. Since Azrom has conquered entire planets with merely those numbers, the masses probably see it as a sign."

"No doubt, Lord Romnus feels the same. Like they have met their match." Lord Graggor added.

"Not a match," the secretary of defense replied. He grinned. "A worthy opponent." He turned to Lord Pondur. "When was the last time they had to fight with their full armada?"

Ah! How long ago was it? Five hundred years, maybe? Lord Pondur thought back to the great war that almost crippled Azrom, throwing it into poverty. The population began starving and their infrastructure fell apart. Halfar had only been in reign less than a century, having taken over the fight after his father met his demise in battle. The start of the succession process where he rose victorious over all the participants.

Because Romnus refused to throw his claim into the arena.

From the windows, they watched the enemy being escorted back to their ship, surrounded by the full might of an entire battalion. As the ship lifted off, the land to space cannons swiveled to track their departure. Once they reached the satellites, the defense systems would activate there as well. They had no moment of opportunity to attack.

Lord Pondur stifled a grin.

Four: Seeing Stars

Galactic War

Multicolored beams of light crisscrossed in the bright skies of the neutral zone. A spectacle of beauty rained devastation on each planet. Everywhere those beams hit, a structure fell, citizens died, and military units answered in kind. They blocked most of the enemy's bio-weapons. Where the red tendrils struck made for a gruesome sight.

Four factions of Dreridian forces went planet side, defending what they could while their ships held steady against the enemy bombardment in space. Victory meant nothing, seeing the damage already done to the neutral zone.

After days of constant fire power blanketing the system, the enemy finally got bored with not being able to advance any further, running out of energy. They retreated in a hail storm of Dreridian might, their ships damaged as they disappeared through a vortex.

And there was silence.

All three planets' surfaces smoldered, coated in fire and death.

Trade again came to a halt.

⁓

The situation at hand found Lord Pondur too incensed to the point of assaulting his assistants when the news of the neutral zone attack reached him.

He regained his composure while taking a stroll along the palace corridor, then sequestered himself in his chamber for a few hours. There, he took out a long smoking stem, loaded it with a calming liquid, and pushed on the tiny power button to activate the heater coils inside. He lounged on a plush chaise and drew long drags.

Satiated, Lord Pondur got up and dressed in his most austere suit. Charcoal grey vest, pants, and jacket with a black tunic and ascot. His black boots shined like mirrors. Tugging the jacket down to make sure it set right, he headed out to the meeting room where his military leaders had set up the interstellar feed. A slew of squares filled with representatives from over a hundred nations across the five systems covered the holoscreen.

And here we are yelling and screaming with no actual solutions on the table.

Waving a hand to the soldier handling the feed, the mouths moving with outrage accompanied the now muted audio. Lord Pondur didn't care to hear any of it.

He had opted to stand for the first ten minutes of the meeting until the shouting began. Now he sat at the head of the conference table with his six military leaders, seated three on each side, not paying attention to the holoscreen. They, too, were disinterested in the screaming matches.

He gestured to the soldier in charge of the feed to unmute it. The deafening flood of voices filled the room. His General winced at the onslaught.

"If you are done," Lord Pondur said. The noise died as if severed. The faces on the screen turned their attention to him. "I understand your frustration. But let's be clear." His eyes narrowed as he scanned each one. "This is a declaration of war."

"They seem to be good at catching planets off guard," a planet lord said.

"Yes. Emerging from a vortex and spewing their weapons down onto the surface," another planet leader added.

"Cowardly," the Yaos emperor snapped.

"I must divulge something to you all." Lord Pondur made eye contact with Lord Kraznan, Chardon, and Romnus.

He could make out half of Halfar's body behind Chardon's right shoulder. They nodded in approval. "I have joined in a new alliance between Razzna, New Lassa, and Azrom." He heard the whispers and anger build amongst the other races. "That also includes the Dreridian faction."

Every leader on the screen seemed to pause. *Yes, you know what that means.* Lord Pondur stifled a smirk. He watched the realization take hold. Dreridian power would be one hundred-fold. The enemy had awakened a galactic giant.

∽

"I don't need to tell you the magnitude of this situation," Chardon began, addressing his council in the conference room. No one had spoken so far in the ten minutes they had all been sitting on their cushions with drinks in hand. "We agreed to this alliance long ago."

The head of engineering set her drink down. The heaviness of her eyes told him she had been up since his return, contemplating the outcome. She glanced over at the science leader, then turned her attention to Chardon.

"Ship production will need to be ramped up. In addition, we have to create new defense systems in case the enemy unleashes another full attack on New Lassa." She let out a loud sigh and retrieved her drink. "We don't have much time."

"Morale is also an issue," the head of politics said. He looked close to haggard. "We agreed to this alliance, yes. We never consulted the masses. The last thing we want is another rebellion."

Chardon felt Modas' tension from behind him in the room's corner. That would never happen again. Bringing it up would always be a sore subject. Even Ganna frowned with distaste.

"Our race is the only one who needs ship production," Ganna stated. "Azrom, Razzna, and the Dreridians are superpowers. We have yet to see their full arsenals."

The head of politics slammed his fist on the table. Once again, the carafes shook. Liquid from those and their cups sloshed about before settling.

"I do not want Lassa to become a military force! Why do we have to forgo our peaceful existence to engage in a galactic war?" He turned to Ganna. "You hid us before. Why can't you do that again?"

Chardon stared at the man in surprise. Hide? He saw Talas' body tense in anger, his brow knitted. Jaron balled her fists in her lap beneath the table, her shoulders stiff. Ganna slowly took a sip from her cup and set it down gently.

"We could not hide forever. We needed resources. Chardon's father knew that, and Sestis brought forth the means to gain them." She raised her head towards him. "I don't want to be known as some mighty military, either." Her eyes narrowed. "Stop pretending you don't know why we have to do at least this much."

Silence fell on the room. Heads hung low, while a sense of seething followed. Chardon's stomach knotted from the anxiety as it went on for longer than normal. The head of science sniffed loudly, getting everyone's attention.

"The enemy stripped Lassa of most of her resources. I don't believe for one moment they did not recognize our race when they attacked us." He glared into space. "I want vengeance." To Halfar sitting in the back with Modas and Trinon, he said, "Neither of you are forgiven either. The enemy comes first on the list."

"I understand more than you know," Halfar replied, bowing his head.

"What's the status of the new weapon derived from our foe?" The head of engineering asked. "Are we in mass production yet?"

"Not quite," Ganna answered. "Some minor tweaks are required. I say by next year, we can start. The real work will be planetary defense, as you have brought up."

"Then let's dive into our needs."

The head of engineering drained her cup.

Chardon sat quietly, mulling over the logistics being presented as the meeting went on, interjecting every so often. He understood in that moment that as a leader, he needed to listen first and not yet push his own agenda. After two hours of discussion with heated arguments in the mix, the council decided on their own to adjourn.

They cleared out except for Chardon along with his close cabinet members and Halfar. Talas still sat with a stern expression; his arms crossed with both hands tucked under his armpits. Ganna mindlessly traced her fingers on the table. Jaron seemed shaky, almost nervous. Chardon looked around behind him to see Modas and Trinon, deep in thought. Halfar met his gaze with worry in those eyes.

"Now that that's over, how about we say what we truly feel?" Chardon said.

They all looked over at him. Ganna averted her attention to Halfar.

"How mighty is Azrom? From the intel I pieced together, you have somewhere around what, five hundred thousand ships?"

Halfar appeared to struggle with his answer. Even with an alliance, divulging Azrom's true number of ships would be foolish. His hands clasped together at his waist, he met her gaze and simply replied, "More."

Ganna nodded. "That means Razzna is the same."

"Is it true?" Trinon asked. "That the enemy recognized us even though we have physical bodies now?"

Jaron ran her fingers through her hair, messing it up.

"Lassa's core kicked out an energy signature that covered the entire planet. It dwindled with the rape of its resources, needing another century to recover enough to sustain life again." Her brow furrowed. "There's no way they didn't feel it when they entered New Lassa's space."

"They probably find it intriguing," Talas snorted.

"A twist of fate they see as an advantage," Halfar added.

"They're wrong."

Chardon heard the rage in his own voice.

⌇

The massive fifty-foot-high corridors of the Razznian palace bustled with foot traffic from servants and soldiers hurrying to complete their tasks. The entire planet prepared for war. This did not compare to the battles they engaged in with Azrom. Razzna had not raged such an offense in over a thousand years. The royal council in the upper halls remained in constant conversation with the emperor.

Sars and his unit made their way through the crowds towards the elevators at the end of the main corridor. He had never seen so many flowing within the palace. From what he gathered from random conversations, neither had the elders. An all-out war! Are we truly up to the task? Sars took in the scene as he turned around in the lift.

Since the last mission, the emperor promoted his unit and himself, moving him one step closer to being a head commander. Anything after that would be the upper echelon of generals. Most of them would have to die off for him to even be considered. Not likely. He snorted. Beldur, his second in command, gave him a curious side glance.

The lift reached the upper level, then sped sideways, stopping at the midsection. Its doors opened to a throne room full of advisors and servants moving about in frustration from lack of room. The emperor sat fanning himself while a group of councilmen argued with each other between giving him updates. He caught sight of Sars' and motioned for the councilmen to be quiet.

"Commander Sars! What took you so long to arrive?"

The councilmen all turned their heads over their shoulders and glared at him. Sars felt his mouth twitch with amusement. How they hated him! Keeping his composure, he went past them at the bottom of the throne and bowed to one knee, his unit doing the same. He raised his head.

"My apologies, my lord. The halls are full of life these days. We had to maneuver the masses." Sars stood straight, meeting the emperor's gaze. "Preparations are going well, I assume?"

"Yes." The emperor's tongue vibrated, making the word hiss. "It is time we show the enemy what true power looks like."

The four military advisors turned their attention back to the emperor. One of them opened his mouth to speak. Sars beat him to it.

"My lord, if I may be so bold. I'm sure the advisors at present have suggested that we have not seen the enemy's full range. For all we know, what we witnessed could be a small fraction of their forces."

The military advisor hissed at him so loudly that others in the room halted their movement for a split second. A hush fell over them. Sars stiffened. The emperor's glare bore down on the advisor. The reptile hung his head, shocked at his own sudden outburst. His associates gave him surprised expressions.

"What is the meaning of this?" Emperor Kraznan barely contained his angry tone. "Do we not have more important tasks than showing your status for the sake of bullying?" His reptilian eyes grew dark. "I would have thought you were better than such pettiness."

"I beg your forgiveness, my lord." The advisor bowed with one hand on his chest.

Sars relaxed his stance. "I'm sure we are all feeling anxiety." He wasn't trying to incite such a response. "It was my fault for speaking out of turn." He turned his head towards the offended advisor. "Please accept my apology."

"Hmph!" The emperor smirked. "Our new commander seems to have more grace."

Sars winced, seeing all four military advisors' frown. The only reason for his unit's attendance was their firsthand contact with the enemy. One hundred ships should have done the trick. The emperor now understood how Azrom felt when their mission failed. Sars could see it in his eyes.

"What are your recommendations?" Lord Kraznan addressed his advisors.

The four military leaders looked over at the other five councilmen standing opposite the throne. They remained silent since Sars had arrived. Each one mulled over the situation from their respective expertise. Science, politics, agriculture, trade, and infrastructure. War affected every part of their race.

The head of agriculture spoke first. "We ramp up food production for the ships' inventories. This fight may take years. No need to have our troops starve midway."

"We have increased mining production as well," the head of trade said. "The contract for our ore has doubled. Not only New Lassa requires ship building. The planets they hold under regency have requested a few as well."

Lord Kraznan looked down at Sars. *Ah, I know what he wants.* Sars hid his skepticism. He didn't enjoy speculating on things without all the components. The leaders glanced at him.

They're all waiting for me to say it out loud.

"In my units' observation of the enemy and the way they attack, I estimate their numbers to be astronomical. They appear to be part of an empire." The military advisors nodded in agreement. "Also, their bioweapon is a recent addition."

"This empire somehow smelled blood in the water of the five solar systems." The second military advisor stated. He tapped a thick yellowed talon on the scales of his chin. "If we could find out the catalyst."

"They're opportunists!" The fourth military leader snapped.

"Yes, that is clear." The head of science raised his arms out, palms up. "The counter weapon is nearly complete."

"Unless we have cannons similar to theirs, there is no

point," the first military leader said.

"I am proposing we equip a thousand ships with them." The head of science grinned. "What do you take me for? I'm no budding tadpole."

"That's all?" The first military advisor scoffed.

Sars agreed. It seemed too little. As if sensing their disappointment, the head of science continued. "That is only the start. Please have patience. This is a delicate project."

The meeting went on for another hour before Lord Kraznan dismissed the council and Sars' unit. They all crammed into the elevator. An uncomfortable silence ensued all the way to the end of the rail until it dropped towards the main level.

"We understand your unit has lived this long because of your cunning leadership," the second military advisor addressed Sars. "You're encroaching on our territory."

"I only want Razzna to retain its dominance," Sars said.

"There are better ways to do it." The advisor said sternly.

"You say that even now?" Sars replied heatedly.

"The commander has a point," the head of politics added. "We can no longer go about this as the status quo." Her eyes became vertical slits. "An empire needs to be brought to its knees. The more outside the box with our thinking, the better chance we have."

The lift reached its destination and opened to the crowded halls once more. This time, the masses made an opening for the entourage. The council leaving the throne room made Sars uneasy. At the front entrance, the guards opened the giant doors.

"You're probably wondering why we all left," the head of infrastructure said. Sars nodded. "Even we occasionally need a breath of fresh air."

"I'll be clearing my head in the mountains for the next moon cycle," the second military advisor announced.

"I heard the swamps are revitalized," the head of agriculture said. "I may join you." His tail swished with anticipation.

A period of rest before the slaughter, huh? Sars could see the same look on his units' faces. Their offspring in training centers had an upcoming break. Not a bad idea, he said to himself. Because once the fighting began, Razzna may be in danger.

⌒

Razznian engineers accompanied the three regent leaders on the envoy ship carrying entering the Rendal II system. On approach, they caught sight of the giant repair planet, Barrima, with its swirls agitating different atmospheric conditions along the surface. Beams of pale light appeared to pierce through it at strange angles. Directly in their path lay a monstrous area of blue, white, and green. That's their destination.

The leaders stood in the main cabin, staring in awe at the scene. The four Razznian engineers were already taking notes on their tablets. Their ship resembled a dot against the planet.

"There are no security features," the first Razznian stated while tapping data into his device. "Now I understand why they said ships just come through and land."

"That is not acceptable," the second engineer said. "They need to implement some protocol immediately."

"I agree," General T'Halgar from planet Andal, said. "I realize they don't want to turn away potential profit. It's different now."

"Yes," Ambassador Lombis added. "With support from our regent, they no longer need to be beggars."

Past the clouds, they could see the palace looming over the terrain. Previously a hunk of charcoal grey stone with no appeal, it now sat almost majestic. The cleaning to remove build up from harsh weather and neglect revealed light grey stone. And view ports. Large bay windows overlooked the horizon.

"At least they made the place presentable after the atmosphere generators were repaired." The ruler of planet Nasfir, Emperor Xanic's tail swished across the floor, almost hitting the Razznian engineer standing next to him. "Apologies."

The engineer looked sideways, down at his tail. "Yes, be more careful, please."

Docking at the transport hub close to the palace, the crew clamped down the ship. A waiting party of six soldiers met the group at the end of the ramp as they debarked. Their uniforms had not changed. Still wearing the dingy jumpsuits, they were an eyesore amongst the new environment.

Why must they continue this farce? Ambassador Lombis silently berated them. They seemed to sense his thoughts, tensing up with resentment. He shook his head.

Habits are hard to break, I guess.

They escorted the group to the large conference room inside. It also had a makeover. Modern, neutral colors replaced the drab walls and furnishing, making the room more appealing. Master Adan sat at the center on the left. One leg lay bent on the table with the other's foot planted on the seat, his head bent over a small handheld device.

Beside him sat his two commanders, Ryben and Veris. Both men appeared to be mentally elsewhere, not in the present. They wore ill-maintained uniforms that only came out on special occasions. The masterful tailoring hinted at former glory. Adan's attire told the same tale.

The head escort cleared his throat loudly. "Master Adan! The guests have arrived."

And like that, the three men, startled out of their reverie, looked over at the group. Adan swung his leg off the table, dropping his foot off the seat to stand. His commanders jumped up as well.

"My apologies. I didn't hear you come in." Adan gestured towards the table. "Please make yourselves comfortable. Some drinks and food will be here shortly."

General T'Halgar gave them a once over.

That hair!

He found the unkempt mess disturbing. He knew it came from wearing their work gear. They could have at least done something with it. Their lack of care for their appearance bordered on insult.

"You obviously weren't prepared to entertain us," the third Razznian engineer said haughtily. "Three leaders and four Razznian royal engineers have come, and you greet us," they spread their arms out, "like this?"

Adan inhaled, rotating his head with eyes closed, then stared at them.

"I prioritized getting the atmosphere generators back online. What does it matter what clothes we wear? We're still mechanics by trade."

"It matters!" The Razznian snapped, causing everyone to flinch. "You represent a planet with ties to a Regent and trade. Would you dare show such shoddiness to the royal leaders of this quadrant?"

"They have, unfortunately," Ambassador Lombis coughed.

Seeing the comical way the Razznian's beady eyes went wide made Veris snort. He clamped his hand over his mouth in terror, looking over at Adan.

"These are our best uniforms," Ryben said angrily. "We don't bring these out for just anyone."

"This is also a failure on your Regent's part," the first Razznian engineer added. They turned to the liaison leader. "You should remedy this. Your empire is known for their clothing merchants and skills."

"You are correct." The leader sighed, then addressed their hosts. "Those uniforms are outdated. I won't say anymore on the matter." Pitiful, really. His lips pursed in agitation. "I will have our tailors come for your measurements."

A line of soldiers entered the room carrying trays of food, liquor bottles, plates, glasses, and utensils. Their faces conveyed the disdain they felt for being used as servants.

They set it all down the length of the table and left without saying a word.

"Thank you!" Adan called out after them.

"And you need servants too." Emperor Xanic didn't acknowledge Adan or his commanders as he reached for a thick cut slice of meat. "Soldiers are for fighting. Workers are for the sake of commerce."

"Are you all done?" Adan's expression contorted with anger.

"Of course," the first Razznian replied. "Shall we get to the matter at hand?"

Their nonchalant response took Adan off guard. His demeanor faltered.

"Yes, that would be ideal." He leaned back in his chair; arms crossed.

"The shipment of Razznian ore will arrive shortly. Since it will need to be delivered to a specified region, we want to know if you have determined the building material."

Adan tossed the small communicator onto the table. It spun a half turn before laying still. He laced his fingers against his abdomen.

"Razznian ore is top of the line material. Its malleable characteristics are above all others. That said, we are going to work with it in the tropic climate."

"Interesting." The first engineer rubbed their chin. "I would have thought a high temperature area would be best."

"That's what every raw materials trade worker does. And most times, they're wrong." Adan gave them an egotistical grin. "It's why we are the best builders in the five systems."

❧

Full armadas of combined alliance forces gathered across the system under Lord Pondur's leadership to prepare for war. Logistics became a nightmare as each race's military general argued over who would take command over which sectors. He pinched the bridge of his nose with a thumb and ring finger while exhaling slowly. His other hand held a small teacup half full, the content now lukewarm. They were trying his patience once more.

The holoscreen on the back wall displayed the faces of forty generals bickering at each other. Lord Pondur again directed the soldier nearby to mute the audio. He uncrossed his legs in the high chair centered in the room and stepped down. Setting the teacup on the side table, he walked closer to the holoscreen. The generals saw his movement and stopped talking, focusing on him.

"Turn it back on," he ordered the soldier.

"Since it appears you are not ready, I will send our alliance forces to intercept the enemy at their next target." The expressions of indignation and hostility made his mouth tug at the corners. He wasn't sure if he should laugh or be angry. "That should knock them down a few pegs, and there may be no need for war. Only a negotiation of terms for future ventures."

"How ideal. I hope that is the case," the emperor of planet Halios said. "Though I am excited to show the might of my species."

They can't contain their bloodlust!

None of them can. Lord Pondur saw it spread like a contagion across the faces on the screen.

"They may still refuse even in defeat," another general said. "If they are anything like our race, pride is involved."

"Then we are still needed." The Yaos general lowered his head so that his gaze became sinister. "To keep them in line."

"I don't have any more time to waste on this matter." Lord Pondur turned and headed back to his chair.

"Figure it out amongst yourselves and send an update when you have a plan."

He nodded at the soldier standing by the feed and the holoscreen winked out, the audio cutting the last words of angry insults. Lord Pondur stared at his teacup, knowing his drink would be cold. *I need something stronger.* He walked past his chair and tapped the commlink on the desk.

"Bring me a bottle of distilled spirits." He didn't wait for a reply.

He retrieved his favorite chalice from the nearby shelf and set it on the table before stepping back up into the chair. His body relaxed. Propping an arm up, he rested his head against the back of his hand.

A servant came carrying an ornate red bottle, its clarity showing the liquid's medium viscosity movement. They hastily poured some into the chalice without letting a single drop stray, then set the bottle down and left.

Lord Pondur grabbed the chalice and took a long sip, letting the harsh liquor course through his body. He sighed heavily.

"Open the feed." He gestured to the soldier.

This time, only six squares populated the holoscreen. Lord Graggor and his general entered the room while each feed finished connecting. Chardon, Romnus, Halfar, Lord Kraznan, Emperor Xanic, and His Majesty Cogar Wenthril stared out at him. They all appeared weary, and rightly so. He understood Dreridians weren't subjected to harm like the others in the alliance, simply because his race saw no reason to engage. The enemy's pitiful attack on the home world enraged them more than anything else.

They need to be taught a lesson.

"My trusted new friends," Lord Pondur began. Frowns and scowls immediately formed at his greeting. "How about we wrap this tiresome issue up and not have a galactic war on our hands?"

"What did you have in mind?" Cogar Wenthril asked.

"I wanted your input on the matter." Lord Pondur took another sip.

"The counter weapons, I assume, are being installed per specifications?" Lord Graggor asked.

"Yes," Chardon replied. "We only have five of our ships built, but all are equipped with it."

"We should keep them on standby," Emperor Xanic said. "No need to send out brand new ships, only to have them crippled or destroyed during their maiden run."

"Each part of the alliance needs to be represented." The general tapped on his tablet set before him on the table. "Due to the difference in size for your races, there won't be an even division."

Halfar leaned forward, his fingers from one hand rested under his chin. Those murky green eyes seemed to smolder, the brighter spots having a glow.

"My apologies for speaking when I am no longer ruler."

"Your expertise is more welcomed than you think," Cogar Wenthril replied.

Halfar pursed his lips. "I have spoken with Lord Romnus and would like Lord Kraznan's take on this as well. Azrom, Razzna, and the Dreridians have far more forces than the others, as stated. I propose we three bring the bulk of it with the other races as support." He leaned back.

Chardon's expression, along with Emperor Xanic's turned sour. Seeing this, Cogar Wenthril's eyes narrowed.

"What did you expect?" He bellowed at them. "Are you saying your might is equal to theirs? I am not so delusional as to think that of my own. My contribution of one hundred ships means little compared to their numbers."

"I didn't mean it to be disparaging." Halfar raised a hand in defense.

"You said nothing wrong." Lord Kraznan scratched the side of his face with a single talon. "The idea is sound. Hmm." He looked away, contemplating.

"Ten thousand," Lord Romnus blurted out.

"Oh?" Lord Pondur halted his chalice midway.

"We each send ten thousand with one hundred counter weapons," Romnus said.

"And what are you basing these numbers on?" The general asked.

"With every assault, their forces are in the ten thousand range, sometimes half that," Romnus replied.

"Yes, but we believe they may be part of a much larger empire," Lord Kraznan added. "If that is indeed the case," he trailed off.

"Tripling that number along with more to make it five-fold should do the trick," Chardon finished for him. "Thirty thousand ships, three hundred with counter weapons, and another few thousand for support sounds good." Chardon frowned again. "But…"

"If the size of their empire is on par with Azrom or Razzna, let alone the Dreridians," Cogar Wenthril interjected, "then we are in trouble."

The heavy silence that followed lingered for close to a minute. Lord Pondur resumed sipping his drink. Lord Graggor got up, went to the shelf where more glasses sat, and retrieved one. He poured some of the liquor in his glass and sat back down, sipping as well.

"And here I told the other leaders we were going to stop the enemy and have them beg for leniency." Lord Pondur smirked.

"That is still on the table," Romnus said. "Apart from the leniency. I won't grant them such a thing."

"I would recommend eating them to near extinction, but their hides are not appetizing," Lord Kraznan added. "I'm sure Emperor Xanic would agree."

"Fine." Lord Pondur set down his chalice. "Let's see how far we can bring them down." He addressed Halfar. "As usual, your input is exactly that of a cruel and powerful ruler, Lord Halfar. Your battle experience and lack of mercy alone are frightening."

And why we leave Azrom to their own devices ninety percent of the time.

Lord Pondur warily eyed the former ruler. Poking that monster was to no one's advantage, not even for Azrom itself. Planet bombs. A project commissioned by Halfar in response to the Dreridians' decision to no longer attack with troops unless the situation proved dire, using the tactic of launching assaults from afar. The overreaction had floored Lord Pondur.

Halfar left nothing to chance.

Out of the corner of his eye, he caught a nervousness in Lord Romnus. *What are you hiding?* For him to try so hard to keep his composure, it must be something heinous. Lord Graggor's spies were bringing a report on Azrom soon.

"I am sending the logistics I feel promising to all of you. Please let me know what you may need altered." The general swiped an icon on his tablet.

"We can adjourn this meeting." Lord Pondur nodded towards the screen. "I look forward to hearing your thoughts on our plan." He gestured to the soldier. Again, he cut the visual and audio. "You may leave." The soldier gave a salute, pounding a fist on his breast plate before exiting.

Another soldier tapped on the door frame.

"Lord Pondur, the Azrom scout has returned and awaits your command to enter."

"Send him in." Lord Pondur watched the scout nearly push his way into the room, having no regard for his fellow soldier. "It is best you know your…"

"My apologies, my lord, but this matter requires desperation!"

Lord Pondur reared back in awe. Lord Graggor and the general stared, astounded, at the scout. The soldier at the door placed a hand on the butt of his weapon in the holster.

"What is so dire…" Lord Pondur again didn't get to finish speaking.

"There was a rebellion on Azrom!" The scout blurted

out. Lord Pondur stiffened. "Some royal faction made a deal with the enemy." He tried to catch his breath. "They stole two planet bombs!"

The chalice fell from Lord Pondur's hand. He eyed at the scout in disbelief. He heard the sharp intake of breath erupt from the others in the room. The scout knelt deep, extending his hand and caught the falling chalice. Liquor spilled onto this hand and dripped down to the floor. He stood, holding it in both hands.

"What did you say?" Lord Graggor asked, eyes wide.

Lord Pondur came back to his senses and held a hand up to stop him from asking anything further. The general clasped his hands together as if in prayer. Lord Romnus, how irresponsible of you not to divulge such news.

"Where are they?" Lord Pondur asked.

The scout, having calmed down a bit, took a slow breath. "They are still being traced. Opinion is they are hidden inside an uninhabited quadrant to be retrieved by the enemy when ready."

"That's not the issue," Lord Graggor snapped. "I want to know about the ones still intact on Azrom? Their containment would have been breached."

"Their scientists currently sealed them while repairs are being completed," the scout replied.

"The dimensional forces alone could tear apart an entire system," the general whispered.

"This… puts a wrinkle…" Lord Pondur stopped, his eyes mere slits. "I am not amused."

Bigger Picture

SSars watched the Razznian fleet forming an arched blockade around their neighboring system from the bridge's main viewport. There were more than the promised ten thousand. The general sent an extra four thousand to assist alliance forces in other quadrants. Azrom armada ships came out of vortices amongst the fleet, with a slew of Dreridians following suit.

Let's try this again.

"Look at that," his commander said in awe. "Who would have ever predicted such a thing!"

Sars nodded. "It only makes sense. We all fight each other like estranged relatives until an outsider comes to harm us."

He turned from the viewport and headed towards the dais in the center. The bridge crew maintained their duties while catching glimpses of the scene outside. Don't blame them. He hissed with amusement. What a fascinating sight.

"What do you think the other side looks like?" His navigator asked.

Razzna sat on the far edge of the five systems. The Dreridian home world lay in the center. On the other side, Azrom made itself known. Trade planets saddled the outer edges.

"If I were the enemy and saw this, I would think twice." His arms specialist leaned on the dais rails, resting his chin on folded arms. "Live to fight another day."

Sars let out a small laugh.

He looked over at the newbie standing beside him.

"What is your take on this?"

Prac squinted at the viewscreen.

"They won't back down that easily. They will attack with fervor."

"Hmm." Sars nodded a few times. "I feel the same." He relaxed in the captain's seat. "Hopefully, this works to our advantage."

❧

Dreridian might knew no rival in the system, yet their fleet sprawled throughout appeared to be nothing special. Their show of force, as expected, gave confidence and security to the trade nations. Lord Pondur thought nothing of it, either. Until he saw the feed of the blockade near Azrom. The frozen image on the holoscreen practically screamed at his psyche. He shivered.

The Razznians impressed him. He sipped from his chalice, savoring the hot brew. His floppy lace sleeve, spilling from the maroon and gold brocaded jacket, grazed the sides. With legs crossed, and an erect posture, he personified grace.

Except for his crude expression.

Lord Graggor entered the room carrying his tablet. He pulled a chair from the side and sat closer to Lord Pondur, his girth filling the entire seat. Glancing at the holoscreen, he did a double take, his eyes wide.

"Speak." Lord Pondur heard the tenseness in his own voice. He felt irritated.

"Azrom indeed handled the matter of tracing the planet bombs. There is no way to retrieve them without consequences."

"Why is that?" Lord Pondur snapped.

"One of them appears damaged and enclosed in a temporary barrier."

"How long can it hold?"

"Possibly three years. The level of devastation it can

cause depends on the damage." Lord Graggor breathed slowly, then turned to him. "About that." He gestured a hand towards the holoscreen.

There were Azrom forces mixed in with the Dreridian fleets, as were Razznian across the system as planned. At the inner edge where the trade planets began, Azrom dominated the alliance forces. Twenty thousand armada ships blanketed the blockade, dwarfing the others. A massive message that thundered 'do not cross'.

"Yes, they are overcompensating."

"The moment the enemy gets their hands on one planet bomb, Azrom will have no choice but to stop it at all costs." Lord Graggor raised his craggy brow in surprise. "You have not addressed this matter with Lord Romnus?"

"Why must I pursue information from him? He should have the decency to report matters that affect trade and, more importantly, lives."

"My apologies. I didn't mean to assume." The left side of Lord Graggor's mouth rose, creating a lopsided tight lip. "I wonder what punishment he administered to the rebels?"

"If he were any kind of Supreme Ruler, he should execute them all." He sipped from his chalice, then set it down. "That is what Halfar would decree."

Lord Graggor agreed with a snort. He stared at the holoscreen again. Lord Pondur knew he thought the same. Azrom might won't be enough to remedy the situation.

⌒

Chaos filled the fourth royal house right after Lord Romnus left, having spared every household. They all knew that grace would be short-lived. Tension rose within its walls as the occupants became wary of each other. Who had done such a thing? Infighting between royal houses spanned over millennia. Yet, not once had they sabotaged the planet itself or the entire trade system. Fealty to Azrom remained absolute.

Lord Elendar walked with slow steps down the long, marbled halls of his abode. The corridor lay open near the gardens, bringing in the scent of multiple floras. Giant marble columns that reached the ceiling stood twenty feet apart for nearly half its length. His feet faltered, forcing him to stagger towards one to lean on.

His closed wounds had yet to be healed, taking longer because of Romnus' poison laced claws combined with the deep puncture. He placed a hand on his abdomen, then gripped the fabric of his waistcoat. I feel dizzy. Using the other hand to steady himself, he let his head rest against the cool marble.

No one else had been present in the massive hall. Its fifty-foot width lay empty, the silence broken only by his labored breathing. The moment he felt another presence, he forced himself off the column and morphed one arm into a barbed insect limb.

"Please, your grace, I beg you." He recognized his personal guard's voice approaching from behind. "Let me escort you back to your chamber. You need to rest."

"I need to clean up my house." Lord Elendar heatedly replied. He winced at the tightness in his midsection. "I will punish the wicked myself."

"That's commendable," his guard said. "Weeding them out takes time. You must use yours wisely." He offered his hand. "Come," he pleaded.

Lord Elendar slapped his hand away.

"I'm halfway to the gathering hall. I will see this through."

Defeated, the guard's demeanor shrunk. He let out a soft sigh and waited for him to continue trudging down the long corridor. Guilt for mistreating his trusted companion filled Lord Elendar.

"I'm sorry," he whispered.

"Never apologize to me, your grace."

His guard kept in step with him.

As a royal house of cousins twice removed, their characterization spread throughout the kingdom. He despised the rumors of cowardice, overambition, and deceit. This new situation only proved them right. Interfering with the rebels' asinine plans, he found unworthy of his time. Simply because he knew nothing would eventually come of it. Until now.

Was I a fool? How could I not have seen the difference?

The sentries at the hall entrance opened its double doors for him. He noticed their grim expressions. Slightly disturbed, he entered the room and stopped a few feet in. His personal guard halted beside him with a hand rested on the hilt of his longsword.

Standing together further in were the rulers of the second and third royal house. Lady Haldris wore a heavily embroidered off the shoulder dress with puffy half arm sleeves. Her blond hair, fashioned in a large ball of intricate braids, set away from her face. The handheld fan blocking the view of her ample bosom matched the dress.

How gaudy! He met those murky green eyes of hers.

The third house ruler, Lord Kel, resembled Romnus, except in size. Slenderer, with lean muscle, his frame conveyed its agility and strength even beneath the dark navy robes accessorized by multiple silver-colored sashes. Being older, he gave off a distinguished air. His jet-black hair, slicked back, ended past his shoulders in deep curves. The same green eyes met Lord Elendar.

"What is the meaning of this?" He demanded, glancing back at the sentries who refused to look at him as they shut the door. "Where are the people I summoned?"

"We sent them away," Lord Kel replied.

"You don't dictate the orders of my house!" Lord Elendar stepped forward, wincing.

"Were you really going to dirty your own hands with this matter?" Lady Haldris asked.

Her disappointing stare bore into him, scanning the condition of his body.

"This will solve nothing." Lord Kel's lips went thin. "You let this go on for far too long. Now your house has no choice in the next succession battles."

Lord Elendar frowned. The real reason his house did not participate smacked at his pride. A house full of noncombatants. Less than ten percent of them were battle seasoned, himself included. He tried numerous times to persuade his people to do ten-year military stints to get the bare minimum of combat experience. There weren't many takers and of those, a handful had shown their asses, inciting the current rebellion.

"Is it not my responsibility to punish as I see fit?" He cried out angrily.

"If that's the case, you should have stood by and watched Romnus murder your entire house," Lady Haldris answered. "Is it not his right as Supreme Ruler?"

The two moved to the table behind them where drinks and platters of finger food and fruits sat along its length. They sat across from each other, waiting for him to sit at the head. His guard sat next to him on the left.

"This matter no longer involves just your house, cousin." Lord Kel began while taking an empty plate and filling it with food. "We must come together and figure it out…"

"Discreetly," Lady Haldris chimed in. "Romnus was out of line."

Lord Elendar watched them partake of his food and drink as if they were at their own palace. Lord Kel halted his drink midway to his mouth.

"You have complaints?"

"No," he replied with tension.

"No need for this to go to waste." Lord Kel took a few sips, then set his cup down. "I'm sure you are aware of the rebels' close-knit network in your house. They will not divulge their members so carelessly."

"My spies have information that Halfar has asked Romnus to wait." Lady Haldris said. "That the enemy would make fools of them in due time."

"If that's true," Lord Elendar gasped. His family members dying at the hands of the enemy was the last thing he wanted. "There must be a better solution!"

His personal guard leaned towards him while sliding him a cup of the spirited brew.

"It will help with the other pain as well, your grace," he whispered.

"I understand how you feel, cousin," Lady Haldris said after taking a drink. "I truly do."

"But this is of their own doing. They should make peace with the consequences." Lord Kel met his gaze once more. "Let it be."

"Didn't you just say we need to work this out together?" Lord Elendar tersely asked.

"Yes." Lady Haldris finished chewing the small piece of cured meat she had picked from her plate. "It's simple. We isolate them."

"What?" He asked, confused.

"Don't act stupid! You know exactly what she means," Lord Kel snapped.

He went erect, slamming into the back of his chair. Part of the rumors of deceit stemmed from the fourth house's strategy of trade and complex resolutions. That's also how the rebels pulled off such a stunt.

"They would know why," Lord Elendar protested.

"From you, yes." Lord Kel deadpanned.

Lord Elendar felt his eyes go wide with realization. The sanctions would not come from him. That would only strengthen the rebels' resolve.

"What would our Supreme Ruler think?" He suddenly asked.

Both Lady and Lord stopped drinking, turning to him with looks of disdain and shock. Lady Haldris' face contorted into an ugly frown. Lord Kel tilted his head slightly in surprise.

"What we do with our houses is none of his concern when it does not affect his rule." Lady Haldris replied.

"As stated before," Lord Kel said. "Romnus stepped out of line." He eyed the cup still sitting untouched before Lord Elendar. "Drink that. You'll need more."

Lord Elendar took hold of the cup and gulped half the content. His throat burned for longer than normal. He shook his head, feeling the heat and numbness creep in. The pain subsided to a manageable degree.

"And get to the main palace for treatment." Lady Haldris' mouth down-turned. "You should know our healers aren't sufficient with such a wound. How could you go this long like that?"

"It shows weakness." Lord Kel resumed eating and drinking as Lord Elendar became angry, making a fist on the table. "Walking around wounded does not convey might. Ask General Kur how he feels after returning half dead."

Lord Elendar downed the rest of his drink. His guard reached for the nearest carafe and refilled it to the brim. Lord Kel was right. He needed a lot more.

～

A vortex opened on the outskirts that lay closer to Azrom. Thousands of enemy ships emerged, blasting away at whatever came into view before them. Waves of fire power washed over the darkness of space, creating a river of light. Their steady advance appeared dead-set on plowing through any obstacle.

They were denied.

The enemy assault met the barriers formed by the allied forces' blockade. Not one blast touched its mark. As the last enemy ship came out of the vortex, the entire fleet closed in on them and laid their own onslaught. Red and blue beams exchanged, with neither letting up. A frightening display of power had begun.

Smaller combat ships swarmed out of the main enemy vessels to meet the alliance's own fighter cruisers. Clusters of multicolored dots littered the area, silent explosions erupting within. The alliance outnumbered them, yet the enemy still pushed for dominance.

The Head Commander second to General Kur, stood with arms crossed in the center of his armada ship's bridge. His red cape, attached to the shoulders by black alloy clamps, flowed down past his knees over the black body suit armor. With a stern expression, he watched the display as it went on for more than he liked.

"How much are our weapons depleted?" He asked the weapons engineer concentrating on his station's screen. "This can't go on much longer."

"We are down to sixty percent." The weapons engineer turned to him. "Which means so are they. I think they may bring out those."

The Head Commander snorted. "Good. I want to see how our new counter weapon fairs against it. Give them a taste of their own dastardly deeds." He squinted at the space behind the enemy forces where the vortex sat open. "Can we not get close enough to destroy them from behind?"

"Unless you are volunteering us to go in and see where they came from, it would not be ideal," the navigator said. "The choice is yours, of course."

"I will not condone a suicide mission!" The Head Commander snapped. He calmed himself. "Switch to the main cannons after we fire the counter weapon."

That plan came from Lord Halfar. A strategy he knew well. Many worlds fell to their knees at Azrom's might because of it. The generals no doubt agreed without hesitation. He had attended the meeting where the other leaders stared, listening in shock at General Kur's suggestion. His loyalty to Supreme Ruler Romnus did not negate his admiration and tactics of the former, now living on a different planet as nothing more than a royal family member.

"Here it comes." The weapons engineer sighed.

The enemy assault ebbed around the bigger ships and the red tendrils spewed out towards the alliance. Angry red tendrils reached for their target with greedy anticipation. The alliance ships carrying counter weapons moved forward and the ships on the frontline receded, giving them a wide berth.

Blue light crackled around the device, creating an irregular web of electricity. The strands thickened until only small openings appeared. A sudden flash caused a white out, followed by wide blue beams shaped like cylinders shooting out into the fray. The Head Commander raised a forearm to shield his eyes, but that didn't stop the searing pain in his retinas. He barely made out the tubes of light engulf the red tendrils whole, gaining strength as each one slammed into the enemy ships. The gaping holes in their hulls spread, eating away what remained, leaving nothing.

The Head Commander dropped his arm and stared at the horrific scene. Within moments, the enemy began their retreat, reversing engines towards the vortex. He noticed the cluster of ships blocking the way move. They protect their transport route at all costs. He took note, certain the other leaders were doing the same.

"Should we let them go?" The weapons engineer asked. "We are at thirty percent."

"We bombard them until they are no longer in this system." The Head commander turned away and sat down in the captain's chair. He watched the retreat with amusement. "They would never let up if they were on the winning side."

Then he frowned at the scene. Thousands of enemy ships had come through with the obvious intent of spreading through the system. Starting from the first section and moving towards the outer rim where Razzna sat as the last planet. No. That's not right.

"Pull up the feeds from our forces in the center and near Razzna."

The communications technician brought up footage

from each sector on the main screen, overlaying battle views identical in nature. The enemy had indeed sent sizeable forces across the five systems. Each met the same fate. The only difference being Azrom took out more enemy ships than the others. Their relentless assault matched the enemy's. Even at thirty percent, the Azrom armada could conquer an entire planet.

Behind the holoscreen he could make out the last of the enemy ships backing into the vortex, their damaged in tow, before it shut. The alliance ships ceased firing.

"Send for replenishments," he ordered. "They will be back." And this time with even more might than this. He templed his hands before his lips. For the first time in over a century, he felt a slight moment of dread. "Move us back into our original formation for now."

"As you command," the navigator replied.

"I will need the damage report as well." He rested his head on the back of the chair. "Hopefully, there were no casualties."

⁓

Talas stifled his dismay at the deployed counter weapons' effect on the enemy ships. He had volunteered to command one of the new Lassian battleships near the mid-section of the Dreridian home world. Seeing such an onslaught of fire power unleashed from both sides made him cringe. The brutality of it all. Why?

The red tendrils alone were a bioweapon of catastrophe. To see the combined resources of each race's scientist resulting in something more monstrous terrified him. To go that far. He had never witnessed a level of war this intense. By the looks on the Azrom soldiers, it didn't warrant much thought.

When the enemy attacked New Lassa, they brought less than a hundred ships, thinking their race would dominate as usual. We proved them wrong! Looking back, he realized how naïve his people were. We have no choice now.

"Commander Talas," the weapons technician called out.

Talas winced at the title. He scanned the bridge. Sleek, newly installed, and the most advanced technology filled every inch. He stood with his hands resting on the curved rail of the center dais that came up to his waist. On the main screen, the enemy retreated.

His rust red leather jacket and leggings were in glaring contrast to the alliance soldiers' uniform body suits. Some of them even scrutinized him with disdain.

"Yes. Go ahead."

"Do you want to continue firing?" The technician asked, uncertain.

What is that about? "How are we on depletion?" The technician, an Azrom soldier, seemed to already know the answer.

"We are currently down to fifty-two percent."

That's all! Talas marveled at the efficiency of the ship's weapons.

"Then cease fire. They are running. We can conserve our resources."

"Of course." The technician frowned with disappointment.

The other ships did the same except for the Azrom ships. Talas tried not to roll his eyes in exasperation at their show of might until the last enemy ship disappeared into the closing vortex. The look of pride on some of the Azrom soldiers on board angered him.

"Is that all you strive for?" He asked heatedly. They turned towards him, eyes burning. "Do you think depleting all our weapons is something to be applauded?"

"We are sending the message that we will not take defeat." One of them retorted.

"Do you think they're not coming back?" Talas raised a hand and gestured towards the main screen. "I don't see any replenish ships out there. Do you?"

He watched them all avert their eyes in anger.

They knew he was right. The other soldiers on board kept to themselves, not engaging in the issue. The Razznians' expression said as much. Their relentless enemy would return ten times harder.

Debatable Outcome

Lord Pondur stared at the holoscreen crammed with reportThe holoscreen crammed with reports and data from the war's first battle found it glaringly obvious to Lord Pondur that the enemy didn't fully engage their forces. Another test? Their numbers increased yet, they still seemed cautious. He wondered what they could be after. He glanced over at his general and the accountant sitting at the table.

"What do you think of our counter weapon, general?"

The general straightened his broad shoulders, making his uniform jacket taut. He looked at the holoscreen for a moment before answering.

"Efficient, deadly." He paused. "Wholly unnecessary. Weapons such as these are beyond cruel. Overkill, you might say."

"Yes." Lord Pondur sipped from the tiny teacup in his hand and placed it on the matching saucer held in the other. "It does not sit well with me." He addressed the accountant. "How much in resources did we use for manufacturing?"

The accountant stayed in his usual position, bent over his tablet, scrolling as he spoke.

"Two hundred billion units of energy to power the replicator machines that mass produced the new raw material. Eight million kaldirons of Razznian ore combined with four million from Yaos to make the alloy. One billion hours of labor force and transport."

Lord Pondur tsked. He set the saucer on the side table, then laced his fingers, resting them on his knee as he crossed his right leg over. Well within budget. Still, quite costly. He let out a deep sigh.

"Are there any currently in production?"

"No, my lord. The foremen await a second round of orders," the accountant replied.

"Hah." Lord Pondur tapped his right foot in the air. He turned back to the general. "By your estimate, how many of these weapons do the enemy have in comparison?"

"From the way they scramble to retrieve them at all costs, I would gander we have twice the inventory."

"So, we have the advantage."

"Not quite." The general frowned. "They still have their trump card."

The planet bombs! Lord Pondur's eyes gleamed a bright red. Would they really use them?

The holoscreen switched to a communications feed. A soldier appeared, his face contorted in what they could only describe as distaste mixed with panic. He leaned forward.

"My apologies, my lord, for forcing into your personal feed. A mass communication array has swept the five systems."

"What? How?"

"I am uncertain as yet. My team is researching." He glanced away, appearing nervous. Bringing his attention back to look dead center at the screen, he said, "It is the enemy, my lord. They have something to say to all of us."

For three moon cycles following the battle, there had been nothing. Not one response from them. The alliance sat on pins and needles for the first few weeks, expecting a response.

A blanket array? That piqued Lord Pondur's curiosity.

"Let it through."

"Of course, my lord."

The soldier's image blinked out and replaced with a dark grainy feed. As the quality improved, Lord Pondur made out huge enemy ships moving in the background. Larger than the ones previously seen so far. Their weapons bays, mini black holes set prominently along the sides of the hulls, showed red glows pulsing in the center.

They're showing their hand.

The enemy leader the alliance had talked with before stood back on the left of the screen. A far more menacing creature stared out from the center view. Lord Pondur almost flinched, his fingers tightening on instinct. As a send only feed, it meant the enemy could not see or hear the recipients. The translator system kicked in right as the enemy spoke.

"We tried negotiations in good faith. You spat on our ideas. We attempt to claim territory just as you. We were patient. Gave you time to turn over your territories and resources. Instead, you declare war. Steal our technology to use against us."

Lord Pondur raised his brow. The general sat with his mouth gaping. The audacity!

The enemy continued. "My empire will respond in kind. What is yours we shall have as ours. As ruler of our mighty race, these five systems shall fall by my decree."

The feed cut right as the camera zoomed out, filling the screen with enemy ships of various sizes making their way into multiple open vortices.

"What do you think?" Lord Pondur asked the general after they both regained their composure. "How much time do we have?"

"I say they will show up throughout the system like before in less than two years." The general placed both hands on the table. "Plenty of time."

"They tried to conquer us like we have others?" Lord Pondur shook his head in disbelief. "That's not how we achieved our goals."

"It's more clinical than they think." The general smirked, the crags on the lower part of his face rubbed together. "None of this messiness. My grandfather told me of it."

"Yes, your family has served the Dreridians for millenniums. My predecessor also talked of the great cleansing." Lord Pondur narrowed his eyes. "Yet, we never got Azrom or Razzna under control."

His head jolted upright. The feed went system-wide, meaning every leader would see the enemy empire's declaration of war. How will Azrom and Razzna respond? A tiny bit of anxiety crept in. Both races conducted war selfishly. Never showing their full might. Would they now? Have they truly met their match? Lord Pondur watched his general turn on his tablet with the tap of a talon. Time to get serious.

###

Romnus stared blankly at the holoscreen floating midair in the center of the throne room. His head, slightly tilted, rested against one hand as he leaned to his right. Beside him, Farin chewed on a piece of fruit, her comical expression that of childlike wonder.

"Hmm?" She uttered while chewing.

The royal council, the generals, and his own entourage stood below with their eyes glued to the feed. They were in a mandatory meeting regarding the state of Azrom and the planet bombs when a communications soldier came rushing in without bowing and displayed the message. Now over.

Romnus' fingers rested on his temple. His right eye twitched. He had consumed three of the poisonous fruits to remain calm during the session, feeling somewhat lethargic. The enemy feed drained most of their effects away. Rage boiled to the surface.

"That was…" the first advisor muttered.

"Outrageous!" Another royal advisor yelled.

"I concur." Batis stared at the holoscreen before it blinked out. "Those disgusting," he didn't finish as a small orange blur whizzed past him, barely missing the side of his face.

Farin caught it with her left hand and smashed it into Romnus' mouth right as he opened it to speak, his head pushed back from the assault. Stunned, he didn't move. Farin kept her hand over his mouth. The squashed fruit slid down his throat, the juices having nowhere else to go. He swallowed the mess. Farin removed her hand. A servant brought a wet cloth for her to wipe his face. She did it without looking, then after cleaning her hand, returned it.

"Let's think about this calmly, okay?"

Farin forced a big smile.

She's just as livid, if more, than any of us. Romnus eyed her as he sat upright.

"My apologies, Supreme Ruler!" The communications soldier bowed ninety degrees. "I had no choice. The feed hit everywhere. Even the commlinks in the villages were bombarded."

"Say what?" Romnus felt his mind conflict between his rage and keeping calm as the fruit kicked in. "What do you mean?"

The first royal advisor turned and stepped forward.

"My lord, I was analyzing the feed. It appears this went system-wide." He paused, glancing around. "All five systems, to be exact."

"This is their declaration of war?" Kur stood with arms folded, one hand propped up. He ran a finger along the bottom of his chin. "If you would allow, General Rass and I have a few remedies we can implement."

"As long as we don't have to use full force, do what must be done," Romnus replied.

"Never." Rass grinned, a touch of evil in his eyes. "No enemy deserves Azrom's full might."

⌒

New Lassa's communications array displayed giant holo-screens, blemishing the early evening sky. The entire population stopped their tasks and stared in awe. The manbeasts atop the hills got a clear view. While the gate technician tried to contain the feed, the audio boomed. His counterpart on the other side of the planet attempted the same.

"What is happening?" Chardon cried out, running towards the gate console. "Where is it coming from?"

"Everywhere." The gate operator slammed his fists on the console. "It just came through and took over. The entire planet can see it."

Halfar frowned at the sky along with the rest of Chardon's cabinet members who came to stand beside him. The enemy image appeared, and their message spewed forth. Jaron's eyes went wide, her mouth gaping open. Ganna appeared to rear her head back as if smacked. The enemy's words confused Chardon. Halfar held no such confliction. His eyes burned with intense malice.

When the feed ended, the holoscreen shut down, a hush blanketed the area. The breeze and the rustling of grass suddenly seemed too loud. Small creatures holding conversations usually not heard were now being eavesdropped on.

"Good faith!" Talas' fists clenched tight at his sides. "Patient?" He yelled.

"Well," Ganna smirked. "That was surprising. They got a lot of nerve. May Lassa's light burn their hides to a crisp."

"I don't…what is…" Chardon had a hard time conveying what he felt.

Halfar took hold of his shoulders and turned him around. Their eyes met. He placed both hands around Chardon's face.

"All you need to do is send them back to where they came from. Less in numbers and mortally wounded preferably."

Chardon gazed at Halfar's serenity. War ran in his blood. This situation registered low on the scale for him. That said, there was a new wrinkle in all of this. Every being on New Lassa now knew what they were up against. Sound returned to normal, and he could hear the village resume its activities.

Talas gave Jaron a look of disdain. "Come! We have work to do!"

Chardon watched the two head back to the temple where they had been conducting a meeting. Ganna's face twitched, distorting for a moment in anger. *She's cracking.* He saw Modas and Trinon scan the hill tops. Something in their expression. Resolve? Understanding? Of what? Halfar dropped his hands.

"Let's continue your meeting. You need an annihilation strategy more than ever."

Chardon gave him a tiny smile.

He liked the sound of that.

〜

Lord Kraznan fanned himself on the throne placed outside on the mezzanine built behind the throne room. The humid night air felt clingy this time of season. He glanced at the holoscreen being held by a servant, their head bowed low while their arms shook from holding it up.

"Enough." He waved it away. The servant bowed even lower, then stood, tucking the device away in their robes after the screen disappeared. Lord Kraznan addressed his advisors. "Do you have our answer?"

"Of course, my lord," the military leader replied. "We will get it done with minimal effort, as always."

"Are you still against my choice on who rides the helm?"

The military leader balked. "No, my lord. I am merely worried our reconnaissance will not be as solid without Commander Sars' expertise."

"You cover your scales well," Lord Kraznan scoffed.

The other advisor stared dubiously at the military leader. His confident demeanor seemed to waver as he looked away. Lord Kraznan had seen many leaders come and go over the centuries. This new round had become stagnant, set in their ways. Commander Sars, and his entire nest tobe fair, brought new ideas to battle.Razzna needed a fresh approach. His eyes turned to slits. And the resurgence of a few old ways.

"Bring him up to speed on our true battle plans. His brood lacks knowledge of our previous ones before their hatching."

"I will personally secure him under my wing, your majesty." The military leader bowed.

Lord Kraznan halted his fanning. The enemy. If they didn't taste so bad, he would eat them into extinction.

෪

The crew of the first Azrom rebels' ship moved around with nervous vigor as their vessel sat in a minor planet's orbit near the center of the five systems. Directly ahead lay the planet bombs constrained inside barriers, preventing their expansion. The second one crackled and spit energy leaking from the thin fractures along its casing. Beyond it, the other rebel Azrom ship also kept watch.

Every few days, the ships conducted a scan of the bombs to check their stability. While another began, the head of the rebellion leaned forward in the captain's chair. Both his hands rested flat on his thighs, his fingers twitching as he tried not to let anxiety grip him. Transporting the deadly weapons was no small feat to begin with. A damaged planet bomb made it close to a failure.

The enemy broadcast meant they were ready to address their end of the deal. Once the war ended, the fourth house would replace the current monarchy and allowed to trade outside the five systems. In exchange, the enemy would get two planet bombs as a deterrent for future rebellions. The rebel leader scoffed, thinking about it.

Of course, he had no intention of handing over the bombs. His house may be ambitious, but they were not insane. The plan entailed renegotiating with the enemy to have the bombs delivered after his house took over. They would then hide the weapons, their location revealed to them only if truly needed.

With the scan complete, showing no change, he sat back, breathing a sigh of relief.

Warning lights came on, covering the bridge in red light. Klaxons rang out. The navigator and the communications tech attacked their main consoles in a panic. The viewscreen changed, zooming in on the space to their left behind the bombs. A vortex opened near the third planet. Enemy fighter ships flew out like vermin.

The rebel leader lurched forward, his fear and surprise on full display. He gripped the sides of the chair. No! He turned to the weapons technician.

"Protect the bombs! Hail the other ship!"

"No need." The weapons tech pointed to the screen. The other ship changed course and moved towards the vortex. "Enemy ETA four hours."

"Hail them then!" He yelled at the communications tech.

"Doing that now." She frowned. "They're not responding." Her eyes went wide. "Wait!"

A second vortex opened in the space to the right side of the ship. Fighter cruisers came forward, their weapons bays already glowing hot. There was no barrage of fire this time. Instead, their energy combined and to create a web. The rebel leader knew immediately what they were doing.

"Hail them again." The rebel leader seethed, baring his teeth as an enemy soldier's image filled the viewscreen.

"What is the meaning of this?" The rebel leader yelled. "We had a deal!"

"Change of plans." The enemy soldier attempted a grin, showing thin, razor-sharp teeth. "You are no longer needed. We take the weapons."

"No! You don't get to take them until the deal is complete!"

"Then you we remove and take anyway."

The screen returned to normal view, making the crew watch the webbing continue. The enemy ships near the third planet suddenly shimmered out of sight.

"They jumped!" The navigator exclaimed.

Red beams showered the space on the left as the ships reemerged. The planet bomb barriers absorbed the blasts that hit them. A round of fire from the other Azrom ship countered, holding the enemy at bay.

"Target those ships making the harness." The rebel leader ordered.

The ship turned and began a full assault. Where the blasts hit the webbing, it only delayed their work. A new section replaced them. To his horror, four of the bigger ships stopped making the web and trained their cannons on his ship.

Not like this! He refused to die here in the darkness of nowhere. His pride crumbling, he met the communication tech's gaze. The ship rocked hard from multiple blasts. The view screen flickered, turning fuzzy. He could barely make out the other ship being bombarded, its hull breeched on one side.

"Damage to the rear hull!" The weapons tech called out. "Losing ten percent of our shields!"

The rebel leader nodded at the communications tech. She turned away with a shameful expression.

☙

"Is that what I think it is, beloved?" General Kur stood akimbo in the center of the war room staring at the emergency feed coming through. "Are they being serious?" He turned to Rass. "Is it a trap?"

"Not for us." Rass read the message again. "It seems we were right. The enemy stabbed them in the back."

"And we should help them… why?"

"Do you really want Azrom blood spilt like this by those monsters?" Rass folded his arms.

"Not particularly, no."

"There's also that last part." Rass' brow furrowed. Kur could see the anguish. "We cannot let that happen."

Kur looked at the last line of the feed.

The enemy is attempting to take the planet bombs.

An image attached to the feed showed the energy webbing. Further out, he could see the damaged planet bomb. He ran a hand down his face and let it drop back into the fold of his arms.

"Shall we go ourselves?" He asked Rass. When he didn't receive an answer, he turned to find Rass already heading towards the doors. "Ready two armada ships," he ordered the soldier at the console.

"As you command," the soldier replied.

Well, Lord Elendar. What will you do now when these wretched traitors return?

⌇

Two Azrom Armada ships, each commanded by a general, arrived out of the vortex onto a gruesome scene. Both planet bombs wrapped in the energy webbing were being pulled into an open vortex. Even with their prize in hand, the enemy continued to decimate the already crippled Azrom battleships.

Kur stared in fury at the outcome. None had ever destroyed an Azrom ship. Here before him were two beyond repair. He silently cursed the fourth royal house rebels.

"Hit the enemy forces attacking the second ship. General Rass will take care of the other side."

"Of course, General." The weapons tech opened the bays.

Azrom fighter ships engaged the enemy's, pushing them back away from the listless second one with sparks jumping out from the damaged hull. There were no lights present. The enemy backed off, seeing their numbers dwindle rapidly. Twenty of theirs were no match for an Azrom Armada ship.

On the other side, Rass growled in frustration at his failure to sever the tethers attached to the planet bombs. Every time they hit one, another sprang forth to reattach. The bombardment between the two forces made it impossible to get a clear shot. Which he took as part of a blessing since it eased the assault on the first battleship.

Only a few lights flickered along its hull. The ship would need to be towed back. A large beam shot out of the vortex from behind the enemy ships and plowed straight towards Azrom's ships. The space, now free of the planet bombs, gave them a clear target.

"Shields, full power! Turn forty degrees! Cover the battleship!"

He saw Kur's ship doing a similar maneuver to save what remained of the second one. His ship swung sideways, blocking its view. The blast hit harder than expected. Alarms erupted as it knocked his ship off course. The stabilizers struggled to correct its position. Nevertheless, the shields held. The enemy blast clipped the front of the dead battleship, sending it sideways, then dissipated in the darkness.

Rass watched, disappointed, at the planet bombs disappearing into the enemy vortex before it winked out of existence. Luckily, he had a plan for such an event. He tilted his head down and looked up in hostility at the screen.

You won't get away with this.

His mouth turned up in a sinister grin.

Stuck in a Rut

Did they think it would go unnoticed?

Lord Pondur mused to himself while reading the report from the spy he dispatched to survey the planet bombs. He commended Azrom's desperate act to retrieve the stolen weapons. The enemy had proven themselves bold beyond measure. He sat at his desk, chin resting on the backs of his propped-up hands.

The real question would be where or who they intended to use them on. Lord Graggor entered the room, giving him a slight head bow. He seemed weary. As he should. The scientist worked day in and out on a solution to their current rodent problem. The enemy.

"So, you've heard?" Lord Pondur asked, almost jokingly.

Lord Graggor caught on. "Such a farce. They should have notified us of the theft when it happened." He scratched the side of his head with a talon, getting into the grooves between his crags. "What will you do?"

Lord Pondur hit the commlink beside him. "Open a channel to Azrom."

"Of course, my lord," a soldier on the other end responded.

"Oh?" Lord Graggor's eyes widened with excitement. "You're doing that?" He hurried to the seat by the entrance for an unobstructed view of the holoscreen.

Lord Pondur snorted at his childlike display. The blank screen displayed a blue background with the connection icon spinning, each tiny slash blinking out one by one.

"Connection complete. Sending the feed."

Directly across from Lord Pondur, Supreme Ruler Romnus' image filled the wall. While Lord Graggor appeared weary, Romnus seemed lethargic, burned out, and oozing rage from his entire being.

"Lord Romnus." Lord Pondur narrowed his eyes. "You must know why I have contacted you at such a time."

"Unfortunately, yes."

"Care to explain?"

"I was confident we could remedy the situation before it came to this."

"We would have assisted. No one wants one of those things loose in the hands of an incompetent race." Lord Pondur dropped his hands onto the desk. "And now there are two to worry about."

"The situation is worse than that." Romnus' deadpan tone disturbed him.

"Oh?" Is he on some kind of narcotic? Resorting to drug use already? "How so?"

"One is damaged. Its barrier could fail at any time if mishandled."

Lord Pondur pinched the bridge of his tiny nose. He squinted to ease an oncoming headache. The spy said one of them had energy arcing from it.

"Does this mean every planet in the five systems has to be on high alert and prepared to evacuate their home worlds?" Lord Pondur removed his fingers and stared at Lord Romnus. "Do you have any idea what strife you have caused?" He yelled angrily.

"Disruption of trade, I know."

Romnus wasn't allowed to continue. Lord Pondur slammed down a fist.

"Trade is the least of our worries! This is the annihilation of potential planets!"

Something ominous stirred in Lord Romnus' demeanor. His lethargic expression wore off, replaced with an unholy malice, a spark of blue light glowing in the center of his pupils. Lord Pondur leaned back, careful not to show the terror he felt.

Did I poke the monster?

Lord Graggor hid his nervousness by averting his gaze from the holoscreen. The two made eye contact. What now?

"Maybe," Lord Romnus said tersely, "you should tread more lightly, Lord Pondur."

"I only require a remedy for this issue. You owe the five systems that much."

"That is a given. My rule may not be steeped in longevity. I am still ruler of Azrom."

"Then we look forward to updates on the matter."

"Of course. I bid you wellness and good fortune."

The feed cut abruptly, the holoscreen again blank. It winked out, revealing the boring view of the back wall.

"Well." Lord Graggor breathed a sigh of relief. "That took a few years off my life."

Lord Pondur tugged down on the front of his jacket and cleared his throat.

"Harrowing, indeed." He crossed his legs and positioned them so that he sat sideways in his chair. With one talon, he tapped the desk. "Should we trust them?"

"Azrom has planets under their rule. I can't see them forfeiting their conquests." Lord Graggor tilted his head. "Or their trade contracts. Especially with the outer rim."

Lord Pondur nodded. Yes, Romnus has not ruled long. But his shrewd negotiations regarding trade put him on par with the Dreridians.

"Let's see what you do, Supreme Ruler Romnus."

⌇

Loose grass and leaves, swept up by a warm breeze, deposited in Halfar's hair that flowed forward, riding the wind's movement. He tucked one side behind his ear and closed his eyes, breathing in the scent. He hadn't ventured far into the fields for moments of solace in a long time. Once every moon cycle, he came to recalibrate his mood. The current soon to be war effort found him missing three in a row. The visit felt long overdue.

In his left hand, he held a secret communication chip from Azrom. He had gained the trust of a gate operator who delivered it while he sat alone outside the temple. Knowing it could be bad news, he walked to the other side of the building and set the chip on his wrist communicator. He almost yelled out in fury at the message.

Calm.

Halfar took another deep breath, easing the memory away. Rage would not solve the issue. He had a remedy. Commission of the planet bombs creation came with an explicit way to counter them if necessary. As Supreme Ruler, he understood his obligation to safeguard other regions from their potential target.

Romnus must be exhausted. Halfar pitied his child having to take care of that brooding behemoth. With the debacle at hand, including the fourth house rebellion, he could only imagine the level of stress in the royal houses.

"You always keep secrets from me." He heard Chardon's voice behind him. "I get that you can't tell me everything."

"It's not that I don't want to, Chardon." Halfar turned to stand beside him.

"You have to go to Azrom, don't you?"

"If I tell you why, you'll be more than upset."

"Is that so? You still think I'm too immature to handle such things?"

Halfar felt the sting of his words. "That's not what I think at all!" He clenched his fists, giving him an intense frown. "Don't ever say that to me again."

Startled, Chardon leaned away from him. "I'm sorry." He hung his head and regained his posture. "It's a bad habit."

"Yes, it is." Halfar faced him. "I will tell you."

Chardon listened without interruption. Halfar watched his expression drop and turn blank, as if something had ripped his soul out for a moment. His gaze returned with a deep seeded wrath. Chardon's eyes smoldered, the irises now swirling rainbows. When Halfar finished, he took hold of Chardon's shoulders.

"Look at me," he commanded. Chardon's far away stare focused on him. "I will fix this."

"That's not why I'm angry," Chardon whispered, barely containing his mood. Halfar stared at him, confused. He let go of his shoulders. "Those disgusting predators have pissed me off for the last time."

Halfar stepped back, feeling the rage emanating from Chardon.

"Chardon?"

"Go. Be the royal advisor you need to be for Azrom. I will be with the council." Chardon turned away and headed back to the village. "To plan our enemy's demise."

⤳

The two female escorts gave chase after Farin suddenly bolted down the corridor towards the stairwell leading to the palace roof gate console. Her robes wrapped around her legs as her speed increased while the women struggled to match her.

"Lady Farin, please!" The first escort cried out. "There's no rush!"

Farin imagined their defeated looks. Yet, they persisted. She gave them credit. Most of her escorts would have given up by now. The reason for rushing stemmed from her need to talk to her father before he advised Romnus.

She crossed the threshold of the roof right as the gate opened. Her father walked briskly through the dark pathway.

The moment his feet stepped on the roof, she slammed into him, wrapping her arms tight around his waist.

"Child!" He tried to pry her off. "What is the meaning of this?"

"I had my spies copy the message sent to you." Her face, buried in his chest, muffled her voice. "I knew no one would tell me what's going on."

"Of course not!" Halfar pushed her off by the shoulders. "You think too rationally. We need a more devious approach."

Farin pouted. "I can be devious," she retorted. She straightened her posture. "Still." She turned so they could walk side by side. "I need to discuss something with you."

He glanced at her, concerned. "Is that so?"

The two escorts appeared at the top of the stairs, both out of breath. The first one placed a hand on the stone wall to steady herself right as the other slumped against it without shame.

"Lady Farin," the first huffed. "Please do not force us to shirk our duties this way."

"My apologies." Farin grinned. "Let's go to my private chamber."

"Stop being a brat," her father chastised. "You're too old for that."

The corners of her closed lips turned upwards until her cheeks seemed to puff out, her eyes widening playfully. She looked like a disobedient child.

"Maybe, if I wasn't treated as such," she nodded over her shoulder at the escorts, "I would act better." She turned her attention to descending the stairs.

Inside her private chamber, the escorts bowed and left Farin with her father. The room kept a stock of liquors, drinks, and non-perishable foods for snacking arranged on the table. Lighting orbs nestling in the corners of the ceiling floated halfway down to illuminate the room with a soft glow.

"Please, sit, father." She plopped down into the plush

chair. Her father took the one across from her. "A refreshing drink?" She gestured with a hand extended towards the array of carafes. "Or something stronger?"

"Since I have to meet with the Generals and your beloved the moment their guards come find us, I'll stick with refreshing."

Farin let out a disappointed sigh. She didn't get to drink often with her father like the others, despite also being an adult. Removing the lid off one of the metal containers, she used a pair of tongs to retrieve two frosty orbs from inside. Icy smoke drifted around them as she dropped one in each glass, then poured a green drink over them.

Her father reached over and took one, sipping the content as it smoldered. She watched him carefully hold the glass and drink with refined dignity. Royalty permeated every inch of his soul. Something she lacked. He set the glass down.

"What is so dire that you ambushed me at the gate?"

Farin's tongue kept sticking to the roof of her mouth. It hurt each time she dislodged it. She took a big swig of her drink to conquer the dryness. Feeling her mouth regain moisture, she settled in her chair and held her glass with both hands in her lap.

"It's about Romnus." She gripped the glass tighter. "He's not you." She looked up and met his surprised gaze. "I mean to say." She struggled with her words. "Not that he's spiraling. Well, yes, he's losing control, but…" She stopped.

Part of the reason he had to abdicate the throne came from his cruelty towards not only her but others in the royal courts. His corrupt advisors filled his head with royal statutes long discarded for their capacity to cause extreme harm. It took years for her to forgive him.

"No, he's not." Her father said, breaking her out of the fog. "I hurt you. It pains me to see it in your eyes still." Farin averted her stare. "Romnus never wanted to rule. He doesn't have the resolve."

"You criticized him for not killing the entire fourth house." Farin tiltled her head.

"That was not criticism. I merely stated my feelings. If he had done such a thing, the people of Azrom would have assassinated him on the spot. He wouldn't have finished the act."

Farin stared at him in horror. She had a feeling that may be the case. Hearing it out loud was another story.

"The Dreridians are livid." Farin took another swig of her drink, downing half the glass. "There was an emergency communication from them."

"And Romnus is murderous because they hit a nerve in their attempt to make him feel guilty."

"How did…" Farin sputtered. Then she calmed down. Of course, her father knew. He understood how the other rulers calculated each move they made. "I feared your advice could steer him in the opposite direction. I see now how naïve I am."

Her father exhaled loudly and drank more from his glass. "Farin." He sounded exasperated. "You are far from naïve. Your concern is valid. He may or may not listen to me, even though I am here at his behest."

"The Generals will arrive shortly with the rebels they rescued. There are sanctions on the fourth house in place. Romnus has no idea where they are coming from. It's all third party yet only concerns certain factions of the house, causing strife with trade."

"Do you think my father's sister would stand idly by and watch all the royal houses suffer at the whim of some rebels?"

His mention of the second house ruler surprised Farin. She had met the monarch once during the royal wedding reception. A woman of few words, her demeanor demanded respect.

"Ahh." Farin hung her head. "That explains it. Romnus won't like that."

"He does now?" Her father raised his brow.

"There are so many things compounded that he's losing his focus." She paused. "And his grip on the empire. I want to reign by his side. He won't let me."

"Then first you must make your intentions clear. Do not back down. If he feels the need to harm you in any way…" His darkened eyes said the rest as he drained his glass. "It seems our time is up."

Farin heard the unmistakable sound of multiple boots striking the marbled floors outside and finished her drink.

"Shall I go along or bide my time?"

"I would wait for the Generals to return. That's when Romnus will be most fierce," he stood, staring down at her. "Also, easier to manipulate."

Six royal guards stood outside the entrance; their heads bowed towards them.

"My Queen," the leader of the unit greeted. "Lord Halfar." He raised his head, the others following suit. "Our Supreme Ruler awaits your arrival in his study."

Farin tilted her head and gave her father a grin. "Don't drink too much, father."

"That depends on the situation, daughter."

Farin frowned after he left with the guards. Romnus would be drunk again tonight.

The Dreridian spy sat snug in his tiny fighter, powered down among the shadows of a dark moon in an unfamiliar system. He had escaped detection due to size and his long, thought-out calculations. During the last battle, he hitched a ride through their vortex by attaching his ship onto the underbelly of a crippled enemy cruiser. He floated off with the debris and waited until the fleet moved far enough away for him to hide.

Ahead loomed the glowing, angry enemy home world. The orange ball, with grey and white swirls, glared at him. He felt its ominous aura reach out and try to snare any prey within its grasp. Fitting for their race. They were not the only ones who could instill fear. He knew that tactic.

The Razznians hinted earlier about the enemy possibly having a force equal to theirs or Azrom. He couldn't say that, but it was damn close. Thousands of ships littered the space surrounding the planet with more going to or leaving the surface. Their numbers caught him off guard. Conquerors. The council established the term regarding them at first sight. The system itself felt stifling.

Some feeds he picked up told him the enemy was nothing short of oppressors, with no inkling on how to take care of trade. It merely functioned even at the cost of lives or entire planets unable to keep up. That's why they gobble up resources! They go through them like water. An unsustainable business. A waste.

A fleet of ten thousand towed a planet bomb towards a newly open vortex. His scanner lit up with the intercepted coordinates. The center of the Dreridian system would be their target. The spy watched, helpless to do anything. Another fleet had the other one ready to go into the next forming vortex. Time to go.

He eased his ship out and once again flowed with the lingering debris. The enemy seemed to be in no rush to clean up the region. He clamped onto the rear of a nearby ship and powered down. He would send an emergency communication to the home world the moment they entered Dreridian space. If he could get a message out before that, it would be ideal.

The vortex opened a solar system away from Dreridian territory, with the second vortex appearing next to it. The planet bomb crackled and sparked, its shell a spiderweb of cracks. They're checking it! He already knew from its condition it was too late for that fleet. The first seemed to realize it right as a new vortex formed.

Before the vortex shut, he saw the other warble from the force of the damaged planet bomb breaking out of its shell. Bright beams of light shot from the cracks, lighting the entire region in blinding yellow and white. Some of the enemy ships attempted to reverse engines even while the rest coming out were being torn apart inside the unraveling vortex.

The spy prayed for the inhabitants of the system. The bomb may not hit one planet directly, but it would touch at least the three in the vicinity. Madness. He hunkered down in the cockpit.

⌒

Lord Pondur inspected every face on the holoscreen across from his desk. An alert came from the next system over. Within hours, every leader and ruler called for an emergency meeting. He adjusted the ruffled sleeves of his shirt, extending from the arms of his jacket.

"It seems the enemy has made their move. They've unleashed a planet bomb. It is headed for the center of our system." Lord Pondur crossed his arms, standing straight with his legs slightly apart. "This is a dire situation."

He noticed five of the squares were dark. Where were the rulers of that system? Did they think themselves superior? That this meeting did not concern them? He could see the other leaders glancing around the grid as well.

A soldier came bursting in. His face cragged even more as he bowed hastily.

"My apologies, your grace! The spy has sent an urgent message."

"More urgent than the enemy sending a planet bomb to destroy us?" Lord Pondur asked calmly, with an angered tone.

The soldier looked over the holoscreen. "It would explain the missing rulers."

Lord Pondur frowned. The other rulers' expressions changed to fear.

"Show me."

ACTS OF TRANSGRESSION | 203

The soldier produced a small chip and placed it on the data platform for the holoscreen to project. A smaller second screen appeared, along with the spy's barely audible voice.

"One of the planet bombs, the damaged one, didn't make it. Took out an entire enemy fleet and," the spy's message paused. "They were in the next system over. I fear the surrounding planets... are..."

The feed cut off, no longer needed.

They watched the footage of the planet bomb crack open before the image distorted and went black. Yelling erupted from the audio feed. Lord Pondur took a few deep breaths. Remain calm. He turned to the soldier.

"Any signs of communication? Can we reach them?"

"All communication satellites in that system are dead. Either blown out or disintegrated."

"I want a status report immediately."

"Of course, your grace. Lord Graggor is already doing so."

Lord Pondur nodded. He brought his attention back to the quarreling rulers on the screen.

"If you please," he spoke gently. The fighting died out and they stared in anticipation at him. He addressed one of his generals. "What is the ETA for that second bomb?"

"Within years. Possibly two or three." The general pursed his lips. "There's no time."

"So, we're doomed to half a century of recovery after the fallout?" Lord Pondur lamented.

"Not necessarily." A separate feed from Azrom popped up. Halfar nodded to Lord Pondur. "My apologies for the interruption."

No one else could see or hear him. Lord Pondur feigned a smile as he addressed the other leaders. "I believe we need to think a bit more regarding this event. Cool our heads? We shall continue this another day." He motioned for the soldier to cut the feed. The main holoscreen winked out, leaving the spy's and Halfar's up. "What do you mean, Lord Halfar? It is en route. We cannot stop it."

"But I can." Halfar sat leisurely in his seat, one leg crossed over, the ankle resting on the other's thigh. "I would never create something I can't destroy."

Lord Pondur's eyes widened in disbelief. He always knew Azrom could conquer far more than they already had with their advances in war tactics. But this? This! Neutralizing a planet bomb? A new fear gripped him.

"Is that so? Then you will save us all?"

"It won't be flawless." Halfar gave a stern stare. "The procedure is delicate and anything in its path will be impacted."

"Describe, impacted." Lord Pondur braced himself for the answer.

"The usual. Magnetic interference, dimensional distortion, both causing extreme, maybe catastrophic, weather events."

"I can deal with that." Lord Pondur relaxed his muscles. He glanced at the message beneath the spy's feed. "Oh, my spy says he calculates the enemy has over five hundred thousand ships. A sizable force close to yours and the Razznians."

Halfar's face didn't register the information. He was almost...deadpan? Their numbers fazed him not one bit. Which added to Lord Pondur's anxiety.

"Good to know," Halfar finally responded.

"If you had such a remedy, why did Lord Romnus not say so?" Even as he asked, the answer came to him before Halfar replied.

"Because he does not know. Only the scientists who created them and General Rass, along with me, are privy to that. And it will remain so."

"Yet you are telling me this." Lord Pondur raised a hand to his chin.

"As you say, trade must flow undeterred. Azrom has many planets under its wing that rely on Dreridian trade systems. You control it."

"Are you certain you are not willing to retake the throne?"

Halfar's face scrunched in disgust. "I do not." His expression softened. "You need to give Romnus a chance."

"Only if you agree to advise him."

"That is already established."

Lord Pondur eyed the former Supreme Ruler. There hadn't been a more ruthless ruler since the times of Halfar's father. Or his own grandfather, in retrospect. We are in interesting times. He smiled. As big and genuine as his craggy face could muster.

Five: Repentance

New Strategy

RIn the palace's underground secret lab, Rass checked calculations on the holoscreen above his work desk. A wide red ribbon secured his pulled back hair yet, wisps of his dark wavy hair still found their way out, framing his face. Technicians moved around, careful not to disturb him. On the other side of the desk, Halfar scanned the data flow.

"Are we sure these are correct?" Halfar asked. "This is only the second time we've tried to stop a planet bomb."

"And it was disastrous. Did you not tell Lord Pondur the consequences?"

"I did. He agreed to the loss."

"That's fine," Rass replied. "As long as we're not billed for it."

"He has a different compensation in mind." Halfar seemed to be far away in thought.

Rass stiffened. One option came to him. Romnus may be rough around the edges, but given time, he would certainly be a great ruler. Halfar focused on him as if sensing his concern.

"Don't worry. I will not challenge Romnus to regain the throne. I am not ready to meet my death just yet."

Rass' head snapped up at the remark. He almost forgot about the rules of succession. Everyone kept assuming Halfar could simply kick Romnus out and take his place. Romnus would probably kill him this time.

"Of course."

Rass went back to looking at the data stream.

"You lost your way once. That doesn't mean you're suicidal."

An awkward silence fell between them. Rass looked over at Halfar. No!

"Stop," Rass demanded to prevent Halfar from speaking.

"I'm sorry." Halfar met his gaze. "I truly am. Please, don't ever forgive me."

Rass lowered his eyes. The day Halfar came and took him by force after being bonded to Kur still haunted him. He never expected an apology.

"I won't." Rass clenched his fists, then released them. He steered the discussion back to the task at hand. "The timing has to be perfect. The more accurate, the less damage it brings."

"We need to wait for it to show up. Its appearance will strike fear throughout the five systems." Halfar smirked.

He's enjoying this.

Rass relaxed and sighed, resting his forearms on the desk. Neither of the two were scientists by any means. They simply knew what the outcome should be for their many experiments and creations.

"We also need to dedicate a thousand ships for the launch. They will jump the moment they release the neutralizer." He eyed Halfar again. "Speaking of which. The enemy is coming at full force. Are we going to match them?"

Halfar's eyes narrowed. "Would the Razznians?"

"Absolutely not," Rass answered. He bobbed his head. "Maybe a hundred thousand? A show of good faith?"

Lt. Treshur came swaggering into the lab, his cape a couple of inches from the floor flowing behind him like a wave. His easy-going demeanor irked Rass. He saw Halfar tense up with ire as well.

"To think, Lord Romnus would give you such free rein despite being abdicated." Lt. Treshur halted a few feet from them. "Our Supreme Ruler is quite merciful."

"I am his trusted advisor, nothing more," Halfar snapped.

"Hmm. If you say so." Treshur glanced at the holoscreen. "Should we be so lucky that it works this time?"

"It worked before," Rass retorted. "We were just too late."

The memory of Halfar in a panic pleading with him to stop the planet bomb he had sent to Lassa out of rage following Chardon's rejection. It destroyed an entire planet and its second moon, along with two others behind it in one instance.

Looking back, he should have tried harder to deter him. The purpose of the planet bombs was to intimidate, not actually use them. In the history of Azrom under Halfar's rule, they had used four. And that proved too many, Rass thought to himself.

❦

The newly manufactured Lassian ship demanded respect, its specifications putting it at a power level far beyond necessary. A sleek body of monstrous size, its hull a neutral color of the lightest brown with hints of green and white, the build, a work of art. Spanning nearly a kilometer in width and twice that in length, the elongated oval shape made it appear larger.

Adan stared at it, grinning with pride. He stood with his feet lined with his shoulders, one arm folded with the other's fist propped under his chin. His fingers caressed his jawline.

"What do you think?" He didn't bother to look over at the recipients of his masterpiece.

Chardon and Ganna were speechless. Both seemed to have lost their function to think. Adan's mouth spread into a wide smile. He couldn't help it. To have full production back on the planet boosted not only morale. Work quality also increased.

"It's more than I imagined," Ganna finally spoke.

"Impressive," Chardon said slowly.

A dark expression suddenly formed on their faces.

Adan's brow raised for a moment, then he realized what it meant. He understood the concern.

"Do we really need something like this?" Ganna whispered. "I know I said Lassa should fend for itself. This…" Ganna shrugged one shoulder.

"Would put us in a new category of defense for our race," Chardon finished.

"I admire your reluctance." Adan dropped his arm. "But these are war times. No one gets to sit this one out. That includes us." He stepped closer to the ship. "Four more are being completed on the production site. You'll have five high-powered instruments of death." He saw them go rigid. "If you choose to use them that way."

"What's their equivalence, then?" Ganna asked.

"Like two Azrom armada ships or five Razznian ones," Adan replied.

Chardon went pale. Ganna's eyes widened.

Adan's crew put the best materials and highest technology into the Lassian ships at the behest of multiple leaders. They all wanted to see New Lassa elevated and to see how they would rise to the challenge of going outside their planet to defend others.

Dirty bastards!

His crew received compensation far above the requirements. He couldn't really say no without a valid reason.

"Think of it as survival assurance."

Chardon cast him an angry stare.

"Spatial anomaly detected in the third quadrant," the voice of a soldier coming out of the commlink on Lord Pondur's desk yelled.

He could hear the frantic tone under the false confidence. Lord Pondur sat sipping tea in his usual highchair. He glanced behind him at the commlink, taking a sip from a delicate blue and gold teacup with scalloped rim.

A reply from him wasn't necessary. Everyone knew their parts to play. Lord Graggor came in and sat in the closest chair at the table.

"Good, you're here." Lord Pondur set his matching tea set down. "On screen," he called out.

The automated feed system kicked in. The holoscreen appeared, displaying real time footage of the third quadrant. He almost fell backwards from his chair as the image visually assaulted his eyes. Lord Graggor hissed, turning his head away.

The closing vortex served as a backdrop to the swirling, glowing ball of destruction traveling out towards the Dreridian system's center. A shimmering array of colors shifted within the planet bomb, each instance causing everything around it to warp. The feed crackled before it winked out.

Lord Pondur and Graggor sat stunned in silence. Lord Graggor finally straightened his head, looking down at the table's surface. Neither had seen such an in-depth image of the dreaded weapon.

"Looks like the satellites are gone," Lord Graggor said. "We have to wait for the next ones to pick up. The closer it gets, we won't be able to get a good feed."

"The disruption is indeed massive." Lord Pondur tugged the bottom of his jacket down. "Your thoughts on the remedy?"

Lord Graggor's eyes perked up with intrigue. *Ahh, the scientist in him has stirred!* He watched his hands clasp together as if in prayer, touching the fingertips to his mouth.

"If I had the level of spies needed for a mission on Azrom, I would love to get my hands on their process. Not even we would have thought to create such a thing."

"Let's hope it goes as planned." Lord Pondur picked up his tea.

Lord Graggor frowned.

"Yes, this would be unprecedented. I believe they have

never actually stopped one before."

"Why would they? The goal is annihilation. They show no mercy."

⌒

Azrom's seasonal gloom greeted the incoming ships being towed to the shipyards above ground. Another group of ships carrying both rebellion crews made their descension towards the Fourth Royal House lawn. Servants, medical technicians, and family leaders stood with grim faces behind Lord Elendar. He tried to contain his anger and disappointment.

The wind picked up, blowing through the party, sweeping back their robes and hair. A few raised their arms to shield themselves. Lord Elendar stayed firm in his stance, letting the cold air hit him. He wore a dark navy-blue suit instead of his royal robes. His hair flowed however the wind blew, strands webbing across his face.

The report he received stated that once the ships and their crew were out of harm's way, the generals would continue home while another fleet went to evacuate the crippled ships and perform triage. After months of travel, the rebel members had arrived. He hoped their level of shame matched the disgrace they caused.

"Your Grace." The head chambermaid approached him. "The reassignment of quarters is complete. I apologized for only getting it done so close to the deadline."

"No. It's fine. I'm actually impressed you could do it so quickly with such short notice."

He felt something prickly and glanced over at her. The rage on her face said plenty. She gripped the sides of her robes.

"We worked harder and faster to get those traitors out of our midst." She barely contained the anger in her voice. "They lost their privilege to live amongst us."

"I feel the same. Even though they are being moved to the far end and into the lower bowels, they still hold some

ACTS OF TRANSGRESSION | 213

status until their judgement day." Lord Elendar closed his eyes and exhaled. "Thank you for your dedication."

"Of course, your Grace." She bowed, then left to stand in position with the rest of her group.

Spectators gathered along the outside walls of the palace. Lord Elendar motioned to his head of security. The guards dispersed to cover the area in case the encounter got heated. A royal entourage entered the area, a spectacle of pomp and pretense. He gritted his teeth in frustration.

Lady Haldris, in flowing yellow robes, the sheer outer layer covered in tiny, embroidered pink flowers, walked next to Lord Kel, who wore his usual austere black robes with a purple sash at the waist. A troupe of servants and guards followed them.

The last thing I want is them inserting their will in the situation.

Lord Elendar felt his fingers twitch, wanting to clench into fists. He shook them to stave off the urge. Lord Kel seemed to notice; his eyes focused on them.

"Why the anxiety, Lord Elendar?" He stopped before him. Lady Haldris glared down at him. "Are we not welcomed in your house?" Lord Kel's disingenuous smile riled him.

He refused to address Lady Haldris. Only a few inches taller than him, she exuded authority, intimidating him.

"Of course you are. I'm wondering why you are here?" He glanced at the first ship landing. "Considering the occasion."

"That's exactly the reason." Lady Haldris replied haughtily. "Are you really allowing them back into the royal palace?"

"We have moved their quarters away from the main."

"They should be in the dungeons to rot!" Lord Kel spat.

"I must hear their reasons before sending them for judgement! I cannot act as jury and executioner." Lord Elendar stiffened, feeling the eyes of his people on him. "Even in light of this," he muttered, the sadness folding around him, then whispered, "We must remain dignified."

All the rage inside him dissipated, replaced by a weariness. He didn't intend to show weakness. His own guards gave him dubious stares.

"Enough!" Lady Haldris glared at him. "No more of this self-pity. Sadness?" She scoffed. "This was a long time in the making."

"Lord Elendar. Please rest assure, we are only here to witness their return." Lord Kel smiled. "Their punishment to be held in the coming months will be entertaining."

The first ship's ramp extended, and a row of floating stretchers came down. Lord Elendar counted at least two dozen. He caught sight of the injuries as they passed by, their wounds suggesting the medics had brought them from the brinks of death. The other three ships landed and disembarked similarly. At least forty critically wounded.

After the ones needing dire treatment were inside the palace, the guards escorted off the moderate to non-wounded, bound by their wrists with an energy lasso that kept them together. They came down single file, with expressions of defeat. Lord Elendar had no sympathy left.

A royal guard disconnected the lasso from the rebel leader and shoved him forward. He fell to his knees and went face down, turning his head in time so not to eat the grass. With his wrists tethered together, he sat upright, whipping his long, blond hair off to the side as he spat out dirt.

Lord Elendar took one step towards him, ready to haul him up, when Lord Kel's boot slammed into the rebel leader's back, returning him to the ground. His face embedded in the grass.

"You dare to raise your head after what you've done?" Lord Kel's eyes glowed.

Observe my ass! Lord Elendar reached out to Lord Kel and Lady Haldris denied him, smacking his hand away. He glared at her. *This is my house!* The spectators got agitated, chanting obscenities.

"I can handle this, Lord Kel." He kept his tone even.

"Please do not interfere. Let me address my kin as I see fit."

Lord Kel huffed, removing his foot from the rebel leader's back. "You're being too lenient." He nodded to the spectators. "The people demand an appropriate response."

"They want blood," he retorted. "And they shall not get it this day."

"I will agree," Lady Haldris said. "That is for another day. But." She stepped towards the rebel leader and kicked him in the side of his abdomen, sending him into the bushes five hundred feet away to the right of the ship. "A little show of force is required."

The rebel leader coughed up blood, his body spasmodic. With righteous indignation, he slowly got to his feet and stared Lord Elendar down. His display of will took everyone off guard. A lull of silence. He spat blood onto the bushes.

Cries of rage erupted from the spectators. They moved forward, forcing the royal guards to create a barricade. Lady Haldris and Lord Kel turned to Lord Elendar, their expressions conveying shock at the rebel leader's audacity.

Lord Elendar flashed towards him in an instant, morphing one hand into a claw, and pierced him in the chest. He used his speed and momentum to push him further before slamming him onto the ground; the claw impaling him.

"You will not disrespect this house any further." He leaned forward and whispered in his ear. "I alone have shown mercy by letting you return and not having you all executed. You need to show a little more appreciation."

He watched the rebel leader's eyes glaze over, yet still struggling to stay conscious. After a few more seconds of fighting it, he finally gave in and went limp, his eyes closed. Lord Elendar ripped his claw out of his chest and stood over him. Blood dripped, staining the grass. Insects crawled out from the dirt and made their way to the spoils.

"Get him to the medical bay," he commanded his technicians. "We can't have him die before his trial."

The medical team rushed to the rebel leader's side, a floating stretcher in tow. Lord Elendar's arm reverted, and he stood before Lady Haldris and Lord Kel.

"As I said." His eyes glowered. "I have this under control."

Lady Haldris snickered in amusement. Lord Kel turned away in disgust.

"Then you should have done that first." Lord Kel said.

Lord Elendar turned to his people behind him. They had looks of pride. Now for the hardest part. He nodded to the head chambermaid, and they went into the palace.

\###

With a planet bomb leisurely hurling towards them, the Dreridians prepared for its impact. Lord Pondur made a decree to build reinforced shelters. He would not tolerate the loss of life. They could always remedy structural damage. From the panoramic windows of his office, he watched the home world's activity. Supply ships littered the sky while transport units evacuated entire sectors. Automated production slowly phased out the workers to allow settlement into the shelters.

Clasping his hands behind him pulled the dark, maroon crushed velvet jacket tight across his chest. His eyes squinted at the setting sun hanging at the same level, casting an eerie array of colors across the horizon. They triggered his memory of the report on Lassians. Beings of light energy that kept to themselves until the enemy disrupted their peace.

The outer rim. Strange non bipedal beings inhabited that quadrant, becoming more disturbing the farther you went. The enemy system and Lassa's sat near the start of it. Lassa lay deeper than the enemy's, explaining the difference in form.

He also remembered hearing how Chardon's power resembled a planet bomb to a certain degree. Lord Pondur shook his head. The enemy woke a sleeping monster.

I should tread carefully from now on.

He exhaled loudly. Lord Graggor came in and stood by his side.

"You appear deep in thought, my lord."

"Lassians are dangerous." Lord Pondur glanced down at a protective shield being erected over the power plant below. "The surveyors pinpointed their original location,"

"Yes, I also received that report." Lord Graggor clasped his hands behind his back. "Dare we use them for this current matter?"

"No." Lord Pondur turned away from the window. "I have a feeling that destructive power is not something Chardon can easily tap into. Or he hasn't learned how to yet."

"It does seem more like a defensive weapon." Lord Graggor followed him towards the desk. "There was something else I came to address. Regarding the rest of the spy's report."

"Ahh, yes." Lord Pondur brought up one hand and drummed his fingers against his chin. "The trade system in the enemy's territories. Utter chaos."

"Maybe it's time to expand our organization into the dark." Lord Graggor tilted his head, smiling. "Shed a little light on the outer rim, albeit the shallow end."

"Hmm." Lord Pondur nodded. "I agree." He dropped his hand. "Once we defeat them, we'll send a fleet to take control of the planets while they try to recuperate."

"How devious, my lord," Lord Graggor smirked in jest, snorting.

"It's what conquerors do."

"The enemy fancies themselves as such."

Lord Pondur's brow fused together. "They are nothing but parasites. Having a mighty force that can wipe out their prey doesn't make them leaders. Not organizing a stable trade system means no one profits."

"Oh, I agree. Since the Razznians are closer to the rim, I say we tap them for border control." Lord Pondur gave him a quizzical stare. Lord Graggor's smile widened. "I consulted with our general on the matter."

"Of course, you did. Now," Lord Pondur turned to face him. "What about our current issue?"

"Well," Lord Graggor released his hands. "The Lassians have five new ships. Destroyer class, no less."

"So, Master Adan bent to our demands. Good."

"We need to delegate each race better. Their combined forces did not seem efficient. Lopsided may be the term I am searching for."

"They did not work well, strategy wise." One side of Lord Pondur's mouth curved up. "I know who could remedy the problem. We need to convince them to take up the task."

Lord Graggor's eyes went wide. "You would," he stuttered, "give such a massive responsibility to them?"

"They should get practice to strategize on a higher level." Lord Pondur's eyes narrowed. "Look at their track record. Not a single death on their campaigns simply because their strategist and tactician willed it so."

Healing of Wounds

WWhen the gate agent handed Talas a communication chip, whispering it contained a secret message, he became wary. Jaron, already contacted, was escorted to an empty room on the far side of the temple. Talas arrived and set the chip on the table's relay platform. He read the message from Lord Pondur addressed directly to himself and Jaron. The words displayed on the holoscreen glared at him. Jaron sat silently at his side.

Alone together sitting on plush cushions, the two didn't speak for a long time. The heavy tension between them lingered. Forgiveness may not be on the table, perhaps a truce.

"What are you thinking?" Talas tried to minimize the tension in his tone.

Jaron leaned back, placing both hands flat on the floor. She stared at the message.

"That he knows we won't keep this from Chardon. And that he has some strange faith in us to pull off such a massive endeavor."

"True. It being directed at only us doesn't come across as sneaky, but it smacks of not quite trusting our leader to decide."

"This stems from your demand of no casualties succeeding in every battle."

"It doesn't happen without your input as well." Talas turned to her. "Which at the moment I despise." Jaron flinched. "That said, you are right. We have more important issues to tackle before addressing our messy existence."

He tapped his wristband. When the tiny dot blinked blue, he spoke. "Contact the council for an urgent meeting." It winked out and Talas sighed, mimicking Jaron's position. "Shall we make our way to the commons?"

Jaron reached over and picked the data chip off the table. The holoscreen disappeared.

"Yes. Let's. Chardon may not like this."

"Or Halfar." Talas stood, stretching his arms to the ceiling. "I really don't care about that."

"Really?" Jaron also stood, straightening the folds of her robes. "Because I think we need his help with our decision."

Talas lowered his arms. That fact was not lost on him either.

⌒

Halfar burst out laughing. His head fell back, exposing his gaping mouth to the ceiling. A deep, loud bellow filled the small conference room. Tears formed at the creases of his squeezed shut eyes. His bout subsided. He opened his eyes.

"Hah!" He took a deep breath to regain his composure. "Ahh."

He brought his head upright and stared at the holoscreen before him, his eyes narrowed in disgust at the three leaders staring back, confused by his response.

"You should have informed me of your plans to tap Talas before sending that message."

Lord Graggor, attending in Lord Pondur's steed, bowed his head apologetically.

"We are in a dire time crunch. You can't blame us for reaching out."

Halfar tilted his head back at an angle and stared at that disingenuous, craggy face. Emperor Calabra of Jiez and the leader of Yaos seemed to fidget.

"We understand you have your hands full with advising Supreme Ruler Romnus," Emperor Calabra said. "This takes precedence. Any guidance you can give Talas and Jaron of Lassa would benefit us all."

Talas and Jaron despised Halfar for good reason. After Chardon relayed to him what Ganna had done with their cores, their hatred had certainly intensified. Regardless, the leaders were correct. The two strategists would have to put up with him for now.

"Fine. You do realize they may not need my input."

The Lord of Yaos snorted. "They have been lucky so far. This is on a whole new scale. Their minor battles are nothing compared to the current event. I, too, could guarantee no deaths if that were the case."

Emperor Calabra gave him a frustrated stare. Halfar looked at the Lord of Yaos with amusement.

"Is that so?" Halfar smiled. "Then explain what happened two hundred years ago when you lost an entire fleet. Care of the Razznians."

The blue creature's eyes turned red and its bill-like mouth exposed rows of tiny sharp teeth. A loud rattling hiss slowly built, vibrating through the audio. Halfar smirked at success in hitting a sore subject. He had a duty to keep the other leaders in their place.

"I have more important things to do right now. I will consult with them later."

Lord Graggor gave him a knowing look while the other two frowned at being left out of the loop. Because you're not needed, Halfar chided them silently. He reached over and tapped the feed icon on the tabletop. The holoscreen winked out. He leaned back in his seat, crossing his arms as he closed his eyes.

Balls of electricity, talons, and swords were brandished in New Lassa's open fields. The tall yellow grass swayed a breeze, caressing the Lassians' lower half. Sparks crackled from the glowing orbs in the energy users' palms. The manbeasts were ready to pounce, baring teeth. Every warrior present had their swords in striking positions.

What madness is this?

Chardon stood between the energy users and the warriors. Wind wrapped his cream-colored robes and darkened hair around him. In the center of the fray were Talas, Jaron, and Ganna. This will be a bloodbath. Instead of keeping the details of the core swaps amongst the victims, Ganna aired her sins via a world feed presentation.

"That's enough!" Chardon shouted. "I won't tolerate a battle against ourselves. Did we not learn anything from the manbeasts uprising?"

Barbon sneered. "Are we supposed to turn a blind eye to all of this?"

"They chopped our skills in half! And for what?" A warrior yelled.

Kelin lowered his hand with a blue energy orb pulsing.

"How are we supposed to feel, great leader?" He locked eyes with Chardon. "Knowing all this."

Chardon opened his mouth to speak. He couldn't find the words. Jaron turned to Ganna in disgust. He didn't blame her. An urge to throttle that woman for stirring the pot yet again to achieve her own goals filled him.

"I only wanted to come clean. Be transparent." Ganna said. "We cannot be divided any longer. Too much is at stake."

"Then you shouldn't have done it in the first place!" An energy user snapped.

"I know this is my fault," Jaron added. "It was selfish of me. But," she raised her hands in offering, "I only did it to preserve our essence."

"There had to be a better way," Chardon chimed in. "Yours and Ganna's lack of judgement seems to alays cause more harm than good."

"You're going to chastise someone else's judgement?" Another warrior cried out. "You?"

"Our home world sits a ball of burnt decay waiting to go supernova because of your lack of discretion!" One scientist, also an energy user, shouted.

Chardon stiffened at the assault being hurled at him. He thought they were passed that. Angered by their sheer disregard for the situation, Chardon felt his power surge. Multicolored shimmers of light enveloped him like snow and pulsed out to singe the surrounding grass.

"I said," his eyes narrowed, glowing white. "That's enough." His even tone menacing.

The hordes of people backed away from him. The energy users rescinded their orbs as the warriors sheathed their swords. Manbeasts retracted their talons and teeth. Jaron hung her head, standing in place. Talas clenched his fists at his sides.

"Don't," Jaron pleaded softly.

Chardon eased his power back into him. Its original owner, the person before him, was no longer merely his cousin. They were the embodiment of their home. Their beginning.

Lassa.

A sense of shame fell over the field as that realization spread. Chardon saw looks of bewilderment, anger, and elation. He let out a sigh.

"Go home. Take time to process all this. We will try to answer your questions after."

Disgruntled, the crowd reluctantly dispersed. Chardon noticed how they split in three and headed to the villages in their respective regions. Completely divided.

"You see?" Ganna cried out. "This is how we are now!" She waved an arm across the field at the departing crowd. "This is why I tried so hard to..." She stopped; her eyes widening with fear as her voice cracked.

Tears streamed down her face. She tried to wipe them away, horrified to see them. They kept coming. Chardon, Talas, and Jaron were speechless.

"Why?" Ganna yelled out. "Why is this happening?"

Chardon looked away, not sure what to do. To his surprise, Jaron went to her and wrapped both arms around her, pulling her close. Ganna resisted, attempting to get her hands up to push Jaron off. Then she relented, sagging against her with her face buried in her robes.

"You kept so much locked deep inside for so long. There's no reason to do that."

"Forfeiting a mate, advancing our technology, to gain what exactly?" Talas said. "Nothing would have stopped the division of our race."

"No," Jaron said. "But I could." She held Ganna tighter. "And I didn't even try."

Off in the distance, Chardon noticed their families lingering on the outskirts of the field. By their expressions, he knew they had heard the conversation.

"Well, Ganna. It looks like you have made another mess of things." Chardon turned away and headed back to the commons. "Let's wait until the next moon phase to meet again."

Jaron, Lassa. Chardon felt a headache coming. The issue with Talas, actually Laxis, and Trinon, who inherited the great manbeast warrior's skills, also nagged at him. He could only imagine how his people felt.

⌒

"So, let me get this straight," Und raised a hand, palm forward. "Our mother's core is part of Lassa. And her body is that of the great manbeast, Mandra?"

He watched his father fidget before his shoulders slumped. "Correct."

The rest of Jaron's family kept silent. Mara seemed to struggle with the news. Und dropped his hand. He turned to

Trinon standing silent in the family common's corner, arms crossed, with one foot resting against the wall. His head hung down as if deep in thought.

"And my brother over there has inherited her prowess." He pointed to Trinon.

"She must not have been that great a warrior if her skills couldn't bring down the enemy," Hon said in a malicious tone.

Jakar grabbed him by the front of his robes, the two brothers baring teeth at each other. Their father wrenched them apart.

"Stop it!" He pushed them farther away to opposite sides. "I won't tolerate it."

Trinon looked up, his youthful face somehow haggard. "Because I don't know how to use it," he said in a low voice. "You're not being fair, Hon."

"What does that mean?" Mota asked. "Use what?"

Und suddenly remembered when he and their father had to restrain Trinon from going on a rampage. It took everything they had and only barely because he appeared to be incomplete. As if his true strength slowly unlocked like a dial being turned up. They brought him back down after ten minutes of struggle.

He also felt that surge before, during the battle with the enemy.

"It's a dormant power, much like what happened to the warrior clan," their father began. "The scientist who created us felt no need to display our full strength. Yet, still, a select few broke through the limiter. The great manbeast having gone beyond that threshold proved his theory."

"Do all manbeasts have this potential?" Mota asked.

"I would think so," Und answered. "I tapped into it once. Trinon is right. It's hard to maintain."

"You just haven't trained enough," Hon scoffed.

Trinon stared at him deadpan. "And you can?"

Hon gave them all a nasty grin. "Of course I can."

"Then teach me." Trinon said. "Or am I not your brother either whose death you would welcome instead of embracing me?"

Und went stiff at the remark. Hon's expression fell. Everyone felt like they had been sucker punched in the face. He had no words and saw Hon struggle as well.

"I never said…" Hon gripped the nearest weight bearing post. "That's not what…"

"Then, I too, request you teach the rest of us as well." Und finally said.

Mara stepped forward, glancing at her brothers. "I know I am not a manbeast. I'm still your sister. Whatever help you need with your training, I will be available." She eyed her other non manbeast siblings. "I hope the rest of you do the same."

Trinon pushed himself off the wall and exited the room, leaving his family to wallow in the icky tension that permeated. Und followed him.

"Trinon." He waited for him to stop. "I know why you never tried to hone it." Trinon didn't turn around. His hands dropped to his sides. "When I felt it inside me," Und clenched his fists. "Trinon." His brother finally turned to meet his gaze. "It scared the light right out of my core."

Trinon reached out with his left hand and placed it against Und's right cheek. He held it there for a long time before sliding it away.

"I know." Trinon resumed his walk towards the hilltops.

Und fought back tears. A familiar scent wafted in the air, followed by arms of lean muscle wrapping around his shoulders. He leaned into mate Liula's body, feeling her breasts squish against his back.

Talas could smell the despair coming off the manbeast as she approached. Una. He didn't turn around, pretending to focus on wiping his blade clean after a training bout. Most of the warriors had gone home, leaving the arena vacant. Kelin stood behind the weapons table on the other side, eyeing her with distrust.

Neither had spoken to her since the manbeast uprising. Her punishment for harming their children went into effect right after. Talas never sought her out to get an explanation. He tossed the sword on the wood table and let his arms dangle at his sides. Kelin moved towards them, his demeanor one of apprehension.

"Talas," Una said, barely above a whisper. "Kelin." He stopped a few feet from her. Talas still didn't acknowledge her. "I know you don't want to hear anything from me." Her voice sounded shaky. "Or to even see me." There was a long pause. "What I did to your children was inexcusable. I know an apology is meaningless. Even so." Talas heard the sniffling that came with tears and running snot. "I am truly sorry and beg for a chance to make it right."

Talas whirled around and got inches from her face. He bared his teeth; the rage having a full grip on him. Her hunched over position explained the reason he could look her in the eyes. The way her shoulders sagged with her back arched forward in a painful arch.

"You're right," Talas seethed. "It is meaningless." He watched her tears stream down her face. Then it struck him. A child.

She's just a child!

Her ill maintained mane, off colored skin tone, and lean muscle instead of bulk made the rage ebb away, leaving him with a sense of shame. She hasn't recovered. When she realized what she had done, her mind shattered. The fierce manbeast went docile.

"You let the sins of your elders sway you into doing the unthinkable. If you want to do anything for us, try thinking for yourself and do what is right."

"I understand," Una replied softly.

"And stand up straight!" Talas whacked her on the head. "Seeing you like that makes me uncomfortable."

Kelin placed a hand around her left bicep. "We can't forgive you." She nodded. "That doesn't mean we don't care what happens to you."

Una stood straight, looming over them. A tiny spark in her eyes let Talas know she had indeed heard and understood. He stepped away from her.

"We need you in top form for the battles to come. I expect nothing short of magnificence from you."

"Of course." The tone of her voice still bothered him. "Thank you." She bowed her head to Talas, then to Kelin. "I will leave you now."

Una turned and headed back to manbeast territory. Talas squeezed his fists. Kelin came behind him and covered them with his hands, slowly easing Talas' fingers open.

"It's not her fault. We knew that. She'll be fine now."

Talas looked back at Kelin. "That won't be easy." Una's bravery to come and apologize stirred up a new feeling in him. He needed to ask forgiveness from the masses. Modas was in the same boat. "I think it's time to clear the air."

Chardon stared at Talas, then Modas. His vision seemed to expand as he averted his focus from their faces. He took in his study's bare walls, minimal furnishings, and the midday sun shining through the single bay window behind him. His gaze fell back on them.

"Absolutely not." He leaned back in his chair, laying his arms loosely on the armrests.

"A public apology would help us move on," Talas said.

"It would bring anger and chaos. We don't need to be reminded of either incident."

"Do you think it's all forgotten?" Talas asked hotly.

"That the mistrust and rage just went away? It lingers." Talas gripped the arms of his chair. "No, it has festered."

Modas looked up at Chardon. "The manbeasts clans do not consult me as they should for that reason. I have failed as a leader in their eyes. I must regain their trust once more." His eyes grew dark. "We cannot move on without letting our people know we are repentant."

Chardon sighed loudly. He tilted his head back to rest on the chair's edge. The last public apology entailed the deeds of Sestis, resulting in a riot. His own secret relationship with Halfar caused similar events, leading the council to see him as incompetent. The recent core revelation did them no favors.

"I get that." Chardon raised his head. "Still. We are trying to bring our people together, not divide them."

"And this will do that." Talas relaxed. "You think we haven't thought this through? We have heard what the people say about all of it. You, Halfar, Ganna." He pointed a finger at himself and Modas. "Us. It won't get fixed until we address it."

"If this is how it's going to be, I might as well inform Ganna she's going to be explaining what else she's done." Chardon frowned. "This feels like one of those apology tours they do on Earth."

"Nothing that trifling," Talas scoffed. "And it's been over a century. I would hope humans have grown since then."

"Fine. Do what you must. Give the ones responsible for security details a heads up. They may even refuse to help you."

"We know." Modas rose from the chair that struggled to hold his giant frame. A few hairline fractures appeared in the wood along the base. "It will be done with the burden of heavy cores."

～

Not one building smoldered from retaliation after the broadcast. Instead, silence engulfed the planet. As he thought, none of the security advisors from the three clans assisted. New Lassa's stillness heightened Chardon's apprehension. He was not alone in that feeling. His entire cabinet and the council waited in agony for days, expecting the bubble to burst.

Did they accept it? Chardon felt unsure.

Something about the way the people stared at the holo-screens, then went back to what they were doing before. A lack of reaction. As if they didn't care anymore. Yet, from his own feed surveilling the surface, he saw the looks on their faces. Silent rage fueled their movements. Production of resources spiked weeks later, followed by the Lassians moving about in a muted haze of disinterest as they fulfilled their daily tasks.

This is not what I wanted.

Chardon stood from his desk in the study and went to the window. He could see the nearby village resembling a ghost town. No one walked the streets despite it being time for the usual activities before evening meal.

A knock on the door made him look away.

"Leader, Barbon requests a meeting with you," the servant's muffled voice said.

"Let him in." Chardon took a deep breath. Barbon ducked his head as he came through the opened door. "That will be all," Chardon addressed the servant.

The door closed, leaving the two alone in an awkward silence. Chardon gestured to the chair across from him. Barbon shook his head.

"What brings you here, Barbon?" Chardon remained standing at the window.

"We, the manbeasts, have decided." His deep voice sounded passive.

"And what would that be?"

"Not forgiveness. None deserve it. A new start. To move

forward and regain our sense of family." Chardon nodded in agreement. Barbon continued. "Isolating ourselves and our skills from the rest of our people has proved counterproductive. We will gladly teach any who wish to learn from us." He seemed to relax his stance more.

That was a lot of talking for a manbeast. Especially Barbon. Chardon felt impressed.

"You are the first to come and respond to the broadcast."

"From what I have gathered from the other clans, we are in consensus."

"Do you speak for them as well?"

"I do." Barbon locked eyes with him. "The enemy must pay. We can only achieve it through our combined forces. As you have always said."

Relief filled Chardon. Finally! I will achieve my goal.

"Thank you for telling me."

"It will take time." Barbon bowed his head, "Please be patient," then raised it. "I must leave to consult with Modas." He left the room.

Chardon slumped against the windowsill, letting his head rest on its pane. The warmth from the sun heating it soothed the oncoming headache. Loneliness and guilt set in. Halfar had gone to Azrom, their son, Chafar, stopped visiting, and he had not contacted the culprits of the current events. Ganna had remained locked inside her lab since then. Talas did not train in the arena, instead going out at night into the forest. Modas went on another long trek across the planet, returning home only a few days ago.

They all ran.

Chardon didn't blame them. Facing the aftermath wouldn't be pretty. Now their time was up. A battle needed to be won.

All for One

The Lassian ship cruised through the Dreridian checkpoint and continued to the home world. Talas stared out at his seat's viewport in the main cabin. Clusters of activity sprawled across the surface as the ship exited the clouds. He would have preferred a neutral zone. Multiple times, the temptation to slit Lord Pondur's throat arose during a meeting.

He felt the same regarding the other leaders. The disgraceful and infamous food fight over two centuries ago sealed his opinion. Jaron sat strapped in with her head resting against the viewport on the other side of the cabin. Her forehead crinkled.

They had yet to talk about their roles and the core switch. It needed to be addressed sooner than later. One thing Talas knew for certain. The Dreridians were not to be informed. He didn't trust Lord Pondur with the information. Lord Graggor could probably deduce it after some time if he dedicated himself to the research.

"Prepare for landing." The navigator's voice called over the commlink.

"You should get rid of that frown," Talas said to Jaron.

She turned to him. "Are you going to leave your longsword?" She snapped.

"Of course."

Talas' sword lay in the storage compartment above. He opened it to retrieve a dagger in a decorative sheath and attached it to the back of his hip.

"Hmm?" Jaron snorted. The slightest of a smile crept on her face.

"We'll be in closed quarters. I won't need that long of a reach."

"You're always cunning, Laxis." Jaron mused.

Talas slammed the compartment door shut and glared at her.

"Don't."

Jaron's smirk resembled the same look Lassa would have except on the face of the great manbeast. The mismatch jarred Talas. He sat back down and strapped in for landing. It would only be a matter of time before their cores fully awakened. Had Lassa learned their lesson? He doubted it.

Talas followed the guards, expecting them to turn towards the usual conference room, causing him to misstep and almost veer away from the group. Embarrassed, he corrected his mistake and feigned ignorance. This time, Lord Pondur had prepared an unfamiliar room for the meeting. Jaron glanced over at him with a questioning expression.

At the entrance to the new room, Talas stifled his surprise, knowing he shouldn't be that the Dreridians had such a space within the palace. A massive communications room with multiple holoscreens and delegation cubes spread out before him. Technicians working the consoles lined the left and right walls, leaving the entire room's views unobstructed.

Each crystal-clear cube had two seats. There were at least one hundred of them, and many were already full of delegates from every major trade planet.

"I thought this was going to be some small clandestine meeting?" Jaron stated.

Lord Graggor came up behind them.

"Ah, yes. In a way, it is. This is only a fourth of the representation. Only the major players are in attendance."

Jaron frowned. Talas mirrored her sentiment. He too

suppressed his instinct to attack when the scientist startled them by speaking so close. Neither had heard him approach, despite his size.

"I didn't really have a presentation, or anything prepared," Talas said.

"No, no." Lord Graggor waved a hand. "This is merely a hashing out of scenarios. With your expertise at the forefront, of course." Lord Graggor gestured for them to proceed. "Please, find your section. You are across from the Azrom delegates."

Talas scanned the room and found two cubes side by side with Batis and Biandra in one, and Generals Kur and Rass in the other. He and Jaron walked down the shallow ramp towards their own. Sitting, Talas noticed the location of their cube. Dead center. Making him and Jaron the focal point. No pressure. He sighed.

"I'm feeling a bit exposed," Jaron leaned over and whispered.

They nodded to their Azrom counterparts. Lord Pondur and Graggor sat in the cube at the center of the far wall. A position where they could see every delegate. The four giant holoscreens lit up. Each planet's military leader had feeds connected to their strategist who were not in attendance.

"All we all ready?" Lord Pondur asked. "Let us begin." He nodded to Talas and Jaron. "The floor is yours."

Talas' eyes went wide. He gave Jaron a side glance. She gave him one back. Alright.

"Greetings to you all." Talas watched the digital translator displayed in the cubes start. "I am Talas of Lassa. My role is that of a tactician. Beside me is Jaron, whose role is our strategist." He paused and looked around the room. "I'm not sure what you are expecting from us. We are not a mighty empire and do not have what you would call a military force."

"I think you underestimate yourselves," Emperor Xanic interrupted. "You have a unique ability to come out of fierce battles with no casualties. That is an unprecedented feat."

"I believe it stems from your race's stealth," Lord Pondur added. "To be seen only when necessary. And also, when to withdraw."

Talas' lips thinned. He caught General Kur's eye. The two stared at each other for what seemed like too long. Talas severed their connection. Jaron leaned forward.

"That may be true. But, as my counterpart has stressed, we are not a fighting race. We only became one out of said necessity."

"Which gives you a unique insight to battle, unlike the rest of us seasoned warriors," the ruler of Yaos said.

"Or have grown complacent in their victorious conquests over the centuries," another military leader said, glancing over at the Azrom delegates, then the Razznians. "The same tactics will eventually stop working."

"That has been an issue for a while." Jaron nodded, letting out a sigh. "We tried cross training with other races, namely Azrom. It did not go well. There is also some reluctance amongst our own clans."

"Then this is your chance to remedy that," Lord Pondur replied.

Talas looked over at Jaron. "What do you think?" Jaron simply stared at him. He got the message. Straightening his posture, he addressed the room. "Then let's try this again. If the goal is to implement a no casualty plan, we must learn to battle as a collective."

"Isn't that what we were doing?" A delegate asked.

"No." Talas' eyes narrowed.

"That was merely strategic maneuvering." Jaron answered, frowning again. "It lacked the very foundation needed for success."

The delegates and the ones on the holoscreens looked puzzled. General Kur smirked, crossing his arms, and met Talas' stare once again.

"Trust." Talas said.

The room went quiet. General Kur leaned towards him.

"We trust you now, Talas the Tactician." He tilted his head back at an angle, not severing his gaze. "Give us a chance to prove it."

Talas flinched inwardly. All eyes were on him. Now he felt exposed.

I have to deliver my promise. This time on a scale larger than I could imagine.

Jaron placed a hand on his shoulder. He fought the urge to smack it away, not wanting her to touch him. She sent him a telepathic message.

Let's show them might isn't always the answer.

⌒

Sand swirled around the fighters' feet as they stood in two rows facing each other on the arena floor. The venue, much like Azrom's, boasted a larger space. All the major delegates who made the trip to the neutral zone filled the box seats, overlooking it for what would be a three-month cycle of battle assessments between each other.

The organizers decided the first round should be a redo of Azrom elites versus Lassian. Like before, the fight would be twelve against twelve. Only this time, the Lassians were an array of warriors, energy users, and manbeasts, four of each.

"Now this is better than before," General Kur said, grinning, as he leaned over the balcony edge. "I do hope we don't make a bad first impression."

"I believe this will show just how far the mighty have fallen," Batis stated.

Emperor Calabra, on their left, glanced over at them.

"I'm afraid he may be right. Actually, every delegate here is certain the Lassians are mightier and more skilled than even they know."

"I've said that on more than one occasion," the Razznian delegate on their right replied.

Lord Graggor sat further down with the Dreridian General. His hooded expression conveyed his wariness of the Lassians. No one wanted them to become a superpower. General Kur could picture the gears of his mind turning at a rapid pace.

The slight breeze lifted a few strands of his hair and they floated before his face for a moment until it passed. This is the perfect day for an all-out brawl, he thought with a sense of whimsy. Beside him, Batis snorted, ready to enjoy the festivities as well.

The hologram timer in the sky above counted down the start of the bout. Half of the Azrom fighters morphed. Claws, pincers, and razor spiked limbs sprouted. The energy users' hands were lit with various colored lights. Manbeasts bared their talons and fangs while the warriors unsheathed their swords.

The timer hit zero along with a loud buzzer sound. What followed could only be described as a collision of monsters, the sound of their impact reaching the top box seats of the coliseum. Some delegates cringed, curling away at the sight and sounds. Others leaned forward with intrigue, excited by the impending carnage. The medical technicians waited in the wings near the pop-up bays provided by the Folza government.

The fighting had only been underway for twenty minutes and four Azrom fighters had to be taken out of the arena, along with one manbeast and two energy users. The spectators went silent. They all had an image of the Lassians as a peace-loving, humble race. The viciousness on display in the arena negated that. The Lassians surpassed Azrom fighters, known for their cruelty. Partially torn off limbs still intact lay in the Lassian's restraint.

That fact alone made them more deadly in the eyes of the spectators. General Kur's face scrunched in disgust. They're holding back? He screamed inwardly. With four Azrom fighters left against two manbeasts and a warrior, something about the fight shifted.

The Azrom fighters pushed back the two manbeasts

after sending the lone warrior sailing off to the side. As they closed in, the two manbeast already injured bad enough and unable to defend themselves, the warrior dashed before them as a shield. He grabbed his sword by the hilt and pulled. The sword seemed to split in two, replicating itself.

General Kur reared back as did Lord Graggor.

What did we just see?

The warrior's eyes glowed bright silver as he spun both swords once before getting into a dual wielding stance; one sword above his head, the other held across his body below the waist. The Azrom fighters, unable to halt their advance, had no time to reassess the situation. They barreled forward, intent on defeating all three.

With blinding speed, the warrior's swords moved like hand clocks as the fighters approached. Each swing created blurred arcs of light, preventing the audience from seeing where they struck. They only saw blood and pieces of flesh flying out onto the sand. They forced the fighters back towards the other side of the arena.

The momentum slowed, and the warrior swung one leg around and knocked the last standing Azrom fighter into the side barrier. His swords held at his sides, the blades pointed out, dripped with mingled blood. Sweat dripped down into his eyes as they reverted to normal. He dropped to his knees, out of breath, with his head hung resting his chin on his chest, while the swords laid flat.

"Victor of first bout. New Lassa. Warrior class," the female AI announced to a stunned and silent crowd. "The next bout will commence in three hours. Please exit while we reset the arena."

Slowly, the spectators moved from their box seats down to the banquet halls on the first level. General Kur headed for the medical bay to check on his fighters. Batis didn't say a word the entire time. There was no need. Just as before, when Trinon displayed a new fighting skill for the manbeasts, General Kur felt the sting.

The Lassians were hiding much more.

The five trade leaders convened in a small meeting room on the far corner of the coliseum.

"What is your assessment of these events?" Emperor Calabra asked Lord Pondur.

The Yaos ruler, Lord Kraznan, and Romnus halted their drinking and waited for his reply. They had opted to witness the bouts in person after seeing footage from the first that took place on Azrom.

"I think," Lord Pondur paused, his glass close to his lips, "we should all tread carefully."

He took a sip of his drink and set the glass on the table next to him. The others sat frowning, thinking to themselves. They all realized they were playing a dangerous game, bringing the Lassian race up the ranks as equals in power.

Talas stared at the empty arena. He stayed to watch the cleanup, focused on the blood splatter and limbs left behind being collected for reattachment. Jaron and Modas had already vacated their seats to check on their own wounded.

Was this too much to show?

He could feel the tension permeate the arena as the fight progressed. The other world leaders went silent towards the end. Fear. They hurled that invisible force of emotion out into the air. It never occurred to him how much Lassians had surpassed the military might the leaders boasted.

We have learned more than we wanted to or should.

His wristband made a small ting. He looked down and saw the message scroll across the screen. Not surprised, he let his head fall back over the back of his seat and sighed loudly. The words echoed in his head.

All remaining bouts will exclude Lassian fighters. Further assessment not required.

Kur lounged in a curved chair at the far end of the small, empty conference room close to where the leaders had convened. On the wall across from him, a holoscreen replayed the Lassian battle. His brow furrowed the more he watched. The footage had looped five times already. Each time, he found something else vaguely familiar in their moves. Old tricks made new, more advanced, and precise.

A particular maneuver caught his eye, and he reached over to hit the pause icon on the virtual control panel displayed on the glass table. He leaned forward, his expression incredulous. I know that sequence well! There was no mistaking it. The Lassians used an old Azrom fighting technique for one of their deadly blows. Except they had tweaked it to accommodate their bodies.

He rewound the feed and saw snippets of four other races' signature moves. Fast forwarding, he caught several more. And not just any race. These were from military powers of old, with distances close to outside the Dreridian system. Planets conquered through war against Azrom, Yaos, Jiez, Razzna, and the Dreridians themselves.

Now Kur understood how it all began. The Lassians told them why their race needed to defend itself. How else would they learn to do so without first observing potential enemies? He eased back into his chair, his long legs stretched out, one foot atop the table. The fingers on his left hand rested against his cheek as he used his pinky to caress the corner of his mouth.

A sense of dread came over him. Azrom never unleashed their full might. Even if they did, he had a feeling they would meet their match in a proper battle against the Lassians. Though small in numbers, their ability to learn so quickly terrified him.

All the more reason to stay allied with them.

Dog fight

Halfar crossed his legs, relaxed in the laboratory's viewing room large seat in its center. Two images displayed side by side on the holoscreen. The first showed the enemy fleet, looming behind the planet bomb's stream, ready to act when it reached its target. The second tracked the neutralizer heading towards the bomb. A secondary feed set below them switched between views from across the five systems.

His hands clenched in his lap went pale from lack of blood flow. He silently prayed to the universe for his plan to work. If only he had perfected it long ago. Success meant the surrounding space would collapse on itself for what would look like a split second, though in actuality span hours, even days. A wave of disruptive energy sent after regaining its previous state would see the enemy receive the full blast. Giving the alliance forces time for a preemptive strike.

He watched the other sectors' fleets move into position, forming a starlike pattern to cover all sides. No matter where the enemy emerged, an opponent waited to greet them. Talas and Jaron suggested the maneuver. In all his centuries of battle, he had never seen such a thing. From the feeds of other races, neither had they.

Halfar snickered, thinking about Lord Pondur losing his mind at the concept. The Dreridians always prided themselves on being a superior in knowledge. He went deep in thought. There was more to the Lassians. Something about the way Talas observed the delegates at the alliance meeting. He had changed. The same for Jaron. Like the two of them had amassed information far greater than imagined.

The screen flickered. Halfar looked up to see the enemy firing at the neutralizer. A wave of firepower formed a solid bridge, hitting it full on to no avail. It continued on a straight trajectory. The feed changed view to show the neutralizer hit the planet bomb. It melded into the core, creating a pulsating gold and white center. The cracks on the bomb widened, expanding before it folded in on itself.

The enemy relented, stopping their assault, and tried to move out of range. Halfar shook his head, tsking them for staying so long. With their plan thwarted, they needed to move on to another if they had one. A few stragglers, some fifty ships or more, got sucked into the vacuum created by the initial implosion.

Seeing the neutralizer work, Halfar stood and exited the lab bunker. Time to join the battle. This time as a high-ranking soldier, not a ruler. Romnus let him commission an armada ship so long as it stayed within the Azrom quadrant. He would defend their home with his very soul.

⌒

Lord Elendar sat upright in bed with his head hung low, planted in the palms of his hand stifling a cry of frustration. Strands of hair fell across his fingers, nearly touching the covers below. A nightmare and an omen. The enemy would come close to Azrom. Swaths of wounded soldiers littered the surface as he stood covered in blood, staring at a darkened sky.

He threw off the covers and swung his legs over the edge. Time to get ready. From his window, he made out the armada ships rising towards the open gateway that would send them to the battlefields across the five systems.

A page entered his room carrying his battle gear. The ribbed black bodysuit had matching boots and gloves set atop it. His red cape lay draped over one of the page's arms. In one hand, he held a longsword that hadn't been drawn

ACTS OF TRANSGRESSION | 243

for battle in centuries, sheathed in leather. Elendar couldn't remember the last time someone cleaned it before now.

"Your uniform and weapon, my lord." The page bowed and set the items at the foot of the bed. "Lord Halfar has requested that you be part of his battalion. He will await your arrival on the armada ship."

The page bowed again and left the room. Elendar stared at the neat pile, the nightmare lingering in his mind. Azrom had seen too many wars for his liking. The Razznian invasion didn't count. A mere blip in the game the two races constantly engaged in.

This enemy.

Elendar seethed at the thought of those creatures running amok on Azrom. He glanced over at the washing station on the other side of the room. Should I even clean up? What point was there when he knew his fate involved being drenched in blood? With a sigh of defeat, he walked over and wiped himself down with warm water.

He stood naked by his bed and dragged the bodysuit over him. The nanofiber hugged every inch of his body. His personal assistant came in and stood beside him. Neither said a word to each other. He knelt as Elendar sat on the bed to let him put his boots on.

"If you wish to forfeit your position and not do this, I will understand," Elendar said.

"I will fight alongside you until death," his assistant replied.

Elendar eyed the man in his full battle gear. His assistant rose, towering over him while reaching for the cape. He got up from the bed and turned around so he could snap the fasteners onto the shoulder clamps. Elendar slid the wide belt off the bed and put it around his waist. His assistant handed him his sword.

"I have not wielded this in so long." He felt the weight of it as he twirled it one hundred and eighty degrees. "It always served me well." After one last turn, Elendar slid it into the holder at his hip. The tip floated a few centimeters from the floor. He locked eyes with his assistant. "Come. You said you would follow me into the depths of hell."

"Lead the way, your grace." The assistant spread out his arm towards the door.

The two walked out into the hall, where a full unit of royal guards waited to escort them to the shipyard. Elendar felt his chest tighten. No turning back now. His assistant brushed the center of his back, calming him. He took a deep breath and began his journey.

At the entrance of Elendar's royal house, Lady Haldris and Lord Kel, with their full entourage, blocked his way. Lady Haldris' face scrunched angrily.

"Have you lost your mind?" She seethed. "We've paid our dues! Fought in the great wars. There is no reason for you to throw your life into this farce!"

Lord Kel placed the back of his right hand against her midriff, stopping her from getting closer. He, too, looked disgusted.

"Is that what this is?" Elendar asked. "You, trying to stop me?"

"Let the young ones seasoned in battle defend Azrom." Lord Kel removed his hand. "If the enemy dares to land here, then we show them our true might."

"This is the only way for my house to save face. I won't allow the rest of you to call us greedy and weak," Elendar retorted. He tightened his grip on his sword's hilt. "All will see our house still holds the glory of Azrom."

"Stop this nonsense!" Lady Haldris yelled. "No house on this planet thinks that!"

Lord Kel turned away. Elendar balked in awe of her outright lie. Then again, he thought, she may actually think those rumors were in jest. Lady Haldris picked at strands of hair on the side of her face in frustration.

"I'm going." Elendar straightened his posture and

waited for them to move.

Lord Kel came forward, placing a hand on his shoulder. The two men's eyes met.

"May your battles be glorious. Victory."

"Til death," Elendar replied with a smirk.

Lord Kel stepped out of his way, gesturing Lady Haldris to do the same. She reluctantly obliged. Elendar marched past them, his unit close behind. The transport ship came down from the sky and settled on the lawn. Its hatch opened for them and retracted when the last soldier entered.

The rest of the house, along with Lady Haldris and Lord Kel, watched it ascend towards the sky darkened by hundreds of armada ships awaiting launch.

⤳

Rendal Quadrant

Emperor Cogar Wenthril had a plan this time that would not allow the enemy to set foot on the surface. His planet had barely recovered from the first attack, and he refused to let their hard work in progress be in vain. They erected new shields all along the planet to ensure the enemy's demise. A round of tests showed the barriers obliterated anything that made contact.

Ships surrounded the planet like a cocoon, defending it on all sides. The enemy would be in for a dogfight. Cogar had no intention of backing down. He scanned the multiple holo-screens floating before him, showing every ship's position. Mixed in along with his forces were Razznian, Azromnian, Lassian, and Dreridian ships.

He rubbed his chin with one hand. Wearing full royal attire, his battle suit underneath, he wanted to make sure his appearance exuded power. Soft taps on consoles and digital beeps began filling the communication room. He looked around at his men, emersed in their duties. On the far-left screen, the forces moved around the gateway near Barrima. It had to be protected at all costs.

T'Halgar came into the room, the automatic doors sliding shut behind him. His fierce expression let the King know he was itching for a fight.

"My lord," T'Halgar knelt, bowing. He stood and faced him. "We are seeing activity in the far region. I believe the enemy will appear there."

"How long before they reach here," he paused, "if they break through?"

"Only a few days. They would come fast, as usual."

"Are you sure you want to be on the frontline?" Cogar turned his head towards him.

"It would be my honor. I want to stop them there. Then we won't need to defend our world from these beasts."

"You won't be able to stop them all. Many will break through. I know I said if, but let's be realistic."

T'Halgar frowned. "I know. Still." He raised his head. "I will use everything in my power to make the impossible happen."

"Then I wish you great success and a victorious battle."

T'Halgar bowed again, kneeling, then walked out of the room. Cogar let out a heavy sigh. He didn't relish in wanting this battle. He knew two races who were champing at the bit for bloodshed. The Razznians and Azrom.

Ten thousand ships had already arrived near the edge of the system, where Razznian ships sat in stark contrast to the other races. Their black hulls with red lights that resembled insect eyes almost blended in with the darkness of space. Azrom's white ships glowed amongst them.

Sars scowled at the sight on his ship's main holoscreen. The fully manned bridge remained silent for now. A nervousness came over him. Such an unprecedented event would take place within days. The excitement built as time went on.

A second screen popped up in the corner. The newly promoted Prac's face filled it. With his new title came the command of a ship for this campaign.

"Commander Sars. We have detected a vortex signature on the outskirts. The battle is imminent." His smile revealed sharp, pointy teeth.

"Well, they are not wasting any time. Remember, if you can plow them down first before they unleash a single shot, do it."

"What about the planet behind us?"

"It's uninhabited. We can lure them down and leave their corpses there. Eat what you kill," Sars said.

"Leave nothing for ceremony!" Prac and every Razznian on the bridge yelled.

Sars' mouth turned down. If only they had tastier fare, there would be more enthusiasm. The enemy was not appetizing.

He had not yet settled into his command seat on the fourth day when an enemy vortex opened. As instructed, Prac and the other forces fired on it as multiple ships emerged. Their rounds bounced off the shields while others absorbed them. Sars stood halfway down above the seat, both hands gripping the armrests. He couldn't say anything about the enemy's tactics. Razznians had frequently done the same.

Standing back up, he moved to the dais railing. The holoscreens lit up from blasts close to the feed arrays. The enemy ships behind the frontline dropped their shields and started bombarding the Razznian fleets.

"Third battalion, move out to the edge to join the eleventh. They will open another vortex to surprise us." Sars scanned the rest of the holoscreens to determine which fleets needed to be positioned elsewhere. "We need to…"

He pitched forward, flipping over the railing and onto the bridge floor. Other Razznians and soldiers from behind him went sliding towards the main consoles.

"We've been hit from behind!" The Dreridian on the console, watching the ship's integrity, yelled. "They opened a vortex directly on our aft."

The holoscreen for the rear feed showed an enemy ship butted against them. More ships sped forward. Sars heard the harsh grinding of the two ships rubbing together. Then a ripping, followed by a hard jolt as if something had punched their ship.

"They've breached the hull!"

Sars scrambled onto his feet, leaning forward against the steep tilt made worse by the assault. His beady, red eyes locked on the doors. Should we head out? Strategically, not a good idea, although knowing how the enemy worked, they were sitting targets. The bridge had to be defended from the outside.

"Send out a call to the troops in the hangars. I want only the first four to head this way." He pointed to the soldiers crawling up to stand. "You will come with me."

Despite being of different races, they all understood his plan. The bridge doors opened, and they advanced out into the corridor. Sars stopped at the threshold while the rest continued. He turned his head slightly to the right.

"Seal the doors," he ordered. "The only way they get in is if they blast it. And we won't let them get that far."

～

Dreridian Home World

Planets affected by the planet bomb became combat stations to track the enemy as they moved through the system. The alliance fleets hiding in the vicinity had not launched an assault, even though the enemy relentlessly fired upon the one defending the home world.

Lord Pondur, along with his general, watched the show from a bunker in the lower bowels of the palace. He found it amusing. The enemy's strict focus would be their demise. Ships still spewing from the vortex at the end of the system waned. Once it stopped, the alliance ships close by would enter and find the enemy's home. Another would envelop the enemy, blocking them from fleeing.

ACTS OF TRANSGRESSION | 249

"What are they thinking?" His general asked, perplexed.

"They're quite single-minded. Annihilation, no doubt." Lord Pondur clasped his hands behind his back. The black jacket with a silver design stretched at the shoulders. "I'm slightly disappointed."

"They lack strategy. Should we let them go a little longer?" The general raised his tablet and tapped on a feed close to the home world. "Get them close to the third planet out?"

Lord Pondur contemplated the idea. He didn't know what new thing the unpredictable enemy had up their sleeves. To his shock, he watched an enemy fleet veer away from the main and go towards one of the combat planets, their weapons still blasting, catching the alliance ships on the other side off guard.

"We waited too long!" The general cried out. "All fleets, prepare to…"

He didn't get to finish. The alliance forces moved into position, firing on the enemy. Four damaged ships moved back to wait for rescue as the ambushed ships returned fire. The enemy ended up in disarray, maneuvering in different directions to combat the onslaught from all sides.

"That's better." Lord Pondur grinned.

"In the end, it's going as planned." The general cleared his throat, regaining his composure. "The last ships have left the enemy vortex. The mission is a go."

"Excellent." Lord Pondur's eyes narrowed.

Dreridian trade would expand and the enemy crumble under his control.

∽

Outskirts of Razznian Quadrant

Right as the black swirl of stars emerged, streams of laser fire erupted from its center. As it widened, more fire power filled its girth, pummeling the ships arranged in an arc ahead. Some rounds got around the shields while others bounced off, clipping the edges of ship hulls in range.

In response, the alliance ships unleashed their own unholy barrage of power. A kaleidoscope of colors weaved between each other, creating a wall of devastation on both sides. Silent explosions, followed by gaping holes, threatened the ships' integrity.

Talas stood stunned on the bridge of a newly built Azrom battleship. The first wave of attack took him off guard. Luckily, he recovered less than a second after and commanded the fleet to fire. He watched the two forces collide as the vortex bloomed. Now fully open, the enemy ships emerged without wasting a moment, firing those red tendril weapons.

"They really are angry," one of the Dreridian soldiers at the console said. "This is uncalled for." He pointed at his screen without looking up. "Second vortex opening behind us."

"As I thought they would. Open our gateway."

The crew looked over at him in surprise. He understood their confusion. This was not on their list of plans. Talas had kept it a secret, hoping he wouldn't need to use it. Punching in the coordinates, the Dreridian sat back impressed as it connected. A black line spread, spanning the length of the arc from the other side and the middle opened as if being ripped apart.

The enemy vortex formed directly across from it, barely opening before the second alliance force appeared, firing into its core. Their attack widened with the vortex and enemy ships came out already damaged, free falling to their doom.

From the reports coming in on the other battles, he noticed a few alliance fleets caught on to the enemy's sneakiness. Talas used this tactic for one reason. His fleet's location. Beyond Razzna, past its outskirts, lay the enemy's origin.

Fighters rushed out of the enemy ships to engage with the alliance. To no one's surprise, the Azrom fighters were the first to clash, their brutality equaling the enemy. Talas looked up at the outskirt's feed. Would the enemy come, or were they too busy with the Dreridian force that had certainly infiltrated their territory by now?

His ship shook from minor blasts. Out the side view panel, he saw what appeared to be fifty enemy fighters slamming into the ship, puncturing the hull. Klaxons went off. Another group of fighters hit the other side.

Then one hit made Talas instantly turn around and stare at the rear view holoscreen. One of the large enemy battle cruisers had rammed them from behind. The extending ramp punched through.

They were coming in.

Talas glanced over at the Azrom soldier at the console. He scanned the faces of the other alliance soldiers.

"Shall we?" He asked. The Azrom soldier snorted. "The doors will fly off at any moment. Everyone, take your positions and get ready."

All thirty soldiers on the bridge not manning a console formed a perimeter on both sides. Within minutes, the doors blew off, shredded in the center, as they went careening towards the bridge consoles. The energy users formed a barrier, stopping it a few feet away. Down the corridor Talas saw the enemy charging forward, the soldier in front carrying a tendril weapon.

The alliance soldiers behind Talas panicked, moving further out to the sides as the other soldiers abandoned their stations. He sighed, then let out a high-pitched whistle. Right before their eyes, they watched the enemy soldier go sideways into the bulkhead, leaving a gaping hole that smoldered from the glowing hot edges.

A matching hole directly across from it had an alliance soldier standing in a defense stance, holding a projectile weapon in both hands. They lowered it and moved forward. The soldiers behind Talas recovered quickly, advancing on the enemy, who didn't pause at the loss of their front man.

The ship teetered. Talas knew the damage would worsen if the attacks continued. In his distraction, an enemy came in close range, swinging its razor-sharp battle axe. Talas bent backwards, ducking down at an angle. He pivoted beneath them and came around from behind. The enemy also moved faster than he liked, turning to face him as he came up. Its axe met Talas' sword, crossing it.

Talas recognized them as the leader from the first announcement. Why would it come to this quadrant personally? The battle came close to their region, yet they certainly had defenses set up. And why his ship out of all the ones in the vicinity? The enemy leaned closer.

"You are original being from long ago. Your kind," the enemy growled. "Weak with no bodies. We took your puny resources." It sneered. "Evolution means nothing. Still of no consequence in the galaxy."

That's why. Ganna had hinted that the enemy could sense the Lassians' energy flow. Only he had volunteered to command one of the Azrom armada ships for this sector. The other Lassian forces chose to spread out closer to the center.

A burning sensation bloomed inside Talas. Rage. Not the kind he could easily distinguish, flowed through every molecule. Memories flooded in. Ancient, timeless images of a time long gone. In an instant, he pushed the enemy away and cut down the one that snuck up behind him.

Coordinates he had forgotten sprung into his mind. He turned to the bridge and over the din of battle cries called them out to the navigator right as the enemy he pushed away came back for more. The ship jolted violently before jumping through a vortex, sucking five other ships in the area with them.

"We've lost five ships near the Razznian's far side!" The communications tech cried out to Halfar. The soldier scrutinized the data coming through. "They just disappeared into a jump."

The bridge of the armada ship spanned wide, allowing enough room for a fight without the consoles being in immediate danger. On the center dais, Halfar watching the battle raging before him. His own ship laid down a blanket of rounds at an enemy ship hell bent on coming straight for him. The blasts spread across to the other ships flanking it.

"Where did they go? Can you trace them?" Halfar calmly wrapped his hands around the railing and leaned forward. "How many of the enemy went with them?"

"Looks like three battle cruisers and over a hundred fighters got caught in the jump with our alliance forces." The technician tapped icons on his station. He turned to Halfar; his eyes wide. "They seem to be on the other side of the enemy's territory. I can't find where they are."

That made Halfar look towards him. The report began circling the other feeds. Something didn't sit right with him. He couldn't imagine a scenario where Talas would have to flee using random coordinates.

"What do the ship logs say?" He moved from the railing and stepped down onto the bridge.

"Massive damage to our armada ship and the alliance ones in proximity. But," the communications tech looked back at his screen, "nothing dire. They still had enough ammunition and hull integrity to fight."

"Get me the Dreridians," Halfar ordered.

Within the hour, a center holoscreen changed its view. Lord Graggor's bulbous head filled its frame. The enemy ships that had been advancing were in free fall, their hulls covered in holes with chunks missing. One broke in half, the back end bending ninety-degrees and plummeting down.

"Lord Halfar. Don't tell me Azrom has cleared the field already?" Lord Graggor's craggy lips curved into a thin smile.

"You've been holding out on us."

Halfar smirked. "That is imminent. And you always underestimate our power."

"You want to know about the whereabouts of the missing ships." Lord Graggor's face scrunched, closing the gaps along his forehead. "You won't like the answer."

"Tell me where they are." Halfar crossed his arms.

"Very well." A star map replaced his face on the holo-screen. It zoomed in to the sector where the fleet was last seen. "As you can see, beyond the outskirts is where the enemy territory is a mere hop away. The enemy only needs to make a short jump to get home."

Halfar felt his stomach tighten. He stared at the map, not wanting to see the familiar planets in view. There were many times his fleets and entourage passed through, only to be stopped at a checkpoint at the edge of the sector. He calculated the information in his mind, dread creeping the more he thought about the enemy's home.

And next to that system lay the remnants of Lassa.

The coordinates screamed accusatory at him. That is where he sent a planet bomb out of anger, almost destroying an entire race. Lord Graggor came back onscreen. The soldiers at the consoles seemed confused. Halfar didn't dare tell them why he had stiffened.

"What will you do, Lord Halfar?" Lord Graggor asked.

Halfar dug his fingers into his biceps. He addressed the technician. "Send a beacon to monitor their location in case they request assistance."

"Not to sound disobedient, my lord, but if they summoned a rescue, we would get there too late. They are too far away."

"I understand that. Do it anyway." He brought his attention back to Lord Graggor. "I don't want this to get out. You know why."

"Of course, Lord Halfar. We agree. It's up to the Lassians, what they wish to do now."

The holoscreen went back to its live feed of the ship's side view. Halfar dropped his arms at his sides and took a few deep breaths to calm himself. For the first time in a long while, he counted his blessings that Chardon stayed on New Lassa.

$$\backsim$$

The cluster of alliance and enemy ships came out of the jump in a jumbled ball of crossed fire power. Talas' and the enemy battle cruiser still fused together went crashing down onto a nearby moon. The fiery entry burned their connection, and they veered off in different directions, though not far enough to matter.

Both ships dug deep trenches into the surface as they skidded to a stop after their initial impact. Less than a few miles apart, the smoke from their damages mingled in the air. Unprepared enemy fighters lay broken, littering the area.

Talas climbed out of a breach on the side of the armada ship. A sharp smoke scented breeze whipped his hair back, forcing him to take it all in. It felt good despite its warmth. He gasped as it burned his lungs. His swords remained gripped in both hands. Not far behind him, he could sense the enemy commander moving towards him.

No. That's not right. The direction is off somehow.

He jumped down and scanned the wreckage. His eyes landed on the jagged section of the armada ship. The rest of it sat nearly a kilometer away. Emerging from the severed piece, the enemy commander locked eyes with Talas.

The battle became a surface fight as alliance and enemy forces on the moon engaged without the help of their ships still blasting each other in the darkness of space. Talas could see plumes of fire bursting on the horizon.

A pulse of energy from inside his core made him falter as he stepped forward. He clutched his chest, knowing that wouldn't help the pain. His sword tilting away from him, shook

He dropped to one knee, glancing over at the enemy commander getting closer.

Move!

He took a sharp intake of breath and forced himself to stand, only to fall back again. The soldiers behind him gave a worried stare. Talas looked up and gasped. In the darkening sky, he saw another moon. And next to it, further out, sat a damaged, barely visible planet.

Pieces of the planet floated along the right side, making it appear as if it were in a waning three quarter phase. Patches of foliage were in stark contrast to the sections of black where nothing grew. Large swaths of forest sprinkled the surface.

A planet in the process of healing.

Lassa.

The ancient memories flooding through him explained why Laxis became the leader of the warriors. His original form as a scout investigated the galaxy to aid in Lassa's advancement. They brought the knowledge of war to them. The one who discovered sword making and its techniques on how to use the weapon.

With a cry of utter rage and despair, Talas rose to his feet and turned in time to cross weapons with the enemy commander. He saw his eyes burn starlight blue in his opponent, who moved back from him at the sight. Saliva dripped from Talas' mouth as he bared teeth. He stared between the top of the X created by his swords.

"You will not leave here alive this time." Talas' breathy, malicious tone seemed to disturb the commander. They pushed apart to get some distance. Talas would not have it. He went for the enemy relentlessly. As they had done in every battle. "This moon will be your grave."

Talas' assault sped up, becoming a blur of colors, making the enemy's movements desperate to avoid getting struck. Deep cuts appeared on its armor like skin the more it tried. It eventually tried to run to the surprise of the alliance forces fighting its horde.

Keeping his word, Talas flashed forward, his swords cutting the air in a downward cross. He landed mere inches from his opponent, both swords' tips embedded in the ground between the commander's feet. In a kneeling position, Talas looked up into the enemy's face.

Shock and defeat. A glorious feeling came over Talas right as its body crumbled one piece at a time into five parts. The legs were the last to fall away to each side. Talas stood, swinging his swords to flick off any residue. Now he understood how General Kur felt.

The battlefield seemed to have stood still. Talas turned around and saw hesitation in the enemy. Even though the alliance forces comprised many races, in honor of his command, he gave a smile and yelled, "Victory."

The Azrom soldiers didn't falter. With a collective boom of their voices, they replied.

"Until death!"

The other races joined them in an act of solidarity.

And the battle turned in the alliance's favor. The enemy would meet their demise.

Out of the Fire

Halfar cursed under his breath. The barricade of ships across Azrom and its neighboring planets proved not enough as four enemy ships plowed through a section, heading straight for the surface. The blasts from Azrom attacks bounced off their shields. He saw the first one land, creating a gigantic crater near a village.

"Open the feed!" He commanded the comms tech.

"As you wish. It's done."

"Lord Elendar!"

Crackling erupted, a loud hissing sound behind it.

"You summoned, General Halfar?" Elendar's voice kept breaking up. Halfar turned to the technician.

"What's wrong with the reception?" He asked.

"Enemy interference. The region is heavy with fighters."

He went back to addressing Elendar.

"I'm sure you saw those ships break through."

"I did." There was a pause, the crackling taking over.

"Take the rest of your forces and deal with them. Since they want to fight one on one, you need to lead our people to victory down there."

"The pleasure will be mine."

The feed disconnected abruptly. Halfar looked over at the holoscreen where Elendar's forces were engaging the enemy, his ship's bridge taken out. Electrical arcs shot from the ragged edges as it plunged to the surface. Halfar knew that wouldn't deter the royal lord from continuing his fight. If anything, it probably enraged him.

Elendar's remaining ships followed it down, while another Azrom unit blocked the enemy's pursuit. Halfar almost felt a twinge of pity for them. *That's what they get for coming to Azrom in the first place.*

The royal feed came onto the main holoscreen. Romnus stared down at him.

"What is the meaning of this, cousin? Why are enemy ships on Azrom?"

"Stop being dramatic!" Halfar snapped. "It's only four of them. Elendar is handling it." From behind Romnus, he could see an enemy ship crashing down near the palace. He suppressed his anger. "I'm certain you would never let an enemy enter the palace, either."

Romnus glanced back, staring at the enemy ship. He turned to Halfar.

"Do your job properly, General Halfar. I don't want to see another enemy ship coming through." He looked down with narrowed eyes.

"Of course, my Lord." Halfar bowed his head as the feed winked out and the outside view returned. He addressed the communications tech. "Send a message to all forces to tighten the noose. We will not allow another breach."

～

The first one out of the damaged ship, Elendar emerged with his battalion crawling out after him, ready to cut down the enemy as they flowed towards them like insects. Not far in the distance, enemy fire from above bombarded his house while another ship made a pass across the terrain, heading for the next village over.

The initial round caught the house security off guard. A series of holes ran from one end of the lower level to the other. Shields erected after that absorbed the enemy blasts. Elendar tapped the commlink on his ear.

"Battalion four, intercept that ship headed for the village. Battalion three take down the other one. We will handle this one."

"What about the one near the main palace?" A soldier asked.

Elendar turned towards him with a disgusted look.

"Did you really ask such a thing?" The soldier flinched and walked away to head off a swarm of charging enemy fighters.

That monstrosity on the throne would have his fill of carnage. Elendar also pitied the enemy a little. They had not met a being like Romnus before. Their only encounter with Azrom being General Kur and Commander Abras. Who were quite formidable on their own.

His assistant came to his side.

"Do you want me nearby?"

Elendar sighed. The two had always fought side by side. This time, he wanted to prove his worth without help. Stupid thinking, he knew.

"No. You go around and keep them at bay. I will defend the royal houses from here."

His assistant hesitated, his mouth opening, then shut. He bowed to then left without saying a word. He's angry. That said, Elendar knew he would do his bidding.

An enemy baring ugly teeth and a handheld axe in mid-swing to cleave him in half came at him. Elendar morphed into his battle form, the sharp pincers snapping in anticipation of prey. He lunged forward, crouching down almost to the enemy's knees, making them adjust their attack. Elendar's pincers snapped shut around the enemy's calves. Blood spewed across his face and shoulders, staining his cloak.

With a guttural yell, the enemy pitched forward, unable to stop its momentum, and went sailing over Elendar, its legs from the knees down, missing. It flailed on the ground, trying to turn over, its weapon still in hand. Elendar turned around. Using one of his thick limbs with a pointer on the end, he kicked the axe from its hand and stabbed down into its neck.

He waited until the enemy stopped moving, then bent over and snapped its head off.

A breeze picked up, lifting his cloak behind him. Covered in enemy blood, Elendar looked like a crazed tyrant. He whipped the cloak off, letting it sail off as he stared down at his first true kill of the battle. Elation consumed him. He wanted more. Picking up the enemy's axe, he went back into the fray behind him to cut down his prey with their own weapon.

The first one to engage him head on danced around, jabbing and swinging, to get a hit. Elendar got behind it and brought the axe down in the back of its head, slicing it in half. Another came at him from the side, and he used a pincer to snap its face off, leaving the back half to ooze before gushing.

A projectile pierced his torso from behind. The rod protruded out almost six inches on each end. Elendar grit his teeth at the pain and turned around. His arms reverted to normal. An enemy held what resembled a mechanical crossbow. It reloaded, never lowering its aim. The rod hit Elendar right as he came into the enemy's range. With lightning speed, he unsheathed his longsword and swung upwards between the enemy's legs, and continued, keeping his motion.

Elendar ended up falling through the two halves as they fell away, more blood coating his body. He didn't notice an enemy on the other side waiting to do the same. He looked up at the axe coming down and pivoted to the left. The axe went deep into his shoulder, knocking him to the ground. The enemy bent forward, adding pressure to sever his arm.

Its head went sailing off to the side, the grip on the axe tightening before going limp. The body fell to reveal a furious, blood-soaked Lord Kel, his pincers dripping. A smaller version of Romnus and no less vicious.

"You have to do better than that, Elendar," he chastised him. Lord Kel leaned over and unceremoniously yanked the rods out. "Now, get rid of these vermin. I have more important things to do."

Lord Kel walked off towards the royal courtyard. Why was he at my house? Elendar noticed his head maid running out to assist him. Which meant Lady Haldris stayed to defend hers and Lord Kel's houses. Elendar shuddered at the thought of seeing her in battle.

"Your grace!" He heard his assistant's breathless cry as he got closer. The man slid onto the ground beside him. "Are you okay to fight? Shall we regroup elsewhere?"

Elendar smacked his hand away as he reached for him. He angrily stood, forcing himself to ignore the woozy feeling from blood loss.

"I am tasked with ridding the surface of these things. I will not back down."

He focused on his wounds and willed the muscles to compress, stopping the bleeding. With such a temporary fix, he would last only a few hours before the effect wore off, and he bled to death.

"I'm accompanying you this time." His assistant was not up for a debate.

"As you so choose."

They stood back-to-back and let the enemy fighters coming their way on each side get within range for strike. Elendar gripped his sword and got into a defense stance. No one would look down on his house ever again.

∽

New Lassa stayed on high alert even though they pushed back the enemy away from the planet after emerging from the jump point gate. The newly manufactured ships proved to be more powerful than the enemy or the Lassians had expected. Ganna watched the battle feeds from her console with pride.

She hummed joyfully as her fingers tapped commands for the land to space missiles. Let's knock out a few of those nasty things. Her finger hovered over the detonate icon when a bolt of energy hit her, sending her crashing to the floor. The technicians nearby ran to her side.

As her body convulsed, her eyes opened wide to a vision where she saw a planet. She felt Talas. No. Laxis within her core. She was seeing through his eyes. The planet's core reached out to her.

Lassa's light!

The deeper she went, the more she recognized other energies. Jaron, Trinon, Hon, and Chardon. The other part of her, the core she had merged with her own, lit up inside. The remnants of her father. She reached out to Lassa, trying to grab hold of it. Tears streamed down her face.

Lassa was alive. Barely.

It struggled yet still injected what little energy it had into repairing itself. Always a motherly planet draped in femininity, it only knew how to nurture.

Sorrow radiated from Jaron and Chardon. Ganna felt anger. The being who embodied it had denied that part, refusing to create life until they had no other choice. The enemy had once again invaded their system, taunting and belittling their race.

And then the anger faded away, that emotion no longer needed.

Laxis would not permit the enemy to desecrate Lassa twice. The connection ended, leaving Ganna spent. She let the technicians help her up into a chair. Her chest hurt and she seemed out of breath.

"Hit that button, would you, my dear?" she asked the one closest to the console.

The technician tapped the icon, then came back to her.

"Do you need an energy shot?"

"No. I'll be fine."

Ganna sat straight, realizing every ancient core on New Lassa would have felt and seen the same thing. What does it all mean for them now? Lassa was far from inhabitable at the moment. Nothing an infusion capsule couldn't fix in the next fifty years. It must have been lonely, but also understood why it had to be.

Chardon burst into the communications room. His face seemed contorted in a blend of confusion and rage. Dirt and blood caked his robes. Ganna swerved in her seat, checking the feeds for any enemy that somehow got on the surface. When she saw none, she turned to Chardon, perplexed.

"I was helping with triage in the medical bays."

"Oh." Ganna nodded.

"Can we?" Chardon glanced at the console. "Is it…"

Ganna caught on. She found one of their ships near the gate, blocking the enemy vortex.

"Yes. We will send Laxis help to defend Lassa once more."

"Will it get there in time? The other alliance forces couldn't do it because of the distance."

Ganna smirked.

"Because they don't know Lassa's exact location. I do.

She typed in a message to the ship. Using the gate, she sent the coordinates directly to it before it entered. They watched the ship turn away from the vortex and slide through a glowing white swirl directly next to it. Too late for the enemy to notice or give chase. The gate disappeared, causing the enemy vortex to warble, unraveling. Seeing their exit getting away from them, the enemy made a hasty reversal to retreat.

"Should we let them go?" a technician asked.

Chardon contemplated for a moment. He looked down at Ganna.

"What do you think?"

"At least make it look good," Ganna quipped.

"I will let Jaron know." Chardon walked off, then stopped at the doorway, making the sliding doors stay open. "When this is over."

"I know." Ganna turned to her console.

Once Chardon left, she clutched the front of her robe. Father. Her mind regressed to that of her youth. A budding scientist under his tutelage. Everything she had done stemmed from him.

Already drenched in enemy blood, Talas moved forward through their front lines. The taste of them permeated his mouth all the way to the back of his throat. Like metallic bile, it threatened to bring up anything he may have in his stomach. His fighting style deteriorated as the battle went on, fatigue setting in.

He fought in desperation. The enemy before him sneered as two of its ships above ascended towards Lassa.

"This time we kill it. Finish Azrom's work."

Talas brought his knee up and pushed the enemy back, bringing his swords down at its shoulders, slicing both sides off. The fabric of his clothes stuck to his wounds tugged, causing sharp pains. I won't last much longer. He raised his head towards Lassa. Help me!

The sky shimmered. A white out spread across the horizon, pushing the enemy ships advancing on Lassa back. Explosions erupted in space and Talas assumed the ones still fighting out there had met their demise. A lull in the battle allowed him to tap his damaged yet still functional wristband. The hologram of the space between the moon and Lassa came up.

Out of the white out came one of the newly built Lassian ships. Almost equal in size to the enemy's battleship, its pale, neutral colors seemed to gleam. The weapons bays were glowing hot blue light and unleashed a firestorm on the enemy ships in its way. Talas stared in awe at the destructive power.

It shredded the enemy ships apart. Those farther away retreated to get distance from its onslaught. One enemy ship became emboldened and broke past the Lassian assault into the stratosphere of Lassa. And that was its last moment. The shimmer Talas had seen came from the planet itself. He watched the enemy ship dive headfirst into that field and get eaten bit by bit until nothing remained.

Enemy ships fled the battle on the moon with alliance forces giving chase until Talas sent the order to stand down.

"Let them go!" He yelled into his wristband, ending the hologram feed. "Our priority is the wounded and regrouping."

The alliance forces reluctantly backed off. Talas sighed in relief. His body felt heavy. No. Not yet. He faltered and stomped one foot in front to stabilize himself. He glanced up at Lassa, its view now obscured by the Lassian ship.

I want to go!

As if hearing his plea, his body disintegrated into shimmering flecks of multicolor and flowed up into space past Lassa's shield. The alliance forces on the moon stood mesmerized.

⌒

Such a dirty tactic!

Sars stood in front of the holoscreen talking to the Razznian General. He had seen the double vortex ambush on several of the battles and shook his head. His own ship floated with massive damage. His crew had annihilated the first wave of enemy that had invaded through the hull. When the enemy became aware they would not win, Sars allowed their second wave to flee.

"How do we combat this new strategy the enemy has

implemented?" He asked the General. The reptile's eyes damn near glowed red with rage.

"As much as I don't want to, we need to split the forces so at least one can maneuver around behind the second vortex when it shows up."

"Without getting sucked in, of course." Sars stared at the cracked holoscreen on the left.

Whenever the enemy got overrun, they opened a vortex and moved to another sector to ambush the forces already fighting. Even the Azrom ships were getting pummeled.

"I have been in many wars, mostly with Azrom. We need to tap the other races' forces as a first line of defense with the Dreridians in the center while we combine with Azrom to take care of the enemy hopping around."

Sars scratched under his chin, the sound of his talons raking across his scales louder than he liked. He hadn't thought of that. Glancing over at the right screen that showed the enemy's movements, his eyes became slits. It now seemed obvious.

"I am honored to learn from you, General. Your knowledge keeps Razzna in power across the systems."

The General hissed, his forked tongue rattling.

"You have much to learn. For now, we will coordinate our new alliance and send these-things- back to where they came from."

The General's image winked out, replaced by the original feed of the surrounding planets. Balls of light from explosions littered the space. Sars walked over to stand close to the main consoles and addressed the Dreridian on comm duty.

"I want you to relay the plan we just discussed to our alliance fleet. Open a separate channel to the Azrom ships."

"Not to sound ungrateful for this opportunity, but we are more capable of being the frontline than the smaller forces. Dreridian ships have sustained close to no damage, only seven percent."

"I understand that." Sars placed a hand on the tech's

shoulder. "But this is merely an illusion. The center will be the ones laying fire while the frontline attacks."

The Dreridian's face lit up with that realization and the rest of the bridge crew's morale seemed to change. Good. The comm tech sent out their plan.

An Azrom commander came onto the main holoscreen.

"What else could you want after that disgusting plan of yours? Are we to simply sit back and enjoy the show?"

"Are you being sincere?" Sars narrowed his eyes.

The commander glanced off to the side, then focused on Sars.

"Then you want us to get serious."

"I want us," Sars emphasized, "to get serious. This has gone on long enough."

"I agree. You take the far end?"

Sars grinned.

This commander understood without telling him the details. The whole point of this fight revolved around pushing the enemy back into their system, where the Dreridians waited to bring them to their knees once and for all.

"And you will handle the ones moving?"

"It would be our pleasure."

The Azrom commander smirked as the feed disconnected. Sars went back up to the dais, minus the railing that broke during the attacks.

"Move into position. Open the main channel." The comm tech tapped the icon. "Those too deep in the fight, lure the enemy towards the edge of the system. We are changing our configuration. Avoid firing on our own."

The enemy reacted in confusion as the alliance forces moved around them in what appeared to be haphazard. When the new formation became clear, the enemy brought out more of their tendril weapon ships. They fired on the alliance first line, only to have the center counter with their own.

Clusters of enemy ships sped through hastily opened

vortices to get more elements of surprise. The Azromnians were waiting. Before a vortex could open all the way, they fired down into the dark. Some enemy ships avoided destruction. The ones behind them didn't exit the vortex, shutting it to find another route.

Which sent them closer to the Razznians on the far end. Trapped in a cage of Razznian ships, the enemy had nowhere to run from the onslaught. Their ships became moving targets, scattering to get away. Most of their shields held up, giving them enough time to decide their fate.

Backed into a corner with half their numbers depleted, the enemy tethered their damaged ships and fled through a vortex that sent them back to their home world. The system became silent as a tomb. Debris floated around the alliance, remnants of the fierce battle.

A weight lifted off the Sars and he stared at the main screen. It seemed over so quickly once their plan worked. He almost felt cheated for not engaging in the carnage. Then again, he didn't want to eat those creatures.

⸝

Lord Pondur crossed his arms as he stood before his bunker's holoscreen. Next to him, Lord Graggor nibbled on a small piece of pastry. The two had ordered small offerings of food and drink for the show. Filling the wall sized holoscreen, the enemy home world loomed. It had taken months from the time the Dreridian forces entered that system to position themselves around it.

They left behind only a handful of fleets to defend it, which Lord Pondur found preposterous. Some ten thousand ships dared to come against the Dreridians three times their size. The enemy ruler had sent a threatening message, vowing their victory. All communication went dead when the Dreridians opened fire on the planet, hitting the ships in the process.

In a full circle around the planet, the Dreridians annihilated everything in their path. Crippled enemy ships fell to the surface, causing more damage. And they only had to do it once. Lord Pondur frowned in disgust at how easily the enemy seemed to give up. He bent down and retrieved his half drunken glass of liqueur, taking a sip.

"How underwhelming," Lord Graggor said, finishing his pastry. He licked the residue from his talons. "They really are cowards in the end."

A communication technician came through the audio.

"There is a message coming from the surface. I believe it is that ruler again."

"Ha!" Lord Pondur set his glass back down. "Open it. Let's hear what he has to say."

The holoscreen shifted to the outside feed and the enemy ruler's face filled it. Behind him were two soldiers holding tendril weapons.

"You think you can come and take our home? We will take you with us in death."

Lord Pondur's eyes widened.

"Oh, that is not our plan at all. You misunderstand our goal."

The enemy ruler glared at him.

"You infiltrate our system. Destroy our land. What else is there?"

Lord Pondur lifted his head higher, a nasty expression on his craggy face.

"We came to take over your trade system. You will now do business, as we say."

As he spoke, Dreridian ships appeared throughout the enemy system. Negotiations with the trading planets would be underway.

～

Months after the decree, Lord Pondur lounged in his favorite chair, sipping a hot beverage from a gold and blue tea set. The gold and brown brocade suit with a cream ascot made it a perfect accent. His lace sleeves brushed the edge of the saucer.

He watched the feeds from the enemy territories and alliance ships wrapping up their battles across the five systems. Lord Graggor sat on the right side of the table so not to block his view. An alert flashed at the bottom of the lower holoscreen.

"Incoming encrypted message, my lord," the communication officer's voice said through the commlink. "Shall I relay it?"

"Let it through." Lord Pondur set his teacup on the saucer and placed it on the tall table beside him.

"Our spy has something for us." Lord Graggor leaned forward with anticipation.

The spy's familiar face came on screen.

"Greetings Lord Pondur." He bowed his head, then looked straight into the viewer. "I ended up with the alliance fleet near the outskirts. As you know, we ended up jumping past the enemy's system."

Lord Pondur and Lord Graggor nodded. The message continued.

"Right near the center is a planet whose moon we crash landed on." The spy paused, as if trying to contain himself. "Here is the image I captured before a Lassian battleship appeared out of nowhere to block the enemy."

The two Dreridians leaned back in unison as the footage ran. Indeed, the Lassian ship obscured the view. The white vortex mesmerized them. They had never seen a vortex or gateway quite like it. What stunned them the most sat behind it.

"Is that what I think it is?" Lord Pondur asked.

Lord Graggor inhaled sharply. "I believe so."

The message played over the footage.

"I think this is the Lassian's original home world. As you can see, it is healing itself. There's no significant life detected, but the forests and streams are thriving. That is all I have for now. I will wait for any instructions."

The message ended, not before being recorded, and Lord Pondur rewound it to the still image of Lassa. Broken, its pieces floating out like an arm stretching out, yet not dead.

"The fact that the Lassians sent a ship of that size means they are ready to defend it to the death if necessary." Lord Graggor glanced over at him. "You need to tread carefully."

Lord Pondur stared at the planet. This is what Azrom could do to any who opposed them. He needed to get in the Lassians' good graces.

"Send an envoy to those coordinates. We should offer our assistance."

"How many ships, my lord?" Lord Graggor asked, his brow crackling.

"Oh, an entire fleet."

Lord Graggor sputtered. "My lord, are we trying to intimidate them?"

"No, no," Lord Pondur waved a hand. "I merely want to show that we are ready to be a resource without delay."

"I don't think that is what it will translate to."

"Hmm?" Lord Pondur caressed his chin. "You don't think Azrom will feel the overwhelming guilt and come running with a rejuvenation planet bomb?"

Lord Graggor smirked. Azrom had only used them five times over the centuries to rejuvenate what they had destroyed after conquering a planet. They didn't do that with Lassa for obvious reasons. With the planet healing itself, Lord Pondur was certain Halfar would plead its case to Romnus.

And we get to negotiate a way to learn about their planet bomb technology. They would see through that plan, of course. Azrom not only had might, but the intelligence of a superpower.

∽

Laxis opened his eyes to a sea of swirling light around him. A continuous soft hum kept him calm. He recognized the energy as Lassa's center. With utter abandon, he surrendered his soul, connecting with other ancient cores. He watched his body's wounds heal while they all conversed with their home. So much serenity.

Not yet. Lassa's consciousness enveloped them with love.

They understood. Laxis' core swelled with blue light, a sign of his adoration and frustration. The planet was not ready for habitation. He felt his body merge once again with his core and then dissolve into energy.

You must go now. That is what Lassa's emotion told him.

He left as a stream of glittering lights snaking towards the sky into space and passed through the Lassian ship's hull. The bridge crew reared back in fear as he solidified in front of them. At the helm stood Barbon. The massive manbeast came forward, frowning.

"Talas, what is the meaning of this?"

That's right. I almost forgot my new name. He could tell Barbon seemed disturbed by his sudden appearance. The manbeast did not have an ancient core, but he knew where they were.

"As you can see, Lassa is healing."

"Yes. What I'm asking is how you came to be on this ship. I was about to give the order to extract you from the moon when you disappeared."

Ah!

"My apologies. It seems Lassa wanted to talk to me first." Talas inspected the bare skin showing through his tattered clothes. "Lassa healed me as well."

Barbon pointed to his attire. "But not that. You look like a transient begging on Halios." Talas glared at him. That was uncalled for. "By the way, you missed the good stuff."

"What?" Talas glanced up at the main holoscreens.

"How long was I gone?"

"Three moon cycles. The enemy fled. Dreridians have taken control of their home world."

"Lassa's light!" Talas bent down into a squat, resting his arms on his thighs. "Then we won." He looked up at Barbon. "Right?"

"Correct."

Then Talas stood, staring out at the viewport. The Lassian ship blocked what appeared to be a Dreridian fleet. All the alliance ships were gone.

"What has happened?"

"Dreridian spies."

Talas' eyes widened in horror. He counted a fleet of close to one hundred ships.

"What is their agenda?"

"They say they are awaiting instructions from us on how to assist."

"Assist in what?" Talas cried out. His core flared.

Barbon's brow furrowed. "That I am not sure."

Ganna slapped her hands on the meeting room's conference table. The carafes of drink shook, rippling their contents. Around the table sat the entire council, minus Talas. On the holoscreen, Lt. Treshur waited patiently. Chardon lifted a hand, signaling Ganna to sit.

"Offering to help us repair our home?" Ganna yelled. "In exchange for what?" She reluctantly sat down, her fists resting on the edge of the table. "Azrom does nothing out of compassion!"

"That's enough! We know that is not true!" Chardon countered. He turned his attention to Lt. Treshur. "The Dreridians forced your hand, didn't they?"

Lt. Treshur smiled.

"Not so much as goaded us. Lord Pondur showed the image of Lassa to Romnus and Halfar. Of course, we would take responsibility and try to speed up its repair."

"The Dreridians want something for the information?" The head of engineering asked. "When they came to us offering their resources, it sounded suspicious."

"They told us of their plan, then advise if they had one of our planet bombs, it would speed up the process."

Halfar, who sat silent in the back the whole time, uncrossed his arms, and glared out into the distance. After the meeting with Romnus, he hurried back to New Lassa to get ahead of the mess. Within a day, he learned of the upcoming transmission they now attended.

"They want our technology. They're not being subtle about it."

"Just sneaky," Jaron seethed.

Ganna leaned forward. She eyed Halfar across the room.

"This is nothing but guilt! You were the one who destroyed our home, killed thousands of cores. Now you want to make it right?"

"You think I don't know how you all feel about me?" Halfar stood, yelling. "That I don't regret what I have done every waking moment?"

Ganna shrunk back in fear. The council lowered their heads. They had no right to condemn him, then prevent him from making amends. Lt. Treshur appeared uncomfortable. Chardon exhaled slowly.

"I agree with Halfar. The Dreridians are not fooling anyone. That said." He turned to Halfar. "If one of your rejuvenating bombs will help Lassa, we gladly accept."

Lt. Treshur bowed his head, the feed now ended. The council went silent, soaking in the effects of their decision.

Lassa would thrive once more.

To Be Continued…

ABOUT THE AUTHOR

Hi there. I'm Maquel A. Jacob. I have had a passion for the written word since the age of seven, reading everything I could get my grubby little hands on which included encyclopedias and the thesaurus. At twelve, I had my first encounter with a Stephen King novel and was hooked. I then became inspired to write my own brand of fiction. Combining multiple genres to keep things interesting.

I am a HUGE Anime fan, love a great bottle of wine and rock out to heavy metal music. Green and lush Oregon is where I currently reside spinning imaginary worlds in my head and daydreaming.

For cool limited-edition Swag, updates, FREE short stories, Newsletters
...and more, become a Patron
https://www.patreon.com/maquelajacob

Visit:www.majacobauthor.com

Like Maquel A. Jacob on Facebook plus
Follow on Tumblr and Twitter
all @MaquelAJ1
MAJart Works on Instagram
Also find me on Goodreads

Also find me on Goodreads

Buy Direct at https://www.maquelajacob.com